ON ELIZABETH STREET

Catherine Adami

For information contact; address www.catadami.com
Book and Cover design by Tony Frenzel
ISBN: 0692725342
ISBN: 9780692725344
First Edition: June 2016
10 9 8 7 6 5 4 3 2 1

Pool Hustler's Daughter Press
Poolhustlersdaughter.com

CONTENTS

To my parents, Frederick and Theresa Bentivegna, with love.

BOOK I

Friday

1

SUNSET ON ELIZABETH STREET

I t was Friday, late in the month of August, when the sun began to set behind Old Saint Patrick's Cathedral in the downtown Manhattan enclave north of Little Italy, known as Nolita. A fairly fresh real estate term, as one hundred years ago the larger area was simply Little Italy, its borders were considered to be Houston to the North, Bowery to the East, Broome to the South, and Lafayette to the west. It had a reputation for being mostly residential, with quiet, small streets and little traffic.

Despite the trendy retail shops, and restaurants with wait lists, a part of this neighborhood existed in a bubble. It was part of the charm, languages long dead in Italy were spoken on its streets and the same families spanning three or four generations still owned a fair number of the buildings. Just before five o'clock a posse of dark, ancient, women walked to church to attend a Catholic *novena*. On Sundays, a faint scent of *sugo*, or Italian tomato sauce, permeated apartment hallways and outside the open windows. It was a place one might call enchanted, where the passage of time was gentle and careful.

A group of giggling teenagers skipped past a pair of sweat soaked, stylish, forty-year-old men standing on Elizabeth Street, just above Prince. The macho, Barbour Catalog of handsome men were failing to lift a large and heavy Oriental rug into the back of an over-sized pick-up truck.

"Lift!" the taller one ordered.

"I'm trying!" the shorter one answered.

"Not hard enough!"

"You're paying for my Chiropractor!"

"That guy's a Charlatan!"

"Everyone is staring at us!"

"You love being stared at!"

Their guttural moans, followed by boyish banter, could be heard down the block alongside horn honking from angry drivers. Great-grandmothers dressed in black screamed obscenities with matching hand gestures from tenement windows.

At last, a frustrated twenty year old in a blood-soaked apron exited Albanese Meats, the butcher shop just next door, and helped push the rug into the back of the truck in less than five seconds.

He mumbled something under his breath as he walked away.

"I think that's how you say asshole in Italian," Gerald August Baxter II, forty-three, chuckled, as he stood in front of the Girardi Building. His first apartment in New York City was there, on the top floor.

Blessed with soft to the touch, thick, dirty blond hair that crested in the front, Augie, as he was known, had small blue eyes, small ears and an extremely large, wide nose. He barely reached five feet, eight inches tall but was thick, muscular, and easy to squeeze. When he smiled, his cheeks rolled up in layers, like a *Sharpei,* and his eyes glistened. Lately, he seemed distant, and a little sad in photos. In fact, he had stopped smiling altogether in front of the camera which was odd considering Augie, an exhibitionist, loved the spotlight. He wondered if anyone noticed.

He had come to town that day to housesit for the weekend and to help his best friend from college, JR, move out of this apartment. His ultimate bachelor buddy had just gotten hitched at City Hall, last minute, in a Helmut Lang suit to a much younger girl named Stacy. The newlyweds were leaving for their honeymoon in St. Barths late that night and Augie was in charge of seeing that the last of their belongings made it safely to their new home.

Saying goodbye to "Liz Street" was important. The apartment was a museum that paid homage to his youth. He never thought JR would give it up, much less get *married*–but here they were, loading a truck; or, *trying* to load a truck.

Except for a new kitchen and bathroom, the notoriously frugal JR had kept the place pretty much intact since Augie had lived there. Some of his coveted movie posters were still on the walls and vinyl LPs from his college DJ days collected dust in crates in the living room.

The enormity of his sadness didn't hit until he stood there, yelling back and forth with his best friend over a stupid rug. His visits to Liz Street over the years as a married family man with a passionless (but amusing) job were like a quick, guiltless trip back in time. He could shotgun beers and walk around naked, he could watch his favorite movies and listen to his favorite records until dawn. There was a Land Line with a coveted two-one-two area code! He could leave the toilet seat up, relax, and imagine himself younger.

Only his wife's phone calls returned him back to the present day.

"What have you been up to?" she asked, not really caring about the answer.

"Not much," Augie robotically replied, holding back "I found the Tones on Tail twelve inch!" and "I saw Catherine Deneuve shopping on Madison Avenue!"

"Okay, then," his wife would answer, immediately launching into a recitation of home improvements he would be paying for and country club mixers he would be forced to attend before segwaying into, "I'd like to talk about why we're paying your mother's insurance..."

"Gotta go, that's work on the other line," Augie interrupted, lying to her rather than screaming and hanging up.

People needed Augie; lots of people needed him, not just her. She'd never get that sense of loyalty, and responsibility. His marriage was at the point where he felt he could only experience joy privately. He didn't want to have to justify why he liked something anymore. He just *liked* it, wasn't that enough of a reason? Did he have to be self-conscious about what he *liked*?

Not only was he free to do what he *liked* at Liz Street, but also he could ponder the great desires of his youth, especially the ones that didn't pan out but still lit fire under his ass once in a while. His cravings pushed him to buy tickets to the Film Forum that he always ended up giving away to a production assistant in his office at the last minute or convinced him to splurge on expensive subscriptions for photography magazines with beautiful, glossy, color covers that ultimately ended up crinkled and wet on the floor of his bathroom.

How could he spend (what felt like) every minute of the day recording mostly combative and superficial lives of other people? Would that be his professional legacy? Wasn't his life more important than that of Russian Oligarch Mistresses? Or the Pawn Shop King of Queens Boulevard? Or the Booty Doctor of the Bronx? He hated telling people what he did for a living or what lowbrow television he was responsible for producing. But it paid the bills, and *then* some; his wife would fill in when he lost the will to answer.

He didn't feel like the same person who had lived on Elizabeth Street. Back then, he was a young man taking film classes at NYU and writing script treatments on his coffee break from waiting tables. He was the cocky bastard collecting photographs of locations where he would most certainly shoot his first film.

Since he was a teenager he talked about writing and directing an independent feature, inspired by the masters of cinema he adored - like Scorsese and Kurosawa - a modern western in New York City, maybe? Then he could travel the festival circuit, surrounded by other respectable creative types and feed on their energy and momentum. There was too much pressure on Augie's *future* self. It was his *future* self that was going to live off of less money, be a photographer, write and shoot films. His future self would be the one posting selfies at Sundance in a Siberian fur hat outside of a screening, smiling.

Having passed forty, there was now a clear difference between talking about doing something and doing it. He took pleasure in yelling at his younger production assistants about this subject, merely projecting his own insecurities onto them. The last thing Augie Baxter wanted was to be the lost soul cliché at a cocktail party who is asked about the film or novel he talks about year in and year out that will never be complete.

His professional failures and roads not taken were foremost on his mind. He had become much too good at beating himself up. To combat what felt like a low-grade depression, he started looking at himself in the mirror every morning and repeating the words, "I am my *future* self." There was no time left to wait for a stronger, braver person to appear and do all the heavy lifting. If there were sacrifices and changes to be made (that had no guarantee of working out, but that at least offered the possibility of a more satisfying and fulfilling existence) they had to be made *now*. Augie had to start shifting his thoughts and behavior – *now* - before it was too late. The mental beatings had to stop, as they continued day in and day out. They were *exhausting*.

Augie knew what reactions to expect from people who watched his D grade cable reality television shows. The bar was set low. But anticipating the reactions from an audience regarding his own thoughts and ideas up on screen, his attempts to be taken seriously, was terrifying. Putting himself "out there" would force him to face many of his fears and insecurities. Would he have the "goods?" Did he ever have the "goods" or is he just that cliché? Was he okay with failing? Was he okay with just trying?

With three kids and a mortgage in Chappaqua, he knew this dream had nothing to do with a "make a movie, get rich quick scheme." He had been in the entertainment business long enough to know that it rarely happened like that. He just wanted to do it, not just talk about making a film – but to "put it in the can," and complete it.

Was his dream to be an artist selfish? Maybe, his wife definitely thought so, but he had yet to be brave enough to change his life to such a degree to be an artist. With so many arguments at home regarding money and his career there was no way he could justify a *Pied-a-terre* in NYC to his wife. She HATED Liz Street.

He did try to show enthusiasm for his best friend - he did. He acknowledged JR's burst of energy since meeting his new wife, that he appeared younger, and more optimistic than his normally cynical self. He exuded lightness and talked about the *future*. JR's self-imposed rut since graduating college was over, that was a fact. It was selfish for Augie to want to keep the JR from twenty years ago suspended in time. He had to let JR go, he had to let Liz Street go - but *after* this weekend.

Augie was fair skinned, with a slightly wrinkled face covered in a few pale moles. One night after work in Hell's Kitchen a drunken girl, loudly chomping on a hot dog at Rudy's on Ninth Avenue, called him a *dead ringer for Ewan Macgregor*. Easily influenced by the power of suggestion, this chance encounter motivated Augie to dress in a shirtless, glam rock "Velvet Goldmine" costume that Halloween, with lycra hot pants, platform shoes, and glitter covering him from head to toe. (His daughter enjoyed playing with the black feather boa.) Oh, how he still loved to shock people! He loved to pretend he was someone else – a character.

Publicly, Augie was a husband, a father, and a reality television shows Producer, a show-off. Privately, he was a voyeur, a Momma's boy, and a tantric masturbator. He loved to fantasize, and he'd always enjoyed watching others. This attribute should have been leveraged to make him a great film director, but instead it made him emotionally distant during sex. He often imagined himself in a scene from one of his favorite movies, or a new one that he invented on the spot. Unfortunately, his lover was the last to know, as it wasn't a *shared* fantasy. He never thought anyone could comprehend where he was coming from or how his mind worked; so many movies, books, songs, photographs and paintings were stuck in his head, influencing his life constantly. But he was lonelier without an outlet, or person, to share these ideas with.

That twilight signaled the end of a longer countdown weighing heavily on his mind, twenty-four-seven all that past week. It had made him compartmentalize and deny the impending loss of Liz Street. It had made him downplay the excitement of his best friend's surprise wedding. It had made him question himself a thousand different ways.

Men At Work's song "It's a Mistake" played, and then quickly ended, in the stereo inside his brain. Augie's days often progressed with a private, interior soundtrack playing. The stereo was a Technics with a heavy volume dial. *No,* he thought, *it's not.*

"Are you sure you won't be bored?" Jacob Reynolds, (affectionately known as "JR") now a newlywed, asked, entering the driver's seat.

JR was six feet tall with thick salt and pepper dark brown hair and brown eyes. He had bushy black eyebrows and a near permanent five o'clock shadow. He was known in Uptown singles social circles as the "Jewish George Clooney." A "gentleman" in the economic sense, he never had to work for a living, unlike Augie who not only supported a wife and kids, but his mother and sister.

"I'll give the doorman a double to help me bring it up to my new place," JR told him.

"Oh, so he gets twenty dollars out of you and I only get a hernia," Augie teased.

"You've had thousands of dollars' worth of free lodging on Liz Street. You owe *me* buddy. At least now you can't mooch off my good will anymore."

"You're a regular Roosevelt, JR. *Noblesse Oblige!*"

For over twenty years, JR enjoyed his apartment on Elizabeth Street. Augie first found the apartment back in 1993, following their college graduation. Martin Scorsese's family lived across the street, and Augie was in the process of stalking them. Raised by a genteel Southern mother, Augie insisted on helping Nonna Girardi carry her groceries and was awarded first dibs on her large, empty apartment.

"I forgot that term, *Noblesse Oblige.* I promised my mother that I'd get Stacy on some kind of Board soon…maybe the Junior League?" JR answered Augie, sitting in his truck outside Liz Street.

"And that my friend are what's known as *white people problems.*"

"*White people problems,*" JR snickered.

"Hey, I found this place, remember? Cheap rent, no Broker fee, and an endless supply of home cooked meals by Mrs. Girardi."

The brand new, gold band on JR's left hand broke Augie's concentration for a moment. Then he looked down at his own wedding band.

"New York's dead on the weekends," JR added, pulling some keys off of his key chain and handing them to Augie, "Moving truck will be back on Monday, so please let them in. I'll be on a beach."

"On your honeymoon," Augie finished.

"God, that sounds weird!" JR beamed. "Can you believe Stacy spent seven grand on a dress for City Hall? City Hall, Augie! I told her I didn't want a big wedding, because of the age difference and everything, and that I didn't want to make a scene. Seven grand!"

"And to think, all your old girlfriends used to tiptoe over your money. Then you meet a certified *gold digger...*" Augie began.

"Hey, that's my wife!" JR yelled.

"She is, though," Augie joked.

"No. She's honest and real, I respect her. Not that I don't have an air tight pre-nup," JR joked back.

"Well, maybe she was the type of girl you wanted all along? Maybe that's why this has all happened later in your life" Augie said.

"I'm *so* knocking her up in St. Barths," JR boasted.

"Wait, you can still get it up?"

"Believe me, for a twenty-two year old girl you can get it up."

"Oh shit, I thought she was at least twenty-five. Has she even graduated college?"

"She's on the six-year plan at Hunter."

"Well, you went four and a half years."

"She's the one, Augie. It just is."

"I believe you. You've never said that about a girl before, and the fact that you're spending money on her..."

"Oh my God, you'll love this, the bank called me, worried about the *suspicious activity* in my accounts."

"I'm sure they did!"

"Is it wrong that I finally met someone I want to spoil? Other than you? Don't be jealous now."

"No, no – I'm happy for you. Didn't I say that before? HAPPY. Now will you please go home and get your dick sucked by your new wife? Don't call me, even though I know you're going to miss me, everything's under control here."

"Hey, did you take a stroll down sex memory lane, right before you got hitched?"

"*Sex memory lane*? No."

"Lying fucking bastard. I know you did. I did, and you know who came to mind as a top performer? You'll never guess!"

"No idea"

"Louise! Louise from…"

"College?" Augie blurted as this was too odd that JR was talking about college girls, that one specifically this day of all days. "She treated you like garbage, remember?"

"And I fucking loved it."

"You did."

"Don't know why you're defending her, you treated her roommate like shit and she loved you.

What's her name?"

"Benny…" Augie answered. He was saying her name aloud, to JR. Did JR *know* something?

"When someone lets you treat them like that, it's impossible to love them. You could have never loved that girl…"

"*Benny*." What was going on here?

"You have to respect someone to love them, or at least, that's what I've learned."

"You respect Stacy…the twenty-two year old,"

"She nearly broke the Sports book at Caesars Palace, Augie. Of course I respect her!"

13

"But seriously, St. Barths, in the summer?" Augie asked, changing the subject, still paranoid about JR's college reference. Sweat dripped down from his forehead, stinging his eyes. He felt dizzy, he needed to eat something. But it was *so* hot...

"You know I only do off-season with the locals," JR, oblivious, quipped.

"Me, too," Augie agreed; he had to be different, not the *norm.*

"Have fun in the sleepy city. Hey, just so you know, the air conditioning is on the fritz."

"You bastard, why couldn't you get it fixed?"

"I don't live here anymore, remember? I haven't lived here in months! I might be touring *preschools* this spring. I'm trying to grow up. Make my own kid instead of acting like one. Believe me, I'll catch up to you sooner than you can say, "demon spawn." I even stopped smoking pot a month ago, hoping the boys can swim."

"Wow, this girl *has* changed you."

"Has it been so long, Augie, that you can't remember when a girl *changes you?*"

2

Augie first arrived in New York after college to give birth to his alter ego- the city living Auteur. In the end, he felt like he failed. He left a few years later to start over in a new country, which completely pushed his life in another direction. Broke and frustrated he hadn't made any progress as a filmmaker in New York, he decided to teach English in Japan like his cousin had before him. And, just like his cousin, the woman he brought back would become his wife. He had plenty of money now, but he never took the time to invest in his creative ideas – only those of others who were young and inspired and reminded Augie of those first years on Elizabeth Street.

Why was pleasure so hard to allow yourself when you were forty, he wondered? Once you have a car, a house, the kids, the passport stamped, what else is there? Gatsby's green light to Augie wasn't money - it was art - to be an artist - a feature filmmaker, specifically. Just to even pretend to live in New York City (verses the suburbs) brought so much pleasure to Augie that he thought he might explode with happiness.

Sometimes, when JR was out of town, Augie would stay on Liz Street for the night by himself and act like he *was* that artist. When he woke up in the morning he felt energized. The high he received from being on Liz Street was always short-lived, but magnificent.

Since turning forty and then a few years passing after that, the *carpe diem* clock began to tick louder, until Augie realized he was alone and up in outer space. He was like David Bowie's *Major Tom* looking for some hand to reach out and grab him, and offer him a safe landing back to earth. For a few years, he tried to find a purpose outside and greater than the mechanics of day-to-day, and dreamed of earning a living with very little business to it although he was on the business side of things as a producer. Just like waiting to lose his virginity, or taking someone else's years later, he had an idea in his head, based on art, on what love and happiness look like. And for years as he watched his family grow, he knew what it felt like. But that feeling dwindled more and more as his life was more about business and less about family. The gray hairs came in more often than he liked (even on his knuckles) and after a Saturday soccer game, he had to take a long hot bath and Advil and convince himself he could do it again the next weekend without breaking an ankle.

He was convinced there was more to conquer, achieve and experience in his life, there had to be. He was already giddy since a day into hanging out with JR made his abdominals hurt from laughing so much. All he wanted to do was confide in his friend, but he thought he wasn't ready for JR to punch him in the proverbial gut with his disapproval. JR had so much to look forward to. Augie wanted the same thing.

All his couples' therapist told him was, "If you change who you are, your partner might not want to be married to the person you change into." Augie argued that the artist was who he had been all along; the New Yorker, the coffeehouse patron, the street photographer, the *auteur*. "You're not a kid anymore" was all his wife said in response. So he vowed not to speak to anyone about his aspirations anymore. He couldn't bear to hear anymore "no's". There was enough "no, I don't feel like it tonight" in his bedroom. Even his kids were telling him "no thanks, Dad. I've got other plans."

"I used to be a stallion!" he would tell himself in the mirror, "go all night!" "I could flirt with anyone!"

3

When Augie arrived at the apartment, his t-shirt was drenched. Four-floor walk-ups were good for his legs but he wondered if he should take a shower. He kept forgetting there was a working elevator in the building now.

It was nearly eight o'clock on the Grandfather clock on the wall next to a framed **American Gigolo** film poster. He remembered his hero for a moment, Paul Schrader, writer of **Taxi Driver** and **Raging Bull,** both directed by Scorsese. *That's my poster,* he thought, *I'll take it home with me.* Flights getting into LaGuardia were always late. He wondered if he should run across the street to Café Habana for a quick Cuban coffee. *Better not,* he thought. *I already seem a little jumpy...better leave the poster, too, there's no way she'll let me hang that thing in the house.*

The two rear bedrooms were empty except for boxes. The rest of the apartment was sparsely decorated, with only a full-size mattress on the living room floor and a set of high-thread-count white sheets - a gift left by JR's new wife who always insisted on the finer things. Like seven thousand dollar

Vera Wang dresses for five-minute civil service ceremonies or fifty thousand dollar emerald cut diamonds from Tiffany. Everyone from his mother to Nonna Girardi told JR that he could have scored the same ring, without a Fifth Avenue label, from the Diamond District for half the price.

A stereo with turntables and a cheap CD player stood atop a flimsy card table. The flat screen TV and a DVD player rested on the floor. He had insisted that the TV remain while he housesat. Not only was television his line of work, but he was addicted to it. A few crates of records still sat by the brick wall under the windows that faced west and had a glimmer of the sunset left on the worn down, wooden floor. He fingered through the first crate of records until he found something he liked –

Charlotte Dada's cover of the Beatles' song "Don't Let Me Down." *Better than the Beatles,* he thought.

He began to strip off his clothes, bathing in the last few minutes of sun still pouring through the windows of the apartment, his old, now *very* old, apartment that was his to enjoy for this final weekend. It was the end of an era and, maybe the beginning of a new one?

He smelled his armpits, the hair beneath them tickled his big nose and he winced. He threw his sweat-soaked nylon shorts on the floor and remembered that golden morning with JR, kicking the soccer ball on the West side pitch in Central Park beside the French bakery Le Pain Quotidien, feeling so strong. He drifted off, and forgot, for a moment or two, his age. That was the biggest draw of Elizabeth Street – escape and time travel.

He gave a big stretch up to the fourteen-foot ceiling and noticed his body in the giant dressing mirror in the corner that faced the bed. *Do I look the same?* He thought, *would she look the same?* The mention of *she* started his heart racing and he began to feel the first tingles of an erection. The song didn't help. A mix tape, 1995, *hers*. He bought the album, shortly after, at the now defunct Tower Records, not telling her. JR called dibs on the album when Augie moved out and left the country to teach English in Japan. A last ditch effort to "find himself" the life of the artist having been "shelfed" for financial reasons. Since he was about to leave the country at the time, he didn't put up much of a fight. He didn't want to store it at his mom's house. In fact, he never wanted to see it, or hear it, again - until tonight.

Augie pumped the fancy French soap from L'Occtaine, another Stacy plus, and lathered his body. He began to imagine her open mouth. Would there be lines now? Would she notice *his*? He saw pictures of her. *That's what the Internet was good for - pictures.* Lines or no lines, it didn't matter. The thought of her willing, anxious, open mouth beneath him made his blood pump faster. Feeling a slight pain of guilt for the fantasy but grateful for the reliability of his equipment, he started to touch himself.

It was one thing to fantasize about a celebrity; it was another to fantasize about a real person. He imagined himself twenty years younger and suddenly felt his hands stroking her long, soft, hair back as she positioned him in her open mouth while on her knees like at a pew in church, worshipping.

The girl he imagined - *Benny* – was self-conscious. Embarrassed from the choking and the drooling, stymied by his size, this was the first time she had ever put her mouth on it – *Augie's it* –or any man's *it*. He watched her try her best at wanting to please him, without hurting him with her teeth.

She attempted to hide her face behind her long hair, as if that might relieve some of the shame. When he shifted his eyes down to hers in the dark, he could feel her whole body tremble through her hands on his bare thighs. He had given her that name – *Benny*. It was *his* name for her.

The best part of this memory was this act was of her own volition. For once he wasn't forcing his body on hers, she wanted to reciprocate. She even asked, whispered, *can I try touching you now?* He imagined her stuffed full with nervous brown eyes opening and making contact with his, only once; as if to ask if she was doing this right. Then she leaned back, caught her breath and took him into both of her hands and asked, *did that feel good? Did I make you feel good?* (She claimed that all she ever wanted was to make him *feel good.*) As if frozen in time, he squeezed and stroked himself – one final time, letting loose against the granite shower wall, slamming it with his hand while the crisscrossing jets of water washed it all clean. Then he remembered her telling him – in tears, *but I don't ever want to know what it's like to be with another man. I only want to be naked with you.*

He remembered how intelligent she was and how she remembered everything. It wasn't necessarily anything she said, outright, it was the way she carried herself, the way she smiled around strangers and started conversations with them, walked blind people across busy streets and returned missing children to distraught mothers. She had a profound *naiveté*. She always seemed younger and child-like, as if she still believed in Santa Claus. Conversely, she was incredibly self-aware and the words she gifted him were always alarming, pointed, and edgy–sharp as tacks, which secretly caused his heart to race. But he liked that, he needed that. It was almost a contest between the two of them. Who could rile the other one up first? Or get deep into the other's brain? Or into an abstract space where an artist's imagination never ceases and is always looking for both stimulation and release. A lonely place that was hoping for a visitor.

The details Benny noticed about Augie made him feel important, and alive. He recalled his English teacher's lecture, "To name it, is to give it life," and that, that's what it felt like when he was with her, or so he remembered from just a few recent phone conversations and emails – *alive*.

Why had he never said this to her before? JR was right; he had treated her like shit.

Benny had always taken him, and his dreams and goals, so *seriously*. As if he might actually realize them. He thought, *there is nothing more intimate than being in someone else's thoughts, on someone else's mind, in their fantasies. To share thoughts, to share words.*

After a long period of being married, and now in his early forties, he was redefining what being close to someone meant. Maybe it said something about his marriage that he started to imagine something else, something *better*. Maybe that's why he so quickly called Benny after nearly a ten-year absence? She had emailed him a chapter from her novel, about *him*, about *them*. Was she fishing? It didn't matter. There was a story out there – starring *him!* And it was written by Benny, the girl who said she could never love anyone but him, the girl who at one time had been his biggest fan. The girl who knew all of his details, the best ones! The girl who gave her body and even her love to him, first, before anyone else. That girl, the one he thought hated him, was back.

Spending time alone with her, now, as a grown woman, frightened him. Shortly after she was married to someone else he'd called her, not trying to fuck with her head (or so he believed) but to say he would be in her hometown over Christmas, by himself, and could he *take her out for a drink?* And she refused him. Benny never refused him! She told him *I don't think we should speak anymore, Augie, I, I, I don't think it would be appropriate.* After years of stringing her along, she had put the kibosh on his *fishing.*

He thought he would never hear from her again after that call, and correctly assumed that she would never engage in social networking with old lovers. He could hear her patronize that it was *the least romantic thing one could do,* that Jane Austen would be mortified. He respected her for this, too. So, ten years passed and then—an email. Augie received an email, Benny had written a novel!

She had always spoken about her desire to be a writer and now she was one. She had *put it in the can!* When they were younger, she sent him her stories for fun, and now - a novel. The email included a sample chapter with characters more than similar to the two of them in college. She asked, not trying to fuck with his mind (or so she believed) would he be okay with her *publishing it* in the event that she was fortunate enough to get to that point?

Slowly but surely, they became friends again. Even though one had fallen for the other many years ago and it wasn't reciprocated. Even though both appeared to still be married. Benny's book was providing an opportunity to live vicariously through characters that just happened to be younger versions of them.

Augie was known for bringing Benny out of her shell. She "blossomed" from their lovemaking. He knew it, and she knew it, too. He was never really convinced, deep down, that she loved him. He let her say it, but he knew she had never gotten close enough to him to be able to. It was a schoolgirl crush. He may have found a way to get her to open up to him, but he kept most of his own history to himself. He gave her scraps – here and there – to make a point- or to get her to trust him enough to reveal more of herself - to get beneath her layers. The more she struggled to speak aloud her own history, fears, and desires, the more turned on he was by her and the closer he wanted to be to her. Augie wanted desperately to be loved for the person inside of himself that had been hiding through great "performances." He wanted to be someone else's Benny. But he didn't think it possible. He observed her and her reveals and her awkwardness. Every time he pushed her to try something new, he felt the pangs of victory. He felt like her creator. Rather than embracing Benny as a girlfriend once he realized her smiles at other boys made him jealous, he immediately dammed whatever watershed of feeling was about to explode and told her their sexual experiment between friends was *over.*

So, even if she didn't love him, she was attached to him, because he knew and she knew, he changed her life. He gave her a new beginning, her beginning as a woman. He had power over her. Maybe Benny could bring him out of this new shell and he could blossom. He would use her again – just like he was old enough now to admit that he had used her twenty years prior, and in the years in between now and then - to see himself through the eyes of someone who said yes to him–no matter what.

He remembered his English classes, in both high school and college, and the desperate attempts, during carpe diem lectures of lecturers to inspire their class into action. Keats dropped dead before reaching thirty of tuberculosis but at least he left the world with his poetry. The red eyed regret in the eyes of his mature teachers, when hearing a young student recite Andrew Marvell's "To His Coy Mistress," were ever present in his mind now. They knew something he didn't know back then. And now he shared their regret.

So what if those former lovers and former friends wanted to recreate those moments of not only great sentiment, but of pleasure - beyond the printed page? Wasn't that a special and life affirming time in both of their lives? He had been Benny's *first lover*, remember? Taught her *everything*...Well, wouldn't it be worth experiencing all over again? Just for one weekend – *this* weekend – and step back in time? Just like it happened in the book. Just like it happened in college. *How about on Elizabeth Street? I've got the place to myself,* he told her. *I'll buy your ticket...* And just like old times, she said...*yes.* They hadn't been lovers in twenty years. But he asked and she said yes. Neither one questioned why the other one would say yes or what their lives were like apart. They were beginning to exist in a bubble, but in their minds, in their *simultaneous and secretly shared fantasy worlds*, they always had anyway. He asked. She said yes. It was on.

But this wasn't just any girl. It was Benny. The childish and overly sensitive, well-read girl with pin-up curves under messy long hair, glasses and layers of clothing. The girl who said she would "love him forever." Was it possible that she still felt that way? Would they still enjoy one another's company as much as they did when they were kids, knowing just how to get under one another's skin and making each other crack up? When they were friends who just happened to become lovers, and then went back to just friends? Would she ever forgive him for stealing her heart out of her chest and squeezing it like a ripe tomato? For torturing her and not taking her seriously and taking her love and generosity for granted? How could he make it up to her? He was going to try doing just that – this weekend. Perhaps he would reset his karma.

Augie sat on the shower floor and let the hot water push down on his head and run over his eyelids. He tried to not think about his life outside New York for a few minutes. He was a huge flirt and had been given more than a handful of chances to have an affair over the years, but never pursued the offers. He never wanted to be cliché. He couldn't be cliché! Cliché was the slow and painful death of the artist. His life outside of his family and job *had to* be unique...*had to* be one-of-a-kind. Who was more exotic than Benny? A girl who grew up struggling in the subterranean underworld of racetracks, poolrooms and casinos, yet earned herself a full ride to a private university? A girl who was urban to Augie's suburban? She was the fresh, new toy that had given herself to him so willingly at twenty years old, that he was able to mold in his own image and play with as he directed? How did he find a fresh flower such as her that had barely kissed a boy, much less been touched, or had seen a naked body, or shown anyone hers?

Now *that* was unique. *That* was one-of-a-kind. That was the kind of lover *worthy* of a great artist. Definitely not cliché. She would never, ever forget him, and those first times. He was an artist once and he had created something – Benny, the *woman.*

He heard his phone vibrate. It was a text. He turned off the luxury shower, and grabbed a towel, throwing it around his waist. He nervously lifted the phone to see a text from an unknown number "Landed" was all it said. "I'm here" he texted back. He closed the phone and looked at himself in the steam covered mirror. *I can do this,* he thought. *I am supposed to do this.*

4

enny had not eaten more than 700 calories a day for the past 27 days. It was not to lose weight; she had always had a desirable, round figure. She was tall, with boobs, a bottom and muscles. She liked to run and play pick-up basketball games with the boys at the college gymnasium or beside the playground - while her kids played on the swings. The players thought she was crazy. But once they saw past her hot pink leather Nike high tops and how her height benefited a great rebound, they would pick her for their team. She was always competitive with men. She especially liked telling them they were pieces of shit.

Her temporary anorexia was out of nerves. She was addicted to feeling hungry. To Cassandra Bennett, hunger meant *desire*. It meant having a connection to her younger self – the young Benny, who desired everything but did not know how to satisfy herself. All she had was hunger. When someone put their hands on her skin or whispered in her ear, she felt it in more than one way. It wasn't simple. *Who was she kidding*, she thought, *there was no someone, there was just-him.*

Benny had a girlfriend, Tara, who told her that if she held her pee in long enough, she could give herself an orgasm. Holding it in caused her to sweat, tingle and spasm. Once she finally let go, and gave in to her need to pee, Tara would walk out of a bathroom with a smile on her face.

"I told you so," she would brag.

"You're going to get a UTI," Benny chastised.

Benny's reaction to hunger was slightly the same. By not giving in to her hunger and by remaining in a near constant state of desire, once she did relieve herself, she believed that her body would experience pleasure. And this was something she wanted badly. She wanted lightness again and lightness she got from seven hundred calories a day for twenty-seven days.

Benny was grateful for the smooth flight from Miami to New York City. She upgraded her flight with hoarded frequent flier miles. She always told herself, *if this plane's going down, I'm going to be buzzed off Bloody Mary's in first class.* She also had a constant need to collect herself in the restroom. To close the door, any door it seemed, lock it, and be by herself. It was in these tight, safe spaces that Benny felt comfortable, protected and safe. If the ride was bumpy she needed to be close to the bathroom. Fueled by her OCD, she made countless darts to her safe haven. Once inside, if it was dirty or messy, she fought every urge within herself not to clean it.

Feeling slightly more relaxed from the vodka, combined with a low tolerance from her starvation diet, she looked in the First Class bathroom mirror. She admired her straight upper teeth and hidden crooked lower ones and told herself she *didn't look half bad for forty.* Eyes quickly fading into her reflection, she began to remember the night that Augie

Baxter became more than a friend. She imagined lying on her back and the cold creeping goose bumps on her warm skin as he kissed up her bare navel, gently stroking her skin with his fingers as his mouth worked his way up to her large, heavy breasts. She had gone this far. *Let him inside her bedroom! Inside her house, late at night, drunk!* It was too late not to trust him. She kept telling him at the bar, not to come over and that it was *a bad idea.* But he wouldn't listen. He pushed her verbally and showed up anyway, without knocking and just letting himself in as if he owned the place. He walked right into her bedroom, undressed her and turned out her light, even after she told him she was a virgin. She had never seen him smile so wide after hearing that word, *virgin.* It was as if the Rangers had won the Stanley Cup and a sequel to **Goodfellas** had been announced on the same day. He was *that* happy.

Benny caressed his freshly shorn locks with her hands and then glided her fingertips over the back of his earlobes. She couldn't believe how soft they felt. She didn't know if she was supposed to keep her eyes open or closed while being touched. When his lips made it up and onto her upper body, she enjoyed a tingling beneath her belly button and felt a heretofore unknown object forcefully press into her inner thigh, through his clothes which shocked her. Eventually, his hard body would leave bruises on her soft body.

A gentle pulling on her nipple made her breath erratic and made her swivel her hips. He responded by pressing his body down harder on her. He was fully on top of her now, her legs still close together, yet he was pushing them apart instinctively with his knees. She was still too captivated by his sucking to stop him. There was too much going on in her body, to all her body parts and at the same time. Once she acknowledged a touch, or a brand new feeling in one part of her body, he would rub up against another. As soon as she managed to cover a piece of her bare body with fabric, he would remove another article of clothing; unbuttoning buttons, unzipping zippers and unlocking latches. She decided that she was drunk or that he was an octopus. Shocked and trembling, she whispered, *"Augie, I can't believe you're here."*

So this was what it was like to have a man lay on top of her. This is what it felt like to turn a man on. This is what his body felt like: wider, denser, heavier than hers. There were so many muscles – biceps, triceps, quads, glutes – all in top, tight form – *bulging*. As he rubbed his lower body up against her she felt his strong soccer thighs on top of her soft, milky thighs. After a few minutes, she felt something long, thick, and hard between his legs. That object, too, was rubbing up against her. Is it supposed to be *that* big? Something that heretofore had never been a part of this relationship, a part of this friendship, an erection. Her body was turning him on. She could do this to a *man*. She could do this to *him*. She felt like a *woman*.

She was twenty and a Junior in college. She had never had a man in her bed before. She had never been naked or been touched. Kissed, only twice before and in the upright position. Even her closest girlfriends had not seen her naked. No one had. She had made sure of it.

Until then, Benny had no idea how heavy his body was, how dense with muscle or how much it pushed her down, *deep* into her cheap, old mattress. As his breathing became heavier, she sighed as she opened her eyes and looked down at him. Finally, in the dark, his eyes looked up at hers. His smile looked like a mischievous little boy's.

She was astonished that this was happening - not only *to* her, but *by Augie Baxter.* He was looking at her bare chest and she was feeling his *penis.* Twenty years of sleeping in a bed alone, twenty years of changing clothes behind closed doors. And now...*this?* She was expressing herself as a girl yet she questioned if her body was too sensitive, too responsive to his touch. She was ashamed for actually wanting him between her legs. She enjoyed the feeling of him pressing down on her, even with his clothes on. She could have easily gone all the way with him that first night. But she didn't and he didn't try.

Was he really kissing Benny? Was he really in her bed? He still seemed surprised by how the evening had progressed and would stop touching her once in a while just to catch his breath and look at her, looking at him, desperate for instruction and more kisses. Why did he have to get so drunk that night in order to be brave enough to ask if he could go home with her? Although he never asked her specifically– he just told her – and didn't take no for an answer. Why did he make it seem like a joke or like he was trying to shock her by demanding this, when it wasn't a joke. The first time they were introduced, at the start of college, he tried to hit on her, but she was so naïve and shy and clueless that she had never realized it. She had only the most sincere blank expression to offer him after hearing his thinly veiled sex jokes, and gratefully, privately, he had been saved the embarrassment of being turned down. When he did actually get to fool around with her, he would present it to JR, and even to her, as just a drunken, silly night instead of the rehearsed performance that it privately was.

Benny racked her brain trying to come up with an explanation as to why he was in her bed. Friends, classmates, at times adversaries, and now they were getting naked – just like she had read about in **Lady Chatterly's Lover,** just like she had watched in **Body Heat** and just like the lyrics to nearly every Prince song she had ever heard, specifically – **It** from the **Sign of The Times** album. For all of the years, starting with puberty, and up until that night, art was the only means available for her to experience sexuality, although only lightly and vicariously through her imagination. She hadn't even started touching herself yet. But now the real thing was happening and she figured out why so much great art was inspired by it! And kissing! *How marvelous* she cheered privately. I want to kiss every single day! Cheeks sore from smiling so much, she could now concretely argue that flesh and blood was better than art.

Augie pushed himself onto his elbows and brought his open mouth up to hers. Her entire body tingled when his tongue first touched hers. He whispered into her ear, *Benny, I love your body* and then grinded up against her, sweating from his khakis and the heavy down comforter she kept covering herself with. No one had ever said this to her before – *I love your body.* This revelation went right through her, over and over again, moistening and opening her whole body up to his. She couldn't stop trembling as she thought about the enormity of it all. This night, all these first times. How her body could react to another's. He kept saying her name over and over. Panting and excited he unwrapped her like the first present on Christmas morning... *Benny, Benny...*

His wet and heavy breathing against her ear caused her to arch her back even more and he was able to spread her legs slightly as she wiggled beneath him and he completely undressed her. She smiled and did her best to kiss him back. In the darkness of her cold college bedroom, she wanted to feel everything and be in the moment. She also wanted to watch everything that was happening to her. It was her natural instinct to watch and to be an observer. All of those years sitting quietly in a corner honed her talent for acquiring details, the details that impressed Augie. As much as she hated to admit it, she was a *voyeur* just like him.

He gently placed his hand over her pubic hair and then firmly slipped one finger inside, circling within her. He experienced a lot of resistance and the fright of Benny bolting upright on the bed and screaming "WHAT ARE YOU DOING?"

She couldn't believe how good it felt to have something, someone inside of her, but was embarrassed. She also didn't want him to think she was going to sleep with him or that she was leading him on.

He sat up on his knees, laughed and looked down at her bare body that was drenched in sweat.

"You okay there, Benny?" he asked sarcastically. *"You're...getting worked up."*

"That's not funny!" she answered.

He grabbed the fat, black down comforter and threw it on the floor. Then, he took off his t-shirt. She noticed that his *dick* was coming up and out the top of his khakis. It was large and hard and sticking straight out and half-way up his chest. She looked away, she didn't want to think of what she was supposed to do next. He grabbed her hand, led it to the top of his pants, making her feel the head. The skin felt soft and velvety. Then he placed her hand on the top button of his pants and squeezed her fingers until they unbuttoned. Next, he guided her hand to his pant zipper and made her pull it down as he kept his hand over her own. He placed both of her hands on the sides of his waist and together, they pushed his pants off. She shook and her heart raced as she saw him completely naked - despite the dark of her room. She had never seen a naked man before. "*Oh my God*" she mouthed in the dark... frightened...flustered. He pinned her arms down at her sides and immediately buried his face and tongue between her legs. It tickled at first. The more she squirmed, the tighter his grip was on her arms and hips, locking her into place until she eventually settled down and he heard only her moaning. She thought it felt like lying on the beach on your back with the warmest of waves of water covering your body over and over again. She crossed the threshold, of physical intimacy at least, with Augie. He may have frightened her a little with his domi-nance, but his mouth felt so good. *He could make her body feel so good!* She wished she could relax for just one moment and allow herself to enjoy it fully, enjoy him and stop fighting it. There were more warm waves...

Benny's panties were wet now as she stood in the dirty American Airlines' lavatory. Hot from the poorly ventilated closet, and bright red from the Bloody Marys, she patted a bead of sweat that had formed on her chest with a tissue. Hungry for air, her jaw dropped and her mouth widened. She began to take short, shallow breaths like a panting dog does after a long run. For a moment, the mini-metal fixtures seemed to shift out of her line of vision. *Alcohol*, she reasoned as she opened the small door back out to the cabin.

She returned to her first class seat beside a very tan Octogenarian male who wore a solid gold watch and neon white Stan Smith's. He fell asleep, with headphones intact, during an old **Seinfeld** episode. It was the one where Jerry and

Elaine sleep with one another and Elaine makes him choose between friendship or sex. It was Benny's favorite.

Each time the flight attendant made her rounds down the aisle, she lifted her empty glass and the attendant quickly made her way back to fill it. As she sipped, she thought about the Kinko's bound copy of her novel that she had tucked in the seat pocket in front of her that she hadn't shown to anyone yet. She knew she couldn't let anyone who knew her read it, maybe *ever*. It was too revealing, she thought. No, she knew it was. It might get her into trouble. When she was younger, it was Augie who provided the support and encouragement she needed to keep writing. But this go around, no one had read her entire manuscript, and he had only read a single chapter.

Benny had her IPad loaded with The Hollywood Reporter and the snippet on Augie's upcoming one hour reality show *Basketball Baby Momma Bastards*. She wanted to be well versed so that she could effectively tell him what utter crap it was going to be. She would argue: how his work only attracted the lowest common denominator and that he had sold his soul, to all ghastly of occupations - *television*. She would also remind him that she did not own a television, did not watch television except for important sporting events that she bet her much harder-to-earn-than-his-money on and that she preferred storytelling via public radio, and no, that wasn't *pretentious*. This monologue was prepared and rehearsed. The sleeping man beside her could not tell she was talking to herself, reciting it. The flight attendant ignored it.

Benny would also relay how television turns all great minds into mush – including his. Then she would ask him to recite all of the extremely difficult to recall names of **The Brothers Karamazov**. "AHA!" she would remark with a pointer finger pointing up at the sky, "See? MUSH! I bet you know the entire cast of Aaron Spelling's **Love Boat** though, *don't you?*" She would revisit his claim, that no one had ever watched as much television as he had and how that was not something to brag about. He stayed up all night watching TV since he was a young boy, he told her. You could test me, like **Name That Tune,** but with a few scenes of a show, and I could identify it, he bragged.

"And *this* is supposed to impress me?" she'd argue, "I thought you were smart, intelligent. You read *books*! That's why I liked talking to you! But you, and anyone like you, *making television*, should be thrown in jail for poisoning the minds of America - of the world! Thrown in jail! No possibility of parole! Locked in a cold, dark, dank cell for all eternity!!!" Applause.

And this, the well planned Hollywood Reporter, Dostoyevsky and a few obvious Aaron Spelling references was how she planned on telling Augie that she *loved him more than any other person in the entire world–still.* In fact, she would never love anyone more than she loved him. She had tried, but failed. Her resolve was that if there was not some way for them to realize a life together in old age, arguing over *her* books and *his* television, she was going to start sleeping with women. In India. Like if Julia Roberts in the movie **Eat, Pray, Love** was a lesbian. Yes, that would be her. Even though she had had the lesbian dream and it just didn't work. She just stared down at another woman's private parts and put her hands up, "I *tried*." Then she apologized to the naked lesbian, and feeling guilty, offered to give the lesbian a ride home.

Her emotions were always scattered. Maybe the dream could offer her some insight about her relationship with her own body, her fear of being uninhibited and her knowing that she had always kept herself from truly letting go. Single for the past two and a half years, no one had even seen her in her panties other than her aesthetician, much less, taken her for a *ride* of any kind. She knew she was a girl that could go bananas after having sex, like throw shit, scream and have to visit a therapist immediately. Or at least that was her memory of sex before her ex-husband, that was her memory of sex with Augie. As much as she wanted to have sex "for fun," she could never go through with it. She told her best friend and room-mate from Tulane, Louise, "I don't see what's fun about a psychotic breakdown?"

Two opportunities presented themselves since becoming single which she turned down after the first kiss. She thought kissing was more important than sex and if it didn't immediately feel good, it was a sign. Everything up until the sex part was what she lived for. And she wanted sex itself to be just as incredible as all the flirting and teasing preceding. She already knew how to get herself off simply by retreating into her imagination. Someone would have to share that private world with her if she was ever going to have the type of sex she wanted, the type of intimacy she wanted and the type of love she wanted. She knew that shared, private worlds could exist. They had always existed with Augie. This didn't mean he would leave his wife for her, or that he thought this weekend was more than what it was, "fun." But after two and a half years of being single, after tears, identity struggles, and major life changes, Cassandra Bennett needed "fun." She deserved some fun. Augie simply happened to ask to see her at the right time, this time, and she said yes. Writing a novel was an emotional release for Benny, a blueprint for a better life, the architect of her future and of all her dreams coming true, just like she had laid out in that novel. That, to Benny was the power of being a writer, of being a "creator." It wasn't just the means to live vicariously through fiction, it was about creating *hope.*

For a second, she thought the lesbian bit might turn Augie on. If that didn't work, she was prepared with a "Is your dick still so big I can't get my lips around it?" But no, she wouldn't say *that.* He might faint. That wasn't the *old* Benny talking, the sexually repressed girl who thought she didn't deserve anything, who had trouble speaking in public, who wasn't comfortable in her own skin. No, not her. This was the *new* Benny talking–her alter ego-who after twenty years of hibernation, could say "Fuck you, motherfucker!" without batting an eye or demand the seat up front by the window at a restaurant. She had only started experimenting with new Benny in her manuscript, and now, on this trip to New York, she was going to act like new Benny. Or, at least try to act like her.

Benny plugged in her flash drive and downloaded a photo that was almost twenty years old. It was Augie on the Quad at college sporting a crew cut and green, nylon soccer shorts. His x-ray vision eyes made her feel naked and vulnerable. He was flirting with her even in the picture.

5

Augie didn't grow up with a man around the house. His father, a Doctor, divorced his mother for a staff nurse when he was just two. His father would not consider photography or filmmaking practical. His father certainly contributed financially to his home, but the relationship was more of a two weeks every summer thing in a different state, where he watched his new half-siblings get the kind of care and attention he never received. They would have someone in the stands at their little league games. He resented growing up in a single-parent household during the 1970's. His mother was a career woman who didn't remarry and always seemed like the odd person out at any school or church function. He was angry about it as a kid, but as an adult, he respected her and thought her brave.

His mother and even his sister, made up for the absence of his father, with Augie having it within him to truly admire women. He thought them capable of a lot. He wasn't sexist in the least bit. But he did also crave and yearn for that nurturing from his mother and sister that he grew up with. He liked being the golden boy in the house. The way their eyes sparkled with every little thing he accomplished. "Wow! He's riding a bike already!" "First place in the swim meet." "You are a handsome devil!" Their support of him was almost excessive, but for whatever reason, it made him a highly competitive individual, especially in sports, like soccer, and provided hearty rewards in the long run – like his scholarship to a top boarding school. That selfless love and admiration in their eyes reminded him of Benny – the girl who thought he, too, was capable of great things.

Augie was very hands-on with his own children, and it was because of them, that he stayed married through these years of "later-in-life-self-discovery", with little support from his spouse. But his kids were old enough now, where their time required together was less, and so he found himself repeating to them the same mantra, "you know whatever happens, I will always love you and be in your life" and the kids would joke "we know Dad, we know Dad. You're the best."

He found comfort in this. He told his children he loved them all day, every day and every chance he got. He could care less about embarrassing them – but they were okay about this. They not only loved their dad, they liked him. He was fun and playful and interesting. He had an edge which was exciting for them in the uneventful suburbs. For one, he had lived in New York City and taught them about movies. While other marriages split in his affluent suburb over anything from sleeping with the nanny to just plain hating each other's fucking guts, he always told himself that his marriage was solid, and that he would resign himself to his unhappiness both professionally and romantically, if his mid-life transformation failed to take place. He just didn't have it within him to give up on family, especially on the kids.

Augie had fought his prettiness his whole life having been raised by a mother and one sister – also pretty. He wanted to be edgy, not so far as tattoos and piercing edgy, but he wanted to *shock*. In direct opposition to Benny, the last thing he wanted to do was fit in. Under his pretty freckled skin, he *was* edgy. He loved Ska Punk and Mosh Pits and getting his combat boots dirty (which for some reason he only wore out to concerts.) He loved kinky artists – authors like Henry Miller and Baudelaire and filmmakers like Goddard and John Waters. He knew about cafes in downtown New York City and CBGBs from train rides from Westchester. As edgy as he was on the inside, by his taste in art, he was less so on the outside and he always just looked like someone you could trust and build an entire campaign of wholesomeness around. He shaved his head every Spring to look intense–to look different. He wanted to surprise you, but he also wanted you to think. He wanted to find someone's brain because he desperately wanted someone to find his. He was waiting for a fresh perspective or an atypical reaction from anyone and then he met Benny.

Benny did not look like anyone else. In fact not one person had ever said to her "you look just like my friend so and so…" She would have given anything to fit right in and to look like everyone else.

She was an inch taller than Augie. She hovered around 5'6 or 5'7 from the time she was twelve until she was around nineteen when she grew two more inches. To balance her height, she had large feet, not large but long – size eleven. They were perfectly shaped and symmetrical and they were the best looking feet of all her friends. Even during pedicures she would get compliments.

She had thick but slightly unkempt dark brown hair which shined gold and red in the sun. In college, she had dyed it blonde, and her long strands fell half way down her back. Her long hair was known to fall in front of her face. Not only did she twirl her hair with her fingers but she sucked on the bottom strands on occasion like an insecure child. Attending Tulane University in New Orleans only made it blonder until it reached a natural honey sheen that others marveled and tried to replicate but could not. She loved her long honey hair because it was so unlike her idea of herself. Everyone in her family had black or dark brown hair.

Her hands were long and so were her fingers. She was often asked if she played the piano or wanted to. Piano playing seemed like such a genteel hobby, something she was sure Augie had lessons in as a child (he had.) He loved to play the Shaker song "Simple Gifts" on family holidays.

Benny's favorite poet was W.B. Yeats and her favorite poem "Sailing to Byzantium" which had been recently recited by Pulitzer prize winner Donna Tartt on "Charlie Rose." Her favorite lines were "Fish, flesh or foul commend all summer long, whatever is begotten, born and dies." And that's what New Orleans and her college years at Tulane became to her – *Byzantium*. With perhaps a dash of Coleridge's Xanadu from "Kubla Kahn" another favorite poem of hers, both sexy, fertile, utopias. She continuously sought exterior cues to bring her interior world and the art she experienced to life.

A lifetime of solitude, made worse by instability and shyness, provided Benny with an aptitude for hearing loud in the quiet. Giant oak trees, magnolias, crickets, everything alive and in bloom in New Orleans spoke to her. Everything was alive and growing in New Orleans. Tree stems literally broke through cement sidewalks and burst upwards and out of the ground for a breath of fresh air.

Her fantasy back then was to enter a college party with her hair blown dry, straight and shiny, twenty or thirty pounds lighter in a dress that maybe Cindy Crawford or Naomi Campbell had modeled for the latest Vogue magazine. She would enter the party giggling to her girlfriends, sipping a giant red plastic party cup full of cheap keg beer. A group of college boys would check her out from afar and boldly walk over to the crowd of girls and introduce themselves to the group and say "Don't I know you, I'm so and so" and then that would be it! Benny would get NOTICED! Like Cinderella at the Prince's Ball it was always her alter-ego getting noticed, and then that alter-ego would come alive. A boy would notice Benny. A boy would talk to her once she was at her best and then maybe she would know what it was like to be held in someone's arms and what it felt like to open her mouth and be kissed. She would know what it felt like to taste, to touch and to smell another person.

They were all so young and beautiful, the coeds on campus. She felt just far enough from home that it almost felt like her alter ego had a chance to be born. She thought someone would have to fall in love with her then, while she was young and away from home and before the boobs sagged, the crow's feet flew in, the hair thinned and the jadedness set in.

This was the movie about her alter ego that ran in her brain nearly every free second of every day while in college–Ugly Duckling gets discovered maybe? She remembered when there used to be an ABC movie of the week during the day that she would watch with her mother. This was how she saw Stockard Channing as an Ugly Duckling who becomes a brand new, beautiful woman through emergency plastic surgery and casts revenge on all of those who wronged her in her youth. Benny didn't feel like any one person wronged her. She didn't want to cast her revenge on them by killing them as the Stockard Channing character did, but what Benny hated was how she felt so much like Stockard Channing in that damn movie. Even as a child, she felt like the Ugly Duckling in **The Girl Most Likely To**.

The setting of her fantasy, her hair, and her makeup may have changed, but the drama never did. A boy finally noticed Benny, that was it. A boy finally talked to Benny.

She just wanted someone she could be herself with. Her higher, hidden self. She wanted to breathe effortlessly.

6

The Town Car waited outside the apartment building on Elizabeth Street, while Benny nervously pressed the buzzer.

Augie slowly walked over to the speaker by the door. He pressed a button and put his lips up to the mesh wires.

"Hello?" he said, voice cracking. Too much of a buildup, he thought.

"Let me in already!" she joked. Whenever she was too nervous, she became bossy and loud and assumed her Joan Rivers mode. Her heart rate increased and her enthusiasm could be mistaken for mania.

"I'll come down," he said.

"It's okay. Does the elevator finally work?" she asked.

Augie smiled, "It does, actually. The code is 888," he instructed.

"Got it. Get the air conditioner on full blast, I'm dripping."

She started laughing after saying the word "dripping." *I am the biggest dork. Unintentional.* Then she remembered Augie calling her over to his bed back in college, straight faced and highly aroused, telling her - *Benny, you're so wet right now, you're dripping on the floor.* He was a closet dirty talker, classic case. She never knew what was going to come out of his mouth at any time. But whatever he did say, it affected her (deeply, shockingly), and she memorized every word of it. She was a writer, after all.

Augie chuckled, *Try to act cool.*

Benny dragged her suitcase to the old-fashioned elevator that she remembered was always out of order. Fixing it was a low priority for the owners of the building who thought Americans were too lazy to walk up stairs. *Exercise, keeps you young* was their position on the matter.

He smelled his sweaty armpits again and rearranged the fans to give Benny, a little bit of a breeze upon entry. He wondered how he was going to explain the no air-conditioner situation. *Should I offer a hotel room instead?*

As she opened up the elevator gate, she became increasingly fidgety. *This is a very small space,* she thought, *I had no idea how small. Two people, tops.* She closed the gate, locked her and her small suitcase in, pressed the number four, closed her eyes and waited for the elevator to ascend. Nothing happened. *Oh, the code, the code.* She pressed in the numbers 888 into the security panel and the elevator jerked forward, almost slamming her face into the elevator gate. The car began to rise.

Her husband always recognized how happy she was with her bags packed and heading out the door for a trip to New York – to visit girlfriends, to attend a writing workshop, to just walk the streets quietly to dream up stories. *You love it there, don't you?* He would ask her and she would nod yes and smile. After dropping the kids off at his house that morning, providing many hugs and kisses (for both her and them) her husband (now ex, a fact unknown to Augie) noticed that look and that familiar twinkle in her eye, as she headed out the door.

"Please make sure to braid Lilah's hair before she goes swimming!" Benny ranted, working herself up, as she was known to do, while saying goodbye to her children for a few days. The agreement-amicable, respectful and suitable - she was still getting used to; but she wanted the kids to be with their Dad half the time. Even though it killed her a little on the inside, she knew it was the right thing to do. Her father was never around when she was a child, and she did not want her kids to have to live with that kind of longing. Plus, she would never hurt her ex-husband. He was a *mensch*, in the first degree and he also felt a loss on those few days the kids weren't with him. But they both agreed, *this was for the best.*

"You love it there, don't you?" Her ex-husband told her, once again.

Benny nodded and smiled. She felt guilty that she loved a place so far away from her family.

"Yes," she answered him.

"Maybe you should move there," he told her. It came out of his mouth easily, without arsenic, without guilt.

"I would NEVER leave the kids. We share them, remember? Fifty-fifty," she said.

"Well, we can talk about it," he began.

"What?" She asked.

"You wanted it before we met, while we were together, and you still want it. *I want it for you,*" he said.

"I'm too old to start a life in New York...I don't even have a job."

"We'll talk about it, okay? I'm not going to be a dick. You were my wife for Christ sake. Even if I can't be with you, as your husband, you can still force me to take chances that I wouldn't normally take. Maybe I want you to drag me there. You know, we've got a new office in New York. I keep saying no to the move, but maybe I should balls up and say yes. I'm only going to get a promotion if I move. Plus, maybe I want a fresh start, too. I miss *snow*. Why did I drag us to Florida again?"

"Solar Energy futures. And Louise is here."

"Ah, yes, I forgot that."

"Thank you. For being a great Dad, ex-husband, and...*not a dick*. I miss the snow, too," she laughed.

"Not a dick, I like that."

He was the sweetest man. The best of husbands, ex or otherwise. He just, well, she couldn't tell him *everything* and he wasn't one to dig, with anyone, not just her. This was not his fault. She required digging. For this reason she couldn't give her whole self to him. There was an uncertainty about him that made her always hold herself back. Maybe he had to find himself, too. A move to New York? Was that even *possible*? Benny would have to survive the weekend first, "See you guys in a few days."

When the elevator reached the fourth floor, it stopped. In order to open the elevator door she had to readjust her suitcase and reposition her body as the door pulled forward into the car. *Who designed this thing, an elf?* She shifted herself to open the door fully and saw Augie standing there. He was wearing cut off Khaki shorts and Converse low-tops in his favorite color, olive green. Shirtless, his hairless chest was slick with sweat. Steel Pulse was playing low in the background as they stood, speechless, and avoiding direct eye contact. After a few seconds, they hid a smile from one another; Fear, fatigue, anticipation, excitement and the intensity of the heat seemed to immobilize them. They hadn't seen one another in nearly fifteen years, now only a closed iron gate separated them, kept them from finally being together.

Neither he nor she said a word, or moved a muscle for a full half minute. Somehow, Benny regained her sense of time and space and pressed the emergency stop button on the elevator for fear it was starting to descend. They both reached to open the gate at the same time and their hands grazed.

She pulled her hand back and he cleared his throat once and then said, "I've got this."

He opened the door and grabbed her suitcase, pulling it out of the elevator car and into the living room. Benny, who thought she would be talking a million miles a minute, said nothing and continued to stand still in the elevator car.

He looked down at the floor, smiled and said "It's okay, Benny, come in."

She took a deep breath and swallowed before walking ahead of him into the living room. He closed the elevator door and gate behind her. She just stood and stared at the closest thing in front of her. She fixed her eyes on a black and white picture of JR and his new bride that was pinned to the wall.

"Does JR have any idea how serious marriage is?" she asked. She wasn't sure why in a million years she would spill something like that at this moment, their first moment together in the 'bubble'. The '*bubble*' existed only for this weekend, the *bubble* was a safe place in the exterior world where imagination and normally private fantasies came to life.

What she wanted to say was, *I like you. All of you.*

He spoke right up and said, "Your hair smells exactly the same. Please turn around."

She was afraid of a deep analysis of her wrinkles, or of even smelling *him*. *Too close, too soon,* she worried.

He put his hands on her bare shoulders as she stared out the window to the left. She trembled.

"Your hand," he requested, "like we agreed."

She wished she had eaten something that day.

"Of course," she whispered, extending her left hand to him so he could gently slide the ring off of her finger, which was moistened with sweat.

"Your turn," she whispered. He put out his left hand and she gently removed his gold band. She felt an unhappy pang, knowing that she wasn't the one who put it on in the first place. She squeezed the ring in her hand and then opened it. He ceremoniously removed the ring from her palm and walked over to a jewel encrusted box that held JR's old guitar picks. He opened the box and placed the two symbols of marriage and life outside the bubble they were trying to create. He slammed the box shut.

"Wait, one more thing," he added, "rules are only check it downstairs, outside, twice a day."

She pulled her phone out of her purse, "Yes."

She handed her phone over to him and he placed their two phones in the jeweled box.

"Ringers off?"

"Yes. And I hate phones."

"Me, too. I miss..."

"*Waiting,*" she interrupted.

From a distance he eyed Benny, who was fidgeting and pacing up and down, *assessing.*

"You're so – *small!*" he blurted out.

"You haven't seen me since my twenties, Augie. The baby fat, well, *it finally came off.*"

"I liked the roundness, but I like you like this too. A full-fledged woman."

"Oh, I hope you still think I'm *curvy.*"

He snapped his fingers in front of her downcast eyes, "Over here."

She nervously took a Duane Reade bag out of her purse.

"Oh, this too, when do you want to?" she asked.

"We can do it now if you'd like," he answered. "Do you want something to drink? I'm sorry about the heat, air is broken, but it won't be any worse than that August weekend we spent in your place during the heat wave."

"I kind of have mixed feelings about that weekend. Sleeping together all weekend like sweethearts but *not* sleeping together. It was horribly awkward, like, *a disaster.*" she added. Her eyes remained on the wood floor. She wanted to pace but something stopped her.

"That was so long ago," he told her, "Forgotten."

She started to feel hot from more than the heat. She started to feel flushed, and vertigo – weak knees, dizziness, an irregular heartbeat. She feared she did not have the strength to even emit another word from her mouth as there seemed to be no air in her lungs. If only she could run out the door and into the closet or climb onto the bed and hide under the covers. That's what the *old* Benny would do.

They both smiled and she managed to look into Augie's playful, and now saggy, eyes. The eyes that smiled at her in the picture on the flight to New York. *So saggy.* Could she tell him how happy his aging had made her? She always wanted to be with him just like this. When he was older, when they were older. Just like they had fantasized about in her bed, one hot summer night, holding hands and innocently sharing a bed together a few years out of college and supposedly, *just friends*.

"Now, a cold beer?" he suggested.

She nodded and he jumped up and sped to the kitchen.

Her mouth quivered as she placed it over the top of the beer bottle as he watched.

"My God, I can't even drink from a bottle in front of you. What's wrong with me? Shouldn't we hug or something? You and I were never really..."

"Huggers," he answered.

"I know," she agreed and started to laugh, "but I did always love the way you bumped or grazed me, *accidentally*, in a crowd and smiled. And I liked holding your hand, I don't know why. I always felt more connected by our eyes, than anything else."

"Do you want to?"

"Want to what?"

"Hold my hand?"

"Yes."

He raised his hand up and she grabbed it. She placed it to her mouth and kissed it. Her actions were instinctive. She would take any opportunity she could to express her love for him, whether he knew this or not.

"You know, there's this joke in my family about how our men have the most beautiful hands that never age."

"Really, is it genetic?" Augie asked, "mine are rather battered, as you can tell, so I'm jealous. We all have our vanity."

"You've never lacked vanity, as far as I can remember. You like being pretty, don't you?" Benny teased.

"Is it wrong that I don't want to look older than I actually am?" He argued.

"The joke, of course, is that the men in my family have never known a day of hard work in their lives. *That's* why their hands never age."

"Oh." Augie chuckled, not sure if he was supposed to.

"These hands, *your hands*, prove that you have worked hard in your life, maybe manual labor? I'm guessing you help with the dishes, do yard work, maybe you have even scrubbed a toilet once or twice?"

"Perhaps. My Mom worked me to the bone as a kid. Character, she said, but it was really out of necessity. I was the only man in the house."

"I love these hands, Augie, and what they represent," she finished, "Although a manicure wouldn't hurt. Straight guys get them all the time."

"Never," he answered, "They'd kick me off the soccer team, call me Renaldo."

Benny stared at Augie's worn hands, squeezing hers tightly, and took a deep breath. She lifted the Duane Reade bag out of her purse, looked at him and smiled, "Ready?"

7

"Where's the restroom again?" she asked.

"Oh, it's new, here," he answered, walking her into a large, fancy bathroom.

"Wow. This is nothing like I remember," she said, amazed at the upgrades. There was a large bathtub and open shower.

"JR's girlfriend – I mean, wife. She had some work done to the place. We should be thanking her," he explained. The two began sweating, as the windowless bathroom felt stifling.

"It's so hot in here, let's be quick," she told him, handing him the Duane Reade bag. He opened up the bag and removed a box.

"How long do you think it will take?" he asked.

"Find me a towel, that JR won't mind getting stained," she answered.

"Here." He grabbed a towel and placed it around her neck and her bare shoulders.

"I lean over the sink and you pour it on my hair, okay?"

She bent over awkwardly, and put her hair in the sink. He stood right behind her with the bottle, and poured it onto her hair before rubbing it in. He brushed the thin fabric of her sundress with his shorts while leaning over her.

"Your belt, it's pinching my skin!" she yelled at him as he poured all of the dye onto her hair and worked her wet hair into a bun on top.

"You look," he began.

"Great, I'm sure-like a duck after an oil spill. Set your timer for fifteen minutes and hand me your electric razor."

He smiled when she asked for the razor. He washed his hands in the sink quickly and dried them before reaching into a small bag under the sink for his razor.

"Finally!" she sighed.

He smiled widely. So did she.

He turned on the razor and handed it to her.

"On your knees," she commanded.

He obeyed her and knelt down on the soft, plush carpet in front of her. Her hair was slicked with dye.

"Augie, I've never done this before," she confessed.

"I'm glad I'm your first," he said as he laughed.

"Oh, grow up," she said.

He held her hand while she held onto the razor and he helped her shave the first strip of hair.

"See?" he reassured. She tried it all by herself.

"I'm not hurting you, am I?" she asked.

"No," he answered.

She continued to shave his thick, and beautiful hair off in strips until it was as closely cropped as she could get. It was as if he was ready to enter basic training.

"You done?" he asked, from his place on the floor, "intense, right?"

She swallowed hard, shocked by the finished product. It was just like the picture.

"I, I think so," she answered and turned the razor off.

She kissed the top of his shaved head. He leaned forward and, remaining on his knees he wrapped his arms around her thighs and kissed her stomach through the thin fabric of her dress. His thumbs rubbed up and down on her pelvic bone which jutted out.

"I...missed you," she whispered, remembering that she almost always ended a phone call telling him that she missed him. She missed him even when she held her "Save The Date" cards for her wedding in her hands. Moments from placing them with that day's mail, he just happened to call her. Benny was hesitant to mail them as 9/11 occurred just a few weeks prior and was still a harsh memory. She didn't think she should be celebrating anything and she didn't think it was appropriate. Augie told her to send them, he'd demanded she do so. *You deserve it,* he insisted, *Go ahead.*

She stayed silent for a long time, almost crying on the phone that day. She was getting married, but not to Augie. Why would he call her on that day of all days, out of the blue?

She worried that the untimely phone encounter may have contained his hidden agenda. His approach seemed subtle, yet deliberate. Had she mistaken support for sabotage? Overwhelmed by so many unanswered questions, she cleared her dry throat, took a deep breath and said, "I miss you." Someone else inside her hung up the phone.

She leaned her cheek on the top of his head. The two of them, her standing, him kneeling, in silence, in the heat, were surrounded by a pile of hair.

"I...missed you, too," he told her.

"Oh, shit!" Benny began and broke away, "I have to get this out of my hair!"

"How much longer are you going to be?" he asked from the living room where he was playing DJ. Astrud Gilberto was next. The heat was the main driver, first Reggae, now Bossa Nova.

He heard the blow dryer stop.

"Didn't you claim to, like, discover Bossa Nova?" she yelled, from the bathroom.

He snickered – *Benny*.

"No..." he replied.

"Yeah, I thought you were the only one who knew about David Byrne's Bossa Nova album? So it was you who was responsible for spreading the music of Brazil throughout the world. Thank you so much for doing that, by the way. You and Jesus have a lot in common. Like...spreading gospels..." she added.

He laughed and continued to read the back of a Sheena Easton album.

"Yes, Benny, that's exactly how it went."

"I love Sheena Easton," she admitted as she stood in front of him now. "I wish her and Don Johnson got married in real life, you know, just like on Miami Vice?"

He looked up.

"Oh my god...Benny," was all he could muster.

"I forgot this is what I used to look like, give or take a few fine lines."

She stood there, in front of him, no longer a brunette but with long, wavy, golden blonde hair that fell down her back.

"I feel like the **Saved By The Bell** chick after she did **Showgirls**."

"Just like her. And you know **Showgirls** is now a cult classic." he chuckled.

"If this means you own it on DVD, don't tell me," she answered as she looked across the wooden floor of the living room, toward a large mirror against a brick wall that faced the bed, "Look at us," she said as she admired the two of them in the mirror. She was especially proud of her powder pink toes.

He walked behind her and grabbed her by the waist. They looked at themselves in the mirror again, Augie, with his freshly shorn hair, and Benny with her college girl blonde locks. It was like looking back in time. He had a serious look on his face as he pushed the straps off of her dress and watched it fall to the floor. She covered herself with her hands and looked away.

"No," he said and brought her arms back down.

"Oh, Augie!" she said and turned around, "Are you brave enough to kiss me?"

"Are you brave enough to kiss me back?"

"I'm *crazy*, you know that, don't you?"

"I'm *crazy, too*, Benny…" Augie blurted, grabbing her face in both of his hands and kissing her before she said too much. He had known her long enough, and well enough, to fear her talking herself out of this. He didn't want her talking herself out of this, too much was at stake. As he kissed her, he realized that he had forgotten the time in his life when a kiss told you all you needed to know from a girl – a *yes* or a *no*. Her kisses told him, *'Yes, anything, I'm yours.'* But it also told him, *'Please don't hurt me.'*

She forgot what it was like to kiss someone she desired, someone she liked. How she literally wanted to inhale him into her lungs and keep him there inside that deep and lonely place she called her soul.

They started to kiss frantically, rubbing and touching as much of one another's bodies as possible. Panting, he pulled her down to the mattress on the floor. He straddled on top of her as she started to unbutton the top button of his khakis, desperate to feel his erection for herself.

"I hope my spray tan doesn't stain these white sheets!" she blurted as her face flushed.

He stopped kissing her neck for a second to laugh.

"SHUT UP!" was all that he could muster as he panted, "That's not all that's going to stain these sheets."

He squeezed her ass tightly and began to pull down her underwear as she pulled down his khaki cutoffs, leaving his boxers on. His fingers pressed into the outside of her underwear, they felt moist through the fabric.

"Is it okay if I?"

"Yes."

With that response, he tried to slip a finger inside of her and she pushed him off.

"Ow!" she yelled.

"Oh, no, is it too soon?" he asked.

"Maybe," she answered.

"Okay, we'll wait one more day," he reassured.

"I wasn't going to let you sleep with me on the first night, anyway. I want you to wait, just like the first time."

"And I want you to beg for it, just like the first time."

"What? I never begged for it!"

"Benny, you don't remember what you said to me in the throes of passion, but I do."

"Whatever," she laughed.

"More like, *Augie I want you inside me. Do it!*"

"Lies!"

"Okay, I know how we end this argument properly."

"How?"

"On a pool table."

8

Benny and Augie kissed a little more on the mattress and then she stood up, topless. Her long blonde hair touched her closed arms and covered her breasts. He lay there looking up at her with a smirk on his face. He put his hand in his boxers and started to slowly stroke himself while staring at her. She turned her back to him.

"It gives me goose bumps," she began, "not just the size of your....package, I'm pretty sure you crossed into Thomas Jefferson's blood line at some point, but the way you touch yourself like that while staring at me. Especially from across the room. I feel like a girl behind a glass window at a Peep Show. You have no idea how intense that was for me when we were younger, how intense it *still* is for me. My god! We're half naked in the same room together, Is this really happening?"

"Why do you always cover yourself up like that? I like to look," he said.

"Stare," she interrupted.

"Stare at you," he added.

"You're a voyeur. Well, so am I. Why didn't this factor into our list of reasons to be together for the rest of our lives?" she chided.

"I was never privy to this list you speak of," he offered as he placed his hands behind his head and looked up at her. "Please send my attorney a copy, I'd love to read it in the bathroom sometime."

"Unlike you, Augie, I haven't given my body to just *anybody*," she argued.

"I know you have this idea of me as a real player, but you know..." he argued as he sat up.

"I don't think of you as a player. I mean, I know, you actually *like* women, I think it's easier for me to picture you as a player. I want to think every other woman you've been with is worthless compared to me. For this relationship to exist I must feel special."

He seemed to be listening.

"All of them," she emphasized. She was about to throw her dress back over her head.

"Wait! Don't! Not yet!" he begged, his voice cracking. He knelt on the mattress behind her. Her bare back and white lace Betsy Johnson panties faced him.

She felt a flush and a bit wobbly in her legs. She thought, *I love your voice.* She felt his body heat from behind her. As his hands reached up to her waist, he pulled her underwear down. She gasped and squeezed her legs together.

"Augie, I don't think I'm ready yet," she panted.

"Let me try something," he said as he leaned over between the back of her legs and beneath her *bum*. He began to *lick*.

"Oh!" she moaned.

"Did that hurt?" he asked

"Um...No," she confessed.

He pushed her back down with such force that it made it easier for him to stick his tongue inside her.

"Oh my God, Augie, that feels so good. I... think I might... I think you might make me..."

"Not yet," he commanded. He pulled off his boxers from behind her as he grabbed a nubile Benny. He threw her on her back onto the mattress and buried his face between her legs and she buried her face between his.

"Didn't I just say we should wait?" she panted.

"We're not going to sleep together yet. But we are going to get each other off, definitely need to do that. Now, your legs are shaking so badly, *I have to pin them down,*" she heard as he climbed on top of her and her flailing long legs - tongue out.

9

Benny had fallen asleep on the mattress. She was cradled in Augie's arms when she was awakened with a hard slap from him on her bare-naked ass.

"AHH! Was I drooling?" she asked. She decided to keep it comical, for now.

"No," he teased, then laughed, "but if we're going to Brooklyn to play pool, we better leave now."

"A Sixty-Nine? Now I definitely feel like a kid again. Thank you Augie," she complimented.

"Thank you sir," he corrected.

"Thank you *sir*," she emphasized.

"I like hearing you say that."

"It's just like our first night together when you scarred me for life by ripping my clothes off and throwing me upside down into a sixty-nine, not understanding that I HAD NEVER FOOLED AROUND WITH *ANYONE* BEFORE."

"It's like that first night, except you didn't almost sever my penis with your teeth."

"It's not my fault I didn't know what I was doing, or that your dick is so goddamn big."

"Hey, that's not all we did that first night."

"Okay, one thing at a time. My therapist does not take phone calls. Interesting take on downward facing dog, by the way, *Points*."

He handed her an IPod Nano. She smiled.

"Okay, here's yours. Where's mine?" he asked. "I can't wait to hear what you put on your playlist to me."

"I have yours in my purse, Augie. We can listen to our Nanos on our way to Brooklyn if you want. You realize, the playlists we made for each other are a *romantic* gesture?"

He took a deep breath.

"Yes, I know it's *romantic*."

"You weren't really clear on that when you sent me a mix tape from Asia."

He didn't say anything. She decided not to push.

"I loved that tape. I hope you liked mine. I thought about it a lot before I made it, I even used *consultants*."

"Yes Benny, I liked the tape. Very thoughtful, especially The Replacements song."

"My roommate told me to put it on there. She said I told her so many stories about you, she thought it fit the mold."

She was glad they were okay with all that old business, she wanted to talk about tonight.

"We can't know the playlists until we listen to them, like we said, agreed?" she asked.

"Agreed," he replied.

"I am very excited to hear what you put on mine!" she announced as she kissed him on the cheek. He tasted salty and sweet. Then she kissed his big nose.

"I love this nose," she said.

Twenty minutes later, they found themselves in the back of a taxi with the window down, in the dark, downtown New York moonlight heading south.

"I can't believe you wouldn't let me take a shower," she complained.

"I like you dirty," he answered.

"I have cum in my hair, *and I'm forty.*"

He began to laugh loudly, she started to laugh too.

"Keep it down Benny, we don't need all of New York City knowing what a deep throated slut you really are."

"Yep, that's me. My nickname on chat rooms is actually – Deep Throat. How'd you know?"

He poked at the panties between her legs just once, quickly, the gesture surprising her. Since he hadn't taken a shower yet she could still taste, and smell, herself all over his face and chest. They were acting like children. She forgot what it felt like to have someone cum from her mouth, what it tasted like. *Warm,* is all she could think. Although, the flashback of his explosion onto her face, dripping and trickling down her neck sixty minutes earlier, got her wet *all over again.* She wouldn't tell him.

"Not even the taxi has air conditioning!" she complained.

"Hey, you know, I used to drive a cab," he bragged to the driver.

"Oh God help me, not this again." she interrupted, rolling her eyes.

"Here?" the driver asked.

"New York, yes," he continued.

"What he means is New York State," she corrected. "He was a cab driver in the suburbs. Thinks he was a working man."

"I was a working man. Walkie-talkie and everything." He said, feeling like he had to defend himself.

"Oh brother," she interrupted, "Pull over!"

The taxi cab was at the foot of the Brooklyn Bridge.

"What?"

"Please, Cabbie, let us out here. We're going to walk the rest of the way," she insisted.

The cabbie pulled over.

"Seriously, we're walking the Brooklyn Bridge?" he asked.

"Yes, I bet the view is beautiful."

"It will take us an hour to walk to the bar."

"We have our Nanos remember?"

They got out of the taxi and began to walk. He was surprised at how many people walked the Brooklyn Bridge on a late Friday night.

"Did I ever tell you how much I love New York, Augie?" Benny began.

"No."

"How one of my biggest regrets is that I never took the chance to live here as a young woman? You got to do that, with JR. I've always been envious of you for that."

"It looked much more glamorous than it was. I couldn't make enough money to survive. I'm a terrible waiter, that's why I left the country."

Benny preferred not to dwell on his life in another country, so she changed the subject.

"Henry Miller," she chimed.

"What about Henry Miller?"

"You introduced me to him back in college. So *of course* I read all of his stuff,. I became *mildly* obsessed."

"You have that quality, don't you?" he joked.

"Well, *okay*, I love the whole young man in New York **Tropic of Capricorn** thing. But what I *love* is him as an expat writer living in Paris, starving to death and nearly dying of pneumonia on a dirty floor in **Tropic of Cancer**. I go for drama."

"You do, you should have been an actress."

"Oh, I was. I was even accepted into a theater company at thirteen."

"Why didn't you act?"

"Puberty hit and destroyed any and all confidence I did have. Then I went to college and met a boy named Gerald August Baxter II and he gave life back to the *actress*."

He shook his head approvingly.

"An actress I could direct."

"Let's just say artist."

"Yes, *artist*."

"But the best part of **Tropic of Cancer** are the last few pages when he is on a ship heading into the New York Harbor and seeing the Statue of Liberty. I always think of that moment, *his moment*, when I come to New York. And because I think of Henry Miller, the boy from Brooklyn and renowned provocateur whose books were banned, well—every time I come to New York, I guess…by default that also means I think of you."

"I influenced you."

He thought *every time I eat a bowl of pasta or play a game of pool I think of you. Even just buying olive oil, extra virgin, makes me smile.*

She nodded and put her hand in her Le Sport Sac black purse that hung over her shoulder and pulled out the Nanos. She gave him the green one.

"I know how you love the color green," she told him.

She held a pink Nano in her hand.

"That one's yours," he told her.

Midway up the bridge they both put on their headphones and turned on their Ipods.

Excited, Augie smiled widely and pointed to his headphones, "Benny, Sade, *'Never As Good As The First Time'*? Aw, that's sweet."

She began to hear the theme song to the old television show **Hawaii Five-O** and burst out laughing.

"Have I told you I love you before? **Hawaii Five-O** theme song seals the deal," she childishly told him. He never grew tired of hearing Benny tell him that she loved him, even though it wasn't fair, even though he knew he should stop her. He never did, he just smiled, on the inside for him and the outside for her - for Benny, *his* Benny. She was the girl without a category (okay, maybe crazy,) and she was the girl who saw her ideal life beside him for one of her crazy reasons. He even acted *with* her. But she was *totally* okay with that. What was he getting himself into? Why did she lure him back in with that chapter of her book about him? For years she had sent him her writing, but it was never, *ever* about him, about *them*. Until now, why now? She had always told him that he was *the biggest mind fuck she had ever met* but something, some inner sense, kept questioning this…could it be, perhaps…was *Benny* the biggest mind fuck *he* had ever met? Was she also an exhibitionist? Had she given him signs of this when they were younger?

He remembered the bedroom encounter they shared on one hot August night when he had returned to the States. Was he so concerned with his own image, that he was tricked? Was he completely oblivious to Benny's puppeteering? Was she like Don Corleone of Mario Puzo's **The Godfather**, pulling all the strings? Who was this girl, this Benny, *really*? Why was he noticing all of these details about her now? Was this "luring" him at an older age part of her long-term plans all along?

*Am I getting naked with Keyser Soze, from **The Usual Suspects**?* Augie thought, worried, *Holy shit, I just went down on Kevin Spacey!*

Then, Grace Jones's "La Vie En Rose" hit Augie's playlist and suddenly, Benny's Brooke Shields thick and dark brown eyebrows squeezed together as Husker Du's "Diane" began to play for her.

She started to walk quickly, very quickly, away from him. He jogged across the top of the bridge to catch up to her, unaware of the crowd of walkers along both sides of the bridge, grabbing her to make her stop.

"Benny, what's wrong?"

"Why did you put this song on here?"

"It's Husker Du. It's a great song, and it's, I can't believe I'm using this word in a sentence, romantic in a slightly sociopathic way."

"That's the only reason?"

"Yes. Don't you like it?"

"Augie, what's my middle name?

He hesitated, "I don't know."

"Diane, my middle name is Diane. And I don't hate this song, I love it! I always loved it! I always wished it was written for me."

"A song with a rape? And murder?"

"*Alleged* – it's all metaphorical! It's about desire, deep, deep, desire."

"Then why in the hell are you mad at me?"

"Because I've known you for more than half my life and you don't know my middle fucking name! I know yours!"

"Because that's the name I go by, *Augie*. Listen, I'm sure you told me your middle name before, I just forgot."

"How can you forget someone's middle name?"

"Give me a break if I forget a few details, it's not like I've looked over your driver's license or anything."

"Sorry if I'm overreacting, it's just an emotional song. I'm out on the town with you, listening to your music, I'm *overwhelmed*."

"I know we're not huggers, *but...*" he said reaching out to hug her. He loved her crazy, but not so much that it ruined their weekend. Then he held her hand for the rest of their descent off the Brooklyn Bridge.

10

"Finally! We're here," he yelled. "We are getting a car service to take us back home tonight."

Benny thought about it for a second – *home*. The car was going to take them back *home*. She tried not to over think it like she had the Husker Du song. They had one more block to walk. The only storefront with lighting on the whole block of Smith Street was a used bookstore – Ages of Pages.

She stopped in front of the bookstore for a second with Augie trailing behind.

"Why do you always walk ahead?" he asked.

She didn't answer him just yet because she was mesmerized by the rare hard cover of a collection of Milan Kundera's short stories, **Laughable Loves.** "The Hitchhiking Game" was her favorite. It gave her an idea.

"I wish they were open," she said. Her face was stuck in front of the bookstore window.

"It's midnight and I'm thirsty. You know your legs are longer than mine," he complained.

"You're an athlete aren't you? All I do is take hot yoga, I don't understand why you can't keep up."

He caught up to Benny in front of the bookstore. He took her hand and dragged her a few more feet until they both stood outside a bar in Carroll Gardens. He began to open the door for her, but she stopped him.

"Augie?"

"Benny?" he scoffed, widening his eyes until wrinkles appeared over his arched brows and sunk his neck into his shoulders. His thirst and the heat added to his confusion.

"Just wait five minutes before you come in."

"Wait, why?"

"We don't know one another."

"What?"

"When you walk inside here, we don't know one another."

With that last prompt she took a deep breath and walked into the bar, Brooklyn Social, alone. Although he was still sweating, confused and extremely thirsty from the hike into Brooklyn, he stayed put. He patted his shorts and realized that he didn't have his phone on him. He was so used to scrolling through old tweets, email and Facebook to kill time. His phone was sitting in a jeweled box back on Elizabeth Street, hopefully without any emergency messages.

He looked down at his tastefully expensive watch and saw that he had actually let ten minutes pass. He took a deep breath, opened the dark heavy door, and walked into the bar. It was dark and a Frank Sinatra tune was playing. He loved Frank, but he was slightly annoyed as he reasoned, *this is Brooklyn, not New Jersey.* He guessed that these were going to be all hand-crafted cocktails. He took one look at the menu while waiting at the bar and found out he guessed right.

"Water, please," he asked the bartender who wore a black bow tie and a white button down shirt. He felt so underdressed here in his khaki cut offs and wrinkled sea blue shirt. *At least it has a collar,* he thought. The only thing that kept him fitting in were his Converse. He looked across the extremely dark, candlelit hipster bar and saw his shaved head in the mirror. Startled, he had forgotten he just had his hair cut. He always liked looking intense, his nose looked bigger and his blue eyes more sunken than normal. He knew he was supposed to look like he was in his early twenties, but he still appeared over forty. *At least I don't have a mustache,* he thought and laughed to himself.

"I'll be right back," he told the bartender after having finished the water. He wanted to find Benny to ask her what she wanted to drink. He moved through the dark crowd into the center room where a pool table stood. There she was with a vodka on the rocks in one hand and a pool stick in the other. She was flirting with a tall, tattooed, guy who was around their age, maybe younger.

The balls were spread out on the table.

"Benny, what would you like to drink?" he asked, slightly annoyed, from the other side of the pool table. She ignored him.

"Benny, what do you want to drink?" he repeated.

She turned around and walked away from tall tattoo guy and toward a miffed Augie.

"I'm sorry, do we know one another?"

"I guess...we don't?" he answered, not really having any fun with this.

"What's your name?" she asked as she bit on her straw in her rocks glass which was covered in red lipstick. He noticed her lips were covered in a very sticky, very red lip gloss. He didn't know what to make of it, unable to decide if he liked or hated it. The Benny he was accustomed to displayed an innocence about her, reflected in her preference to pale pinks. He had never seen her with racy red lips before, even if they were *sticky*, even if they were meant to look *alluring*.

"Augie, Augie Baxter."

Neither one of them said anything for a full minute. They just smiled at each other.

"Very cute name you have there, Augie. It's one a girl can't ever forget."

"So, what's your name?"

"Diane."

His eyes almost popped out of their sockets and he took a step back.

"REALLY? *Really?*"

Okay, he knew what was going on here, she was getting her revenge. He'd play along, he welcomed the challenge.

"Yes, really. Why, do you know any other Dianes?"

"No, no actually, I don't, but it does make me think of the Husker Du song. Oh, do you know Husker Du?"

"Yes, I know Husker Du."

"Well, you looked a little young, I wasn't sure."

"Thank you."

"You know the song then Diane?"

"YES, I know the song."

"And do you like it?"

"I more than like it, Augie. I *love* it."

He snickered.

CATHERINE ADAMI

"So now that we've met, *Diane*, can I buy you a drink?"

"Sure. Just a beer, vodka goes straight to my head and then I tend to make very bad decisions. Like really, really bad ones."

"Then I'm definitely going to get you another vodka."

"How kind of you."

He started to walk away from the table and then he turned around.

"Diane?"

"Yes?"

"I really like your hair."

"You do?"

"I like bed heads."

She felt self-conscious and patted down her sticky, frizzy, newly blonde hair and tried not to frown. She didn't want him to think he got to her. She rolled her eyes at him from across the room.

He came back to the pool table with the drinks.

"Game?" he challenged.

"By all means," she answered.

"One thing," he insisted, putting chalk on his cue, "I don't ever play a game without making a bet."

"Really, a bet?"

"Did you ever play 'ten minutes in heaven' when you were a kid?"

"Maybe once, but I don't remember being very good at it. I was always kind of a prude."

"I win, then ten minutes of heaven in that storage room over there."

"O-kay?"

"All I ask is that you close your eyes and open your mouth. *Widely.*"

Shocked by the terms of the wager, she turned away from the pool table to blush.

"O-kay." she agreed.

"You win, I'll do whatever you want."

"Whatever I want, huh? How can I refuse a wager like that?"

"You're welcome to break first, if you like?" he asked, pointing to the table.

"You don't need to give me the advantage. I realize we are just meeting for the first time tonight, but you should know, I am confident in my pool game."

"As you wish," he chided.

He stood at the top of the pool table and practiced holding and stroking the cue stick as he looked at her. Finally, he jerked forward and broke the balls - a solid in.

"I really like to, you know, *ram it in there*." he teased. He smiled and walked around the table to set up for a shot for the two ball.

"You like to *ram* it in there?"

"Yes."

"So macho of you, Norman Mailer."

They played down until there were three stripes and the eight ball left on the table. He missed his eight ball bank shot and slammed his pool cue down on the floor. His face flushed, he grit his teeth and took a few short, quick breaths. For a few seconds his eyes appeared wild, he did not take losing lightly, he did not take losing at pool, to Benny, lightly.

"Dammit!"

"Can't finish the job?"

"NO. I guess not. I will, though, trust me. I plan on finishing at least one job, *tomorrow*."

"And what kind of a job would that be?"

"None of your business, Diane. But let's just say, it's been a long time coming and I haven't been able to stop fantasizing about it."

"Fantasizing about it? Lucky girl."

"I feel pretty lucky, too."

Old Benny would have been overwhelmed by this revelation. Augie always attempted to be honest. She knew this and it was why she always took what he said to her so seriously. But the new Benny kept her emotions in check and reminded herself this was just *one* weekend, even though it brought a half smile onto her face.

With her innate talent bolstered by a fresh confidence, she made her way to the nine ball and made one shot after the other, leaving the eight ball on the table.

"Get ready," she warned before she cut the eight ball into the side pocket. At first, he frowned at her triumph, then he smiled.

"Okay, Diane, I said I'd do anything, so, tell me what you want me to do."

This was Augie daring Benny. How far would she go with this?

Far. New Benny would go far.

She laid the pool cue on the table and leaned back against it as she positioned herself in front of him. He wanted to reach over and run his hand up her bare legs and under her skirt, in front everyone in the room. Well, maybe not everyone, but at least the Tattoo guy with the mustache. Instead, he backed off, grabbing his beer and finishing it.

She motioned to him with her finger and placed her mouth next to his ear.

"Meet me in the storage room with your pants down, but not off, and *don't* touch yourself."

She kissed him on the cheek and he responded by pushing his semi-hard-on up against her sweaty dress before walking over to the storage room. Heart racing, he looked both ways in the bar to make sure no one was paying attention before opening the door.

When she joined him in the storage room he motioned to her and stood with his pants and boxers down. She told him to *stay where he was.* She wanted to enjoy her new power. Here he was, a handsome, muscular body, naked and aroused, before her, yet not able to touch himself.

"Hands at your sides," she commanded. He followed her instructions. She walked all the way around him once, taking him in, before moving to stand in front of him again as if he had to pass inspection. It had been twenty years.

"Give me your hand," she demanded. He extended his right hand out. She grabbed it and put his middle finger in her mouth and began to suck on it.

"I like to look at you" she told him. His hard-on became visibly more painful, as it remained untouched.

"Please wet my fingers for me."

He used his tongue and licked her fingers. She removed her fingers from his mouth and walked backwards to a wooden chair. She sat down.

"Augie, I think your body is beautiful. So beautiful, that I want to sit here in this chair and touch myself while looking at you. Would you like to watch me touch myself while I stare at you?" she asked lifting up her dress and pulling down her panties.

"Yes," he answered. He was free to touch himself now. He wouldn't analyze what was happening to him at that moment, or who this new woman was across from him. He just liked it. Hadn't he made her watch him touch himself while looking at her, twenty years ago? He was amazed at the role reversal.

"Yes what?" she pressed. She was free to touch herself now.

"Yes, I want to watch you, watch me," he answered.

"Your body turns me on..." she cooed.

"Your body turns me on, too," he responded.

"Look at me," she directed as she lifted her leg up, "do you see my tattoo?"

She lifted her leg up to reveal the letter "A" written in thick marker on the inside of her thigh.

He wanted to laugh but he was afraid he was going to cum all over his clothes.

"Yes, I see it," he said.

"Do you love it?" she kidded.

"Yes, I love it," he answered.

She put one hand on her breast and squeezed it.

"I can touch you if..." he offered as he stroked himself - faster now!

"No, no, Augie. I want to show you. Look at me! Please, look at me while I... And I'll look at you. *I need you to look at me,* understand?"

"I... need you to look at me, too."

The timing was perfect. They caught their breath and cleaned themselves off the best they could and then exited the storage room separately. He walked straight to the bar to get some beers. She sat down in a candlelit booth. Howlin Wolf's "Shake It For Me" played overhead.

He returned to the booth and delivered the beers. The pool table was still vacant so he racked the balls and broke them apart. He motioned for Benny to join him for a game but she declined and took a big gulp of her beer.

"How old were you when you lost your virginity?" she asked him. He was about to make a try at nine ball corner pocket.

"Whoa! That's kind of personal, Diane. We just met."

"I feel like you and I are connected now. Plus, I have a sense for these things."

"Connected?" he rolled his eyes and smirked. He took a deep breath in and then out, "Sixteen."

"Let me guess. With a townie? In boarding school?"

"Bingo! How'd you know?"

"Telepathy."

"Really?"

"Something tells me I've heard this story before. Maybe in a past life."

"Perhaps on the swings of a playground in college at midnight."

"Perhaps."

"Definitely a past life, then."

"Did you ever, excuse the term, deflower a girl?"

"Yes, I did once, back in college."

"Really? What's it like, you know, for the man?"

"Well, it's exciting... a turn on."

"I bet she was, you know..."

"Tight? Yes, she was."

"Did you hurt her?"

"Very probing questions, Diane."

"When discussing probing, one should probe."

"I think so...I didn't mean to, though."

Augie was coming out of a heat and pleasure induced coma and wanted to be careful.

"Did you love her?"

Taken aback by this question, he took a long drink from his pint glass, '*Careful.*'

"No. But I did like her very much and we were friends. Good friends. We'll always be friends."

"I see. Friends. Did she love you, *the girl?*"

"She claims she fell in love with me that night. You know, after the first time."

"You don't believe her?"

"I didn't at first. But now that we're older, I do."

"Did she cry?"

"No."

"Are you sure?"

"I...I think so."

"Did she bleed?"

"Like in the Godfather II when they throw the sheets out the window in Sicily? Yes, *a lot.*"

"Did you ever think she *did* cry but hid it from you? Like, maybe when she went into the bathroom and looked at herself in the mirror she bawled, running the water in the sink so you wouldn't hear, feeling ashamed for having feelings for you when you told her you could never be more than friends?"

"Benny!"

"Then she asked you to take her home so she could cry some more, even though she wanted to stay with you, to sleep in your arms that night?"

"Benny!"

"Who's Benny?"

"Benny, stop it!"

"I want to know what you think about this girl!"

"I'll tell you anything you want to know, but not like this."

"Like what?"

He grabbed a napkin and held her arm in a tight grip.

"Augie!"

He wiped the red lipstick off of her mouth.

"We're going home."

He said it again, *home*.

11

Augie and Benny sat in the back seat of the Town Car on opposite ends. He decided to ignore her and talk with the driver about the US Open.

When they arrived at Elizabeth Street, she opened her own door and jumped out while he paid the fare. She realized when she arrived at the front door of the building that she was dependent on him to let her in. Once inside the hallway, they walked to the elevator and squeezed in. She did her best to not touch him in the elevator car, but it was so small that their hips kept touching as the elevator made its way up to the fourth floor. Once the car hit the fourth floor, she had to squeeze up against the wall as he squeezed in front of her to open the door. Once he opened the gate, she pushed forward and walked into the bathroom. *Those long legs are sprinting,* was all he could think.

He threw the keys down on the counter and walked outside to the bathroom door. He tried the knob but it was locked.

"Benny. Benny what are you doing?"

"I'm washing your jizz out of my hair you fucking asshole, that's what I'm doing!"

"You keep wanting me to believe you've grown up, *Cassandra,* but when you lock yourself in a room like this, I beg to differ."

He called her by her actual name, Cassandra. He always did that when he wanted to be serious. This fact scared her. She heard what he said and she knew he was right. She wasn't going to tell him this, though. In a way, she felt guilty. She had to stop feeling so hurt about the past; about what they were like when they were kids. If he could forgive her and her immaturity, then she could forgive his, well, she could think of a long list of things.

Benny finished washing her hair quickly and got out of the shower. She pat her skin dry with a towel and put on a brand new, sheer white cotton nightgown. She felt like a Shakespearean lady-in-waiting with it on, and most importantly - fresh, young and innocent. A time-traveler. It had long sleeves and there were two strings hanging in the front of it that you could cinch like a corset. If you untied and pulled the strings apart, the simple, short shift would fall off both shoulders and bare her breasts.

She walked out of the bathroom to find him in his boxers under the white sheets on the mattress on the floor. He had rigged all the fans to face their bed.

"Will you come to bed now?" he asked, "I have some ice water over here, if you want it?

And a present, I wanted to give it to you earlier. I'm not sure if I got the right size..."

She walked over to the mattress and stood above it and above him.

"Please don't tell me you bought..." she began as he gave her a beautifully wrapped box that said "Agent Provocateur" on it.

"You don't have to wear them if you don't want to, it just reminds me of you."

"Lingerie, really?" she asked touched, *hopeful*. This was not the old, selfish Augie talking. She opened the box slowly to find a pair of white, nylon underwear that would cover her entire midsection. She wore them in college and they were affectionately known as "Granny Panties." She never thought anyone would see her in them-until Augie came home with her that first time.

"I think they might even be the same ones."

"Granny panties? You bought me Granny panties?"

"Agent Provocateur does not sell Granny panties, Benny. I explained the underwear you wore when we first got together in college and this is what the saleslady found for me. They look exactly the same as the ones you wore."

"Okay, high-end Granny panties."

"These are panties Joan would have worn on **Mad Men.**"

"Joan is a whore Augie, *and I'm...not...*"

They both had to think about that one for a minute. He was giving lingerie to Keyser Soze.

"I'm just telling you, you in these will drive me *wild.*"

"Okay, Augie, whatever you want. They do look the same. Thank you for the *gift.*"

"It won't be the only one this weekend Benny, I promise. I have a lot to make up for," he told her, offering her a chance to see his vulnerable side. He did like her. He always *liked* her.

Was gift giving a precursor to loving someone? As in, there was a possibility that Augie could love her? She wondered if you can like someone more than love them. Maybe those were her feelings for Augie, just a friend who did not give her gifts, that liked her a lot. This relationship was all about liking. The love part was an afterthought.

She walked over to the mattress and got under the covers. She laid her long wet hair on the pillow and took her glasses off.

"It's okay, Augie." she said.

"What's okay?" he asked.

"The television. I know you're dying to put it on. You can't sleep without it on, go ahead."

"I don't have to."

"No, please. I can accept the fact that television is one of the great loves of your life."

She grabbed the remote from the makeshift nightstand and handed it to him.

"Is there something you want to watch?" he asked.

"It's been a long day and I can't see two feet in front of me without my contacts or glasses."

"Two feet, I'll remember that later tonight," he chuckled.

"The only thing that could get me to put them back on was if you told me Johnny Carson was on."

"I miss that guy" he said.

"I do, too" she concurred.

She turned over to lay on his bare chest. Under the sheet, she tried to stay cool from the fans. The closeness of their bodies made them even hotter. Yet, they didn't seem to care.

"If you feel the need to masturbate on top of me again, don't hold back," he tried to joke. But he immediately knew it wasn't funny and regretted saying it. He was sparked by the memory of the last time they slept in a bed together fifteen years ago. How had they managed *not* to have sex that weekend? Why did he visit her first thing after moving back to the States, a few years out of college, a few years after they had last been lovers? Why did he sleep in her bed with her even though he had a girlfriend? He had never slept in a bed with a woman and not messed around with her, what was different about Benny? Why were they so close? She had sent him two letters a week for an entire year! Why did he torture her like that? Sleep in her bed with her, visit, and then say they were still, just friends when he knew she loved him?

The first night of his visit, in the dark of her bedroom, she was too shy to hit on Augie, who was lying beside her. She asked if he would hold her hand while she touched herself, and he did. This was the one memory of Benny that replayed in his mind the most. It wasn't even a sexual memory, he had just never seen a woman be so brave with him before, trust him so much. He knew just how much strength it took from her to take a risk, especially with him. He knew she hadn't been with any man since him and the guilt he felt that night was overwhelming. He knew asking his girlfriend to move to the States meant they were going to get married. That path had already been chosen, there was no going back.

That night he didn't sleep a wink. Mind racing, he just watched Benny sleep beside him. Wearing a tank top and a thong, she was a woman ready to give him every last ounce of herself, her private self.

Fast forward fifteen years and here he was on another miserably hot night, without air conditioning, and with a half-naked Benny beside him. But this time she didn't have those puppy dog eyes and she wasn't hanging on his every word. This time he was the one who asked her into his bed, he paid for her trip. Over these last years she had been loved, married, she was a career woman, a mother, and now she was realizing his dream by trying to become an artist.

"Try not to snore." She said.

"*I do not snore!*"

"Augie-your nose, like your dick, is enormous. Yes, you do snore."

Both of them laughed.

BOOK II

Saturday

1

"Absolutely not", "Worst idea of all time", "Grave mistake", and "New Coke bad" were just some of the expressions of support Augie and Benny's best friends and roommates, JR and Louise, provided the couple when each discussed the possibility of a deflowering, early that senior year of college in the Fall of 1992.

"Remember when we went to that Frat party freshman year and there was a porn playing on a projector behind the shot bar? Your face turned blue and you started wheezing so badly I thought you had swallowed your tongue and threatened to call an ambulance? That's why you shouldn't have sex with Augie. If that's your response to a dick on a screen, I can't imagine what a real one is capable of!"

Louise had launched an assault!

"We've fooled around a few times now, I'm kind of getting used to it?" Benny wasn't as confident about this statement as she would have liked to be. It was a fact, she was terrified of Augie and his naked body, as well as her own. But she was also grateful that Augie had kind of forced it to happen that first time they spent the night together. They didn't sleep together but there was a wave of relief for her the next day knowing that she had the coming of age experience of fooling around with a boy *finally*. It was her last year of college, and she was starting to think it was a now-or-never situation. If the sex part didn't happen now, when would it? He said he would make it nice for her. He said it was better if she did it with a friend.

"You are not going to be okay with this. Deep down you want a boyfriend and I just don't think he's boyfriend material, sorry. He wants this to be a low-key, "friends with benefits" situation and you're not ready for that," Louise lectured.

"But what about **When Harry Met Sally**?"

"That's well-written bullshit!"

"But you and JR sleep together on occasion, and you're our roommates. That's hypocritical!"

"I don't want a boyfriend! Especially not JR, he's a player! Luckily enough, I'm kind of a player too."

"I don't think of you as a player, you're a serial monogamist."

"I've had a boyfriend since I was twelve, I've had roses, and dinners, and school dances. I'm on a break now that I'm in college. Basically Benny, I'm allowed to just fuck a guy if I want to, no strings. *You* are not. I want you to get the romance. Losing your virginity to someone sets an important precedent. It sets expectations…"

"Do you want to ruin our life? It's senior year. I just want to plow girls the rest of the year, and then move to New York City next year and plow some more, that's it. It's our time to plow. We'll all be married one day, better enjoy ourselves now." JR told Augie while catching a football on Newcomb quad.

"Weren't you ever the first for a girl? I haven't been and, I don't know, I'm turned on by it. I'm turned on by Benny, actually. My first time, it could have been better."

"Don't ever rate sex. You put your dick in a vagina, be happy."

"It could have been better…"

"I've never had a virgin and I have no desire to have a virgin. Clingy, needy, you have to teach them what to do…"

"But that's precisely what I like about it…"Augie began, "I get to teach her. I get to make it – unforgettable."

"I'd much prefer a girl who's already sucked a few dicks before she's sucked mine, you know how I feel about teeth."

"Seriously, Benny's okay with this…I think. You should be too."

"Yeah, she's definitely okay with this. She sent you a dead fish because she saw you talking to another girl. She LIKES you LIKES you."

"I feel like I should deflower a late blooming virgin who sent me a dead fish. Just for the experience."

"You and your silly life experiences. I swear to God, to you today, you do this and she will think she's in love with you and stalk you for the rest of your life. I promise you, what your ego now enjoys, your sensible side will regret later."

"I don't know how she feels about me. As far as I know she's had crushes on other guys and only sees me as a friend, I can't be responsible for what happens to her feelings."

"You sound naïve, but also like an asshole. Just wait, we'll be forty and laughing about this. I hope it's worth it. If I have to actually start going to class because she stops giving you her notes, I'll be furious."

Augie always felt a wave of humiliation when he thought about his first time. He was the one out of his group of friends from boarding school who hadn't had sex. He was nearly seventeen and was teased mercilessly. It was an all-boys boarding school, so intermingling with girls was rare. He was always studying or on a bus with the travel soccer team, so he had to be strategic.

"Pele probably got laid at like nine. You know how those Brazilians grow up fast," his Boarding school roommate Matty, argued.

"So what? Yes, I need to get this over with, but with who? When? Where? I can't bring girls to the dorm?" Augie asked.

"Come home with me this weekend, we'll take the train. I've got the perfect girl for you. A Townie. Her Dad owns the gas station. She's been selling me cigarettes since I was twelve in exchange for pot. I've slept with her a few times. She's a bit older, relaxed. She gets around so just wear a condom. It'll be over in no time," Matty offered.

"Over in no time?"

"You do know what you are supposed to do?"

"Yeah, I'm pretty sure."

He wouldn't admit it to anyone other than himself, but wanted it to be special. Deep down, he was a romantic. How many love scenes had he watched on television and movies late at night that made him smile and how many made him want to recreate that same exact moment for himself? Early on, he was already a director.

The month was December. Augie felt weird on the train ride to ritzy Darien on the Connecticut rail line. He was super horny and ready to explode up until the point they picked the Townie girl up at the gas station and brought her to Matty's freezing greenhouse where the deed was set to take place. He knew he was forcing himself to do something he didn't believe in one hundred percent, but that he wanted to get over with. Once and for all, a release, a life experience checked off, and the ability to move forward, to stop being teased at school, and to hopefully sleep with someone who was actually his girlfriend in the future.

He wanted someone he could hold, laugh with, and call later. Someone in all of those movies and TV shows who kisses you, gives you goose bumps, and takes your breath away. Someone – and an evening – he could sentimentalize until old age. Someone that didn't make him throw up Southern Comfort in a box with peeling pink paint filled with cold, prickly, dead rose bushes. Someone that didn't make him feel shame. But it was over. Mission complete.

But was it? He was fortunate to have a boost of confidence with the girls after losing his virginity. His boarding school friends talked him up plenty upon his return and he appeared less as a Momma's boy. He started dating and having girlfriends, and having plenty of sex. It felt better and his skills improved. He even thought he was in love once or twice. But it never quite removed the vision of him freezing, seeing his breath in the frigid air, pants around his ankles and Matty standing outside within earshot. He lived for details but on that night he wanted to remember the least number of them.

When Benny asked him what his first time was like, he answered her "Great. Unforgettable" and smiled. When Benny revealed she was a virgin, he got an idea he didn't share with her. He'd get a do-over where *he* could control everything.

2

Benny woke up at ten o'clock. The first thing to come into her mind was what to feed her kids for breakfast, and then she remembered that they were in another state, at their father's house. The sun was pouring onto the mattress she slept on. She found herself alone and her abandonment complex automatically kicked in. She knew how to handle it when it arrived, but she never knew how to prevent it from happening in the first place. She had had it her whole life. Then she heard a crash from the kitchen.

"Oh, fuck!" yelled Augie from the next room.

"Augie, are you okay?" she asked.

"Think I just burned myself." he said

"Let me help you."

"No, no, stay in bed. I'll be right there."

She heard him turn the volume up from the boom box in the kitchen. It was the classical station, Delibes.

He walked into the living room with a tray carrying breakfast. There was a bagel, coffee and some strawberries. He placed it on the bed and sat on the mattress beside her.

"The strawberries are from the Elizabeth Street Garden and super sweet," he said.

"I think you need to call an ambulance," she said, as her jaw dropped.

"Why?"

"Because I might have a heart attack."

"Over breakfast?"

"Not just any breakfast. Augie, I don't think you've ever bought me a cup of coffee before and now you're making me breakfast? This meal is a lot more substantial than the half of a Snickers bar you offered me in an airport back in '93."

"Today's going to be a special day and all. I wanted to start it off right. And I have to…"

"Check your phone messages?"

"Yes."

"I was a salesperson for fifteen years. I know when I see the old bait and switch."

He kissed her on the forehead and stood up, putting on his flip flops before grabbing his phone and keys.

"I *wanted* to make you breakfast, Benny."

"I'm so happy right now. Go! Go check your messages. When you come up, I'll go down, myself."

He started to check his messages in the elevator on the way down. He wanted to get this over with, quickly. The only message was from the Executive Producer on his new show who heard he was in New York somehow and wondered if they could meet up for a drink. Definitely *not* this weekend. He walked across the street and bought a decaf. He called home. Everything was status quo except for the fact that he had lied to his wife. He wasn't in town for work and he wasn't still with JR. He didn't stay on the phone for long.

For some strange reason, he decided to call JR. JR was his best friend, but he was also on his honeymoon, in St. Barths. He wondered if JR could even get reception there.

"Dude, I'm on my honeymoon. Is the apartment on fire?"

"No, no." Augie reassured.

"Why are you calling me then? Do you miss me?"

"No... *I don't know.*"

All he wanted to do was dish to JR about Benny – how she looked, how she smelled, how she tasted. She was confident and on occasion, self-deprecating. How she had so much going on in her in life, in her head, that she shared with him in person, not in a letter.

His heart raced as he thought of all the details he wanted to share with his best friend. After all, JR actually knew Benny. He couldn't imagine explaining to JR how different she was than he remembered. How *strong*, how brave and daring she was sexually. How, he couldn't believe he was actually admitting this, *dominating* at times even? How she showed off her body to him rather than hide it. But he couldn't tell JR he was having an affair with Benny this weekend, at JR's apartment while JR was having his honeymoon. It was both a sworn secret and in bad taste. JR was a newlywed, Augie was a cheater.

"What's wrong with you? Are you lonely? I told you not to spend the weekend alone in that apartment. Go to Soho House, my key card is in the kitchen. Stacy made me get it for her, of course.

Just make sure you're there Monday morning for the movers."

"That's a nice offer, but I'm staying on Elizabeth Street."

"Then at least go and use the pool at Soho."

"That sounds like a good idea, today. It's ninety."

"Well, I'm off to go drink a fifty-dollar glass of wine out of a box on the beach. These French bastards fleece you like motherfuckers. Stacy loves it. You should hear her try and speak French. It's awful but it gives me a hard-on at the same time."

"Okay, sorry, I forgot why I was calling."

"Get a hooker," JR suggested.

"What?"

"If you're unhappy at home, which you are, or you wouldn't keep begging to come into the city to visit me. I mean, do you and your wife even *live* together anymore? Please, just be decisive already. This is your life. I love you and I want you to feel as good as I do right now, okay? I'm not a fan of sad Augie."

"A hooker? NO, NO THANK YOU."

"Hey, you know what you can do for me? Go to the track and place a bet. No off tracks in the city, so just take a car to Queens. Stacy Speed is running in the eighth race at Belmont. I should have been a Handicapper. Can you put a hondo down for me? It'd be kind of fun to see if she wins. I'll watch the race on my IPAD under an umbrella."

"Yeah, I'll do it. I haven't been to the racetrack in a while."

"Thanks. My bookie's at a yoga retreat in Costa Rica, no phones."

"Of course he is."

"And I lost a shit-ton betting on your sons' little league game last weekend. The fix was in –

I'm telling you."

"You bet against my sons' team. Against my kids, against me, your best friend!"

"I like when the odds are against me, a bigger payoff."

"You don't respect money, and you have truckloads of it."

"Hey, didn't Uncle JR buy the whole team ice cream in Central Park?"

"You were trying to impress the single Moms."

"Wait one last thing, you'll never believe what I just heard."

"You're a gossipmonger, JR. You sound like a girl."

"No, you'll wanna know. It's about your old friend, *the virgin...*"

"The virgin?"

"There was only one, wasn't there?" JR asked seriously, for once.

"Yes, J.R., *only one,*" Augie agreed.

3

The second Benny heard the elevator go down to the street with Augie in it to make his phone calls, she jumped off the mattress and quickly grabbed her phone out of the jeweled box where it was hidden. She called her very best friend who had been her college roommate, Louise.

"Are you alive?" Louise asked.

"Yes, I'm alive and a full-fledged adulterer."

"You're not an adulterer if you had him first."

"That's not true, but I'll go with it."

"And she's a foreigner."

"Okay, whatever you say Louise. I'll have to go with that philosophy in case we ever actually..."

"You mean, you haven't done it yet?"

"No."

"Wow."

"No, not yet. I'm still sore down there from being *rejuvenated by Dr. Weisman.* You'll never believe..."

"I don't believe any of this, Cassandra. But, but, did you take care of the *other thing*?"

"Yes!'

"Thank God! *An orgasm*, finally! I bet your skin feels softer, do you feel *better*?"

"Better is a relative term."

"Is he like so freaked out with how good you look and how ballsy you are now?"

"Louise, I'm shy."

"Cassandra you are anything *but* shy. That girl, the shy one, went bye-bye, a while ago."

"Fine, you win, I'm not shy."

"You even make me blush, and I'm a girl."

"Please."

"You're my best friend, and I want you to have a second chance. *Everyone deserves a second chance* and you deserve to have fun and to feel pleasure. I know it's been a long time for you since you had either, but I don't want you to get hurt. I just don't see how you're going to be able to handle Monday morning when you have to say goodbye. He's married. This is *wrong*. I mean, you love this guy, or think you do. That's not having an affair. You're not French, like me, I know about these things…"

"You're American."

"My Grandmother lived in Paris before the Nazis came."

"Yes, I know, and you know I love that woman, but can we can talk about World War II after I return home as I only have five minutes left until Augie busts me for talking on the phone. We promised each other we wouldn't use them inside the apartment."

"Fine, what I'm saying to you then is that you can always leave early, *if you need to.* You don't have to do this, because once you start dating again, you know, *available men...*"

"Every time I feel guilty, or think I should just run out of here, I get this feeling from him, *that he wants me to stay,* like *he needs me, Louise.*"

"Maybe that's what you want to think because you're so horny! I get it!"

"Whoa, Louise. It's only ten a.m.!"

"Oh, brother, Cassandra! Augie Baxter doesn't need anybody. He's just a guy who wants to have his cake and eat it, too. He's always been one to get away with shit. Think of everything he got away with...with you."

"Because I let him."

"Yes, you did."

"But not anymore."

"Better not. Even if he asked you for the affair, even if he paid for your ticket...he's *married...*"

"This isn't my perfect situation – no."

"You've played everything by the books your whole life. Above board. Never lied or cheated on anything. Forty years of being an innocent – you're allowed one major *incident.* I get it."

"That's what you're calling this weekend, an incident?"

"Hey, I'm giving you a pass after a spotless forty-year run, but cheating, or, being with a cheater, it's just not you, Cassandra. *It's just not you.*"

"I know, I'm pushing myself – to the edge. I need different ingredients to try and get a different result. I need to put my childish ideas about this person aside once and for all. This is my chance to do that. I miss *our friendship, though.* Sex aside, he was the first man to hold me in his arms, Louise."

" I'm not a Psychiatrist…"

"Although you fancy yourself one," Benny interrupted.

"But, I think you're *regressing.*"

"Didn't you ever want a second chance?"

"Of course, a million times!"

"Goddammit, Louise, I have been celibate the majority of my adult life. Let me enjoy my body, while I've still got one."

"Just do it. I'm serious – just do it. Be selfish. Ayn Rand would insist you do this – and you like her, don't you?"

"I do."

"Your life is so great and promising right now, it's so great even without this weekend!"

"I thought I was the one who changed the most, after so many years, but maybe it's Augie."

She deliberately raised her voice to drown out Louise.

"Or, maybe, you're changing him, this weekend."

"I never imagined I could change him."

"See, only the old Cassandra – *or Benny* – or whatever the hell his pet name is for you, only *she* would say that. You've come so far, Benny, light years. You're on the verge of greatness, you are on the verge of being a novelist. A fucking novelist! Now that's realizing your dreams. NOT seeing Augie again. Augie Baxter's going to have to take a number as far as I'm concerned. It's time for you to get out of the cocoon you've been hiding in for the past forty years and become the colorful butterfly you were born to be."

"Ok, Reiki Master, I get it. I want to be that butterfly, I'm tired of hiding."

"Do you know how lucky you are to have a passion in life with writing? I don't have a passion.

All I have is a husband."

"Who is devoted to you."

"And three boisterous sons who I am smothering."

"A little smothering is okay."

"Anyway, you becoming a published writer, an artist, is my dream, too. I get to live vicariously *through you*. Remember that. I have no natural talents."

"Of course you, do. You're the smartest person I know. You have like *three* graduate degrees and you're that rare breed lawyer/nutritionist/yogi. On top of all that - you taught me how to give a blow job, Louise. I'll never be as good at it as you either, *fact*."

"Well, okay, I will take credit for that. But that is not *a passion* of mine. Although my husband probably wishes it was."

"I've never cheated on anyone before. But now, I've got Augie cheating. Why couldn't we have just ended up together back then? Why couldn't I have been this cool twenty years ago?"

"Shut up! You were plenty cool twenty years ago, *the coolest*. Hello! Who else ran the pool table at every bar in college? You being shy and inexperienced should not have kept him from dating you properly. You put yourself in his hands and he disappointed you. He was a bungling fool and didn't appreciate you."

"I don't know. I don't want to think about the past. I want to focus on *who* I am today. My head is spinning, Louise. I was drinking vodka on the rocks, *of all things* last night. Who do I think I am, *Elizabeth Taylor in Butterfield Eight?*"

"She did win an Oscar..."

"I better get off the phone before I get caught talking to you."

"Okay. I can't believe I am saying this to you because it sounds like I'm condoning an affair here, when I'm not. However, if this weekend is what you need for closure so you can move forward with your future, then do it. I am behind you. I mean, *even I* see and hear things that remind me of the two of you. You both have overwhelmingly annoying personalities. I even had a dream about the two of you. You're on *my* mind!"

"You think, you think, I have an overwhelming personality?"

"Yes *new Benny*, you do."

Benny was shocked to hear even her best friend tell her she was powerful. That she and Augie together left an imprint on others. *'That's the goal of all great artists, right?'* she thought, *' To get into someone's mind?'*

"*New Benny*," she happily conceded.

"I will be waiting for you with Pinot Grigio and peanut M&Ms when you return home *sobbing*. I've already picked out at least ten guys on J-Date that you can go out with next week."

"Louise, I'm not on J-Date. I'm a Shiksa, remember?"

"You can convert."

" Don't fool yourself, Louise. Those are all guys *you* would go out with if *you* were single. By the way, does your husband know you have an account on J-Date?"

"No, I put it in my grandmother's name."

"And you think I'm sneaky."

"Fine, Cassandra. Don't go out with them! Good luck with your married WASP!"

"Thank you. I will try to do just that."

"There is a suspension of disbelief you have going on this weekend. But come Monday, you have to live with the fact that *he is married*. I would give anything for him to tell you that he loves you and his wife is this *awful* woman and that he is going to leave her for you, but that only happens in movies."

"But I love movies, and Augie loves movies, too."

"I love you, you crazy romantic fool. Even if you are an adulterer!"

"Just call me Hester Prynne!"

"God, that's a mouthful. Does Augie know that you're single again?"

"No, he doesn't."

"Okay, *whatever*. It's not possible for this weekend to be any weirder than it already is. You and *Biggie Smalls* deserve each other, you know that? You're both perverted mind fucks!"

"What's wrong with mind fucking?" she asked, hearing the elevator lift, "Oh, shit, gotta go!" she exclaimed running over to the other side of the room to hide her phone inside the jeweled box.

Augie walked in the apartment and looked at her hiding under the covers. He liked the way she looked in the distance with her hair down, smiling at him and eating the bagel that he had toasted for her. He decided not to question her about the divorce JR had just told him about, to just let the weekend continue, *as is*. But he felt badly, as her supposed friend, that something so monumental, had happened to her and that he was unable to ask her about it. He wanted to listen to her story and to comfort her. He felt cheated. The new Benny wasn't playing fair. He wanted to know what divorce *felt like,* if it was what *he'd imagined.*

There was something else nagging in his brain. Why were his feelings intensified? In less than a day, she had won over his heart and his mind. Like one of her scripts she had sent him years ago, like her new novel. Was she supposed to come to him single and available? He was all too aware that he wasn't single and that he wasn't available. But yet he didn't feel married anymore. Not, really. He had changed. For a long time before Benny, before this weekend. Like in all of the important areas of his life, he had trouble…taking action and… moving forward. He didn't like feeling cornered and frustrated, but he wouldn't tell Benny. He was at a crossroads.

"Feel like taking a dip? Cooling off?" he asked her. She nodded yes, beaming.

4

They arrived at Soho House late Saturday morning. As soon as the doorman ushered them inside they sighed in relief over the air conditioning and took the elevator to the rooftop pool.

"I'm in the mood for a swim," Benny told him.

"You know I've seen you naked, but never in a bathing suit."

A Frenchman that was sharing the elevator with them grinned upon hearing their conversation.

"I didn't let anyone see me in a bathing suit until I was like twenty-eight. Now that I'm forty, I'm okay with it."

"I am liking you...older. What about me?"

"Augie, I feel like I've been waiting my whole life for you to grow old so that we could finally be together," she answered.

He didn't respond. He knew that she still lived in a world where they were going to grow old together. She was going to take care of him and push his wheelchair. Her fantasy always included a wheelchair. She told him, '*Then you can't run away from me.*' He indulged this fantasy of hers when they were younger. He couldn't believe such a young girl loved him so much that her fantasy was to be with him as an old man and that she promised to take care of him. He knew this fantasy was one of the many reasons that made her different from any other girl he had ever met.

"Remember," he began, "we have to leave early to make the race."

"Are you sure I haven't been more of an influence in your life?"

The elevator doors opened and they walked down the hall toward the valet.

"I, for sure, have to be the only girl to ever take you to the racetrack with her father. Twice, I think."

"Yes."

"How about them apples?"

"Yes, Benny, you have *influenced* my life."

"Is that on the record?"

"Yes."

"How many times in your life up to now, have you retold that track story?"

"Benny, let's get a chair already."

The valet found them two shaded chairs and laid their towels down. She was impressed that he tipped the valet, she remembered what a cheap ass he was when he was younger.

"What would you like?" asked the valet.

"Arnold Palmer," she answered.

"Make that two," he confirmed.

The pool wasn't very busy, most people were out of town so only tourists dotted the area. They each lay in their chair and sipped their iced tea lemonades.

"Happy?" he asked.

"Very," she answered, "I feel like I am on a vacation."

"We're in a bubble," he said, "We *are* on a vacation, a vacation from our lives."

She was tempted to analyze that last remark but decided not to. Even in the shade, with the cold drink, she was burning up.

"I have to get in that pool," she said. Instead of being self-conscious, she wanted him to look at her body while she took her cover-up off. She wanted him to get a good look at her in a bathing suit. *This is what I look like as a woman,* she thought. *You either love me or you don't.*

She walked up to the pool and he grabbed the green Nano out of her purse while he looked over the Racing Form that he had picked up that morning after the call with JR. Running in the same race as Stacy Speed was a horse named "Shorty Forty." He would bet it. Benny always addressed her letters to him as "Shorty" or "Short Stuff", he had to bet it.

The next song on the Nano for Augie was Sonic Youth's "Moist Vagina" and then Prince's "Adore." He remembered he put "She's Always In My Hair" on his playlist for Benny.

Slightly aroused, he took the IPOD off as well as his shirt and walked over to the pool to join Benny in the water.

"I hope you put on SPF 100," she teased as she treaded water at the pool's deep end, "You're Irish and I love you."

"Yes. We all can't have olive skin," he told her.

He sat on the edge of the pool in army green swim trunks. His feet were on the stairs of the ladder. He began to play with one of his toes.

"I remember you always playing with your feet," she said, "I almost think it's an unconscious habit. Maybe it has something to do with playing soccer. You're obsessed with feet. James Joyce was.

And you share the same birthday."

"How do you know that?"

"He's my favorite writer, remember?"

"And I am?"

"My favorite – *person*."

He was quiet for a moment as he gave her a half smile. He...didn't know how to react to her comment. He stared at her for a few moments without speaking. This caused her to dart her eyes and twirl her hair into ringlets with her finger.

"I like your playlist so far," he told her, breaking the silence.

"Me, too," she answered, "I'll listen to more of it on the ride to Belmont...Oops. You don't mind if we make a quick stop in the Diamond District on the way to Queens?"

"Diamond District?" he asked. For five seconds the thought crossed his mind that she wanted him to buy her jewelry.

"It will literally take five minutes," she answered.

"What on earth do you need from the Diamond District, *literally*?" he asked.

"I have to drop off a package for my father."

"Your Dad?" he half yelled and acted nervous. "Please don't say he knows you're here with me?"

She continued to tread water.

"NO, God no! I've got to see Brooklyn Jimmy, five minutes."

"His name is Brooklyn Jimmy?" he asked.

"Yes."

"Who did he have to whack to get that name?"

"You know, you're way too white bread from the suburbs to be allowed to use the term *whack* in a sentence."

"Oh, Mrs. Girardi warned me all about *whacking*. Who is he?"

"He's a famous handicapper, actually. Maybe he'll give me a tip for the race today."

"I already know who I'm betting."

"You do?"

"Yes, but I'm not telling you yet, you pick your own horse."

"Don't worry, Shorty, I will. You forget I've been going to the track since I was in diapers."

"Fine. We'll drop off your package. Will we be tailed by the Feds afterward?"

"No."

"Good."

"Thank you!" she said and with that, she pushed herself up on the ladder and kissed him on the cheek, "I'm really excited about tonight," she finished.

"Me, too," he whispered.

"No one would ever believe that part of my perfect weekend with you is a trip to the racetrack."

"A girl after my own heart."

"Hey, aren't you going to come in? The water feels great."

"Your lips feel great around my dick."

"Augie!"

"Okay, okay, I'm in."

He jumped in the pool and pulled Benny toward him. He grabbed her legs and wrapped them around his waist and pushed her back up against the swimming pool wall. She tried to push him off of her and then finally relented as his body made her body warm in the water. She rested her head on his shoulder. She let him hold her in his arms and kiss her neck. It tickled.

"Our first time…" she began.

"Yes, what now? Something else I've forgotten?" He whispered back into her ear.

"You saved me from that asshole at the bar, remember?"

"You think I *saved* you that night?"

"Yeah," she said softly, *convinced.*

"That's sweet Benny."

He lifted his face from her neck and looked into her eyes and stroked her hair back as she finished her story. He could tell this story was important to her. She continued to lock her arms around his neck.

"I called you from a pay phone and you showed up ten minutes later. You rescued me that night and that's why I decided to finally sleep with you, to *lose my virginity to you.* It was completely unplanned. I..I thought you were my hero."

He leaned forward, grabbed her face, and kissed her. She sighed. She didn't know that he didn't know that's how she remembered that night. It was her favorite, favorite night.

"You should also know I weigh more when I'm soaked in water," she had to add.

He kissed her even more forcefully this time around and stuck his hand in her bikini bottoms under the water. She quickly retrieved this hand and put it back around her waist.

"Damn you, *Irish,*" was all she could get out and then, she laughed.

5

When Benny and Augie met in the air conditioned hallway, they were both dressed so conventionally that it felt like they *were* on a date. She wore a corseted, peach Isabel Marant spaghetti strap dress over her lightly tanned skin. Her solid gold Cartier watch stood out on her bare arm and her diamond stud earrings sparkled with the slightest movement of her head. She wore a small, cream colored linen hat.

His shaved head and slightly tanned face were covered with a few faint moles. He wore small framed tortoise shell Ray-Bans and a long sleeved, olive linen shirt, unbuttoned, with rolled sleeves. He also wore his prized watch, light-weight belted khakis, and simple slip-on brown loafers.

When she stood next to him she smelled, *cologne?*

"You look pretty," he said as he played with the scruff on his chin that he had not shaved for two days.

"This is a date," she said as they stood side by side inside the shivery lobby of Soho House and waited for their Town Car.

"What?" he asked.

"You're wearing cologne," she pointed out.

"So?" he defended. "It was free in the locker room."

"Okay, you just told me I'm pretty and you're wearing cologne," she continued.

"So?" he teased. He loved any opportunity to get her riled up.

"We're on a date. A *real* date," she finished.

"Fine, yes, we're on a date," he confirmed.

"I'm your *girlfriend*," she said.

He had to hold back from being his normally defensive self. Being designated his *girlfriend* had been a source of contention between the two for twenty years.

"Yes, you're my..." he began.

"Say it!" she demanded.

"My..." he teased, without finishing.

"Say it!" she said, in a voice that was a little too loud for the lobby. Being the exhibitionists that they were, they never cared if somebody...*heard.*

"Girlfriend," he said as slowly as slowly can be.

She leaned over and kissed him on the cheek. This was progress. Twenty years! Progress!

"Miracles do happen!"

"Oh God Benny, lighten up!" he scoffed.

"You called me your girlfriend and lightning did not strike you down! You lived through it!

Amazing!" she said as she lifted her arms in the air as if in a Pentecostal prayer.

"You're my girlfriend this weekend Benny, in the *bubble.*"

The valet opened the door and led them to their well-chilled car. She told herself that he was absolutely right. They *were* in a *bubble.*

118

6

The driver moved from the Meatpacking District over to Houston and down Sullivan into Soho. Augie opened the door for her and they found themselves in front of one of the best Italian sandwich shops in the city – Alidoro – that kept funky hours and that always had a line waiting. The Girardi's recommended it. Because of the heat and the summer travel, the shop wasn't crowded so they were able to walk right in and order. Every sandwich on the menu was mouthwatering. It was hard to choose.

Their eyes perused the assortment of waxy cheese wheels and wedges, pudgy balls of smoked mozzarella, cured meats studded with black and white peppercorns and green pistachios, freshly made pasta noodles and glass jars of homemade marinara sauce. Plump, green, cracked olives competed against wrinkled, black, cured olives marinated in clay crocks filled with olive oil and *giardiniera*.

Augie noticed dried sausages bound in meat netting and tied with butcher's string hanging from a metal scaffold that suspended from tin-tiled ceiling panels. He was ready to eat...

Benny stared at a large glass canister filled with pastel-colored, candy coated Jordan almonds.

Imported *anything* always reminded her of her Nonna who was "steeped" in the ways of the old country. She spotted long, shiny loaves of bread sticking out of a plastic-lined trash container. She hoped the bread was still warm...

"I like it all," Augie said.

"Me too. What's your favorite? Tell me, we'll get it."

"I like Prosciutto," he said.

"*Brashoot?*" she kidded.

"*Brashoot?*" the Butcher asked next.

"Yes, *Bra-shoot,*" he confirmed.

"My apologies. He's *Irish,* we'll take one cut in half. Augie, darling, can you run to the Bodega across the street and get us two Tall Boys? *Bra-shoot* is very salty."

Augie walked across the street and bought the two beers. When he crossed the street, he found her waiting by the door with a paper bag. He opened one of the Tall Boys that was still in a paper bag and he handed it to Benny who took a huge drink.

"How much time until we need to head out?" she asked.

"About forty-five minutes. If your trip to the Diamond District goes according to plan and only lasts five minutes."

"Let's eat these in Washington Square Park."

"It's hot."

"Yeah. But it reminds me of college and all the NYU students. It reminds me of us – in college."

He walked over to the driver and told him to pick them up at the park in forty-five minutes. He opened up his own Tall Boy and the two walked above Houston and over to the park. There were many college kids that were lying on blankets reading books or barefoot and throwing Frisbees.

"It reminds me of the quad," he said.

"Yeah. I love the idea of a patch of college life like the one we had inside this busy city."

"You do love it here, don't you?" he asked as she led him to a patch of shade under a tree where the Baci Ball courts used to be. "New York?"

"Yes, I do. Maybe it's because I've never lived here. But I think it's a place where anything is possible and I can't exist in a world without possibility," she answered as she helped him lay down a small blanket from the trunk of the Town Car.

"You definitely have the outsider's perspective," he said, "wait until you try and get an apartment. Wait until you pay for an apartment."

"I told you, I've always wanted to live here. Downtown, near JR's. New York *is* the heart of the publishing world and I'm a writer. I even think my kids would like it. They already like it," she finished.

He didn't know how to react to any discussion of children. He had children. She had children. They were the same ages. He wondered if he would ever meet her children. He wondered if her daughter looked or acted like her. He thought it would be difficult to replicate her personality.

He started to question her openly by talking of a move to New York City, with her children, without a mention of her husband – or now, *ex-husband*. He thought it odd, but didn't mention it, remembering that he had not uttered one word about his wife.

They sat down on the blanket and she took the giant sub sandwich out of the paper bag. She waited and watched him take a bite before she took hers. His fingers became coated in green olive oil. He licked them while he chewed on and tried to swallow the Prosciutto and Buffalo Mozzarella sandwich.

"Why are you staring at me?" he asked as he tore into and chewed another bite.

"The olive oil," she answered.

"Does it turn you on because you're Italian?"

"Of course. Makes me think of the Roman Polanski film **Bitter Moon**. Did you see it?"

He took another bite but his cheeks were curling up as he flashed a wide grin.

"Yes, I've seen it, I've seen every one of his movies," he corrected with a full mouth of salted pork.

"Of course you have," she said and rolled her eyes. "That scene – where she, Polanski's wife, pours the milk all over her breasts. You know the one I'm talking about?"

He shook his head up and down and continued to eat.

"And Peter Coyote licks them?" he remarked in a garbled fashion as he swallowed.

She blushed immediately and looked out onto the grass and at the other filled, blankets.

"Yes."

"Would you like to coat *me* in olive oil?" he asked.

She couldn't stop blushing. She looked away from him, his hands were dripping in the stuff. She chugged her Tall Boy and didn't touch the sandwich.

"And *lick me*?" he asked again. The smile had disappeared from his face. She was afraid evidence of her desire would leak through her thong. Wearing a thin dress was a bad idea.

"Yes," she agreed, not looking at him as he licked the olive oil off of his fingers, one by one, now that he was finished eating both of the sandwich halves. She held one of his hands in both of her own and licked the tips of each finger. She looked up at him.

"I'd like to touch you right now," she tempted.

"Remember when we flew together?" he roused.

"Yes, of course I do."

"And I put the blanket over our laps?"

She was getting extremely anxious by her memory of that flight. His daring demeanor was one of the reasons why she loved him. He was *brave*. He made her *brave*.

"Yes."

"Sit on my lap. Just for a few minutes."

"Augie..."

"Please. Over here, Now..." he insisted. Then, he grabbed her by the waist and sat her on his lap as he leaned against a tree.

"Oh!" she yelped. She felt his hard-on beneath her, grinding up against her ass.

His hands quickly pulled the bottom of her dress up to her waist. They were covered waist down by the blanket. He turned her face to his and stuck his tongue down her throat, forcefully. She gasped, yet she opened her mouth and legs up to him, naturally.

All she could think of was, *my panties are drenched and they're leaking through to my dress,* and, *I can't believe how goddamn horny I am around this guy.*

All he could think of was, *I can't believe how horny I am around this girl. All-time record for hard-ons in one weekend since turning forty.*

Then she thought, *I am just as much of an exhibitionist as Augie.*

Then he thought, *When did Benny turn into such an exhibitionist? It's usually just me.*

There were people, everywhere.

"Press down," he urged as his voice cracked. She stopped kissing him as soon as he tried to move her thong over to the side and stick a finger inside her.

"NO, NO. This, this, isn't, isn't going to work. You'll make a mess of me before we get to Belmont!" She pushed his arm away from between her legs. She caught her breath and slapped him across his face, in-between gentle and hard. She used to slap him across the face all the time. She loved it, and he loved it. She was Italian and had a violent side. She almost wished she hadn't slapped him because it just made her hornier. God, forty year olds are still horny?

"Damn you Augie Baxter! Why did you ever come home with me that first night? I'm sorry, BEG to come home with me that first night. I told you over and over again NOT to come over!"

Frustrated, she rolled over to the other side of the blanket, beside him. He had his hands over his pants to hide his hard-on.

"Oh, Benny, what am I supposed to do with this?" he asked as if he really wanted a verbal answer. Instinctively, she grabbed the excess blanket and threw it over his lap.

"Just like the plane ride," she said softly. Then she quickly unbuttoned him and placed her hand down his pants. He just closed his eyes for a minute while she touched him. She kissed and tugged on his ear lobe with her lips and whispered into it and licked it as if she were cleaning his fur.

His features stiffened. He squeezed her bare, moist thigh with his hand.

"Please, Augie. Don't touch me, I'll lose my concentration."

"But I touched you, too, on that plane ride..."

"Sorry, babe..."

"Keep doing that," was all he could whisper as she squeezed and pounded down with both her hands, twisting, on his huge erection as quickly as she could.

"Look at all these people in the park, all these students. Do you think they know what I'm doing to you right now?"

"No."

"Look at those girls over there, NYU girls in short shorts talking about fucking their boyfriends. I want them to know what's it like to see a grown man be satisfied. Will you help me show them?"

"Like this," he said and used one of his hands to help her squeeze harder. No one would know better how to jerk off Augie, than Augie.

"I can't wait until you're inside me again..." she began to say while he moaned softly, closed his eyes, grinned, and sweated profusely, "I want to do everything. I want to see everything. I promise you, I'll do whatever you ask. Just please promise me you're going to be inside me soon, Augie, I'm so horny right now. *I want you to make me so sore that I can't walk...*"

With one last stroke, in unison, he loudly groaned and jerked forward in an attempt to contain any spillage onto the blanket, Benny, his hands or his pants. She leaned over and kissed him on his still shaking lips. Then she put the paper bag with the Tall Boy up to his mouth.

"Drink," she ordered.

New Benny, he thought.

7

Augie was a bit drowsy in the back of the Town Car en route to the Diamond District. He put his head in Benny's lap. She loved this. She played with his face and ears and nipples under his chest through his shirt as she read the day's Racing Form with her other hand.

"Who are you betting?" she asked him.

"I'm not telling!" he answered.

"Oh, come on. I'm going to find out eventually. I want to make sure I don't pick your horse. I need to run against you."

"Fine. It's Shorty Forty."

"Oh, really? That's so cute, *Shorty*, I mean *Irish*, I mean *Augie*."

"I'm going to win."

"Sure you are."

"Okay, I normally just pick the number eight horse, but there are only six running. Dammit.

I'm going to ask Brooklyn Jimmy. He'll know what to bet."

The Town Car pulled up to one of many jewelry malls. They all looked the same. So many desperate people stood outside, talking in different languages, trying to coax you inside. Benny got out of the car, went inside a nondescript building and smiled and spoke to an Orthodox Jewish man. She disappeared from the store window as Augie watched her. She was in and out of the store and back into the Town Car in under five minutes.

"I told you, under five minutes."

"Do I dare ask you, what was in that package?"

"It's none of your business, but it's an old army photo, that's all. It's sentimental."

"You were always one for sentiment."

"I think you secretly enjoy sentiment, but don't want to admit it. You like that I paid attention to you when you were young. You were ecstatic about that chapter from my novel I sent."

"Well, I hadn't spoken to you in what, a decade? You told me we shouldn't talk anymore remember?"

"I was eight months pregnant. It was Christmas. I couldn't be....*like that*...and see you. Have drinks somewhere in the city while you were in town like you asked? I had to let you go in order to accept my life. I thought it was for the best. It was for the best."

"Then you send me your chapter and ask me if I'm cool with you publishing *this*? *Us*?"

"I thought you liked it when I shocked you. Admit it. I'm the most exciting woman you've ever met."

"It took me awhile to grasp what you wrote."

"It felt like the right time for us to talk again. And I haven't been as happy as I was writing that damn thing. It brought me back to life, Augie. I love *our* story. Even if we never ended up together."

"Except for this weekend."

"Except for this weekend."

"Not all love stories end in marriage, you know?" she pressed as a matter of fact.

"What horse did Brooklyn Jimmy tell you to bet, Benny?"

"The Girl Who Got Away."

8

Benny was surprised how beautiful the gardens were outside of Belmont Park. She had seen a lot, perhaps too many racetracks in her lifetime due to time spent with her father. But she had to admit that this was one of the prettiest. Thank God, they were there for only one race...

Augie wanted to show off his knowledge of the horse racing industry to her. How he loved to participate in the Triple Crown races. He felt he had designed a near airtight system of winning based on the turf, the jockey, the age of the horse and the previous winnings of the horse. Benny told him she only bet horses based on name or number. That was it. Her magic formula. She wished she treated her relationship with him as lightly as she treated betting on horses.

She felt flattered that he showed such an interest in this world that she had grown up in - a world of sports, gambling and racetracks. Of loud, and boisterous Italian-Americans. He had even gone to the racetrack with her and her father, twice. Who does that? She couldn't figure it out. She always remembered how brave she thought Augie was for being thrown into a situation with her slightly-scary-to-strangers Sicilian father. Augie had seen every mobster movie ever made and his level of paranoia had to be high. He knew her father had some insight into the fact that the two of them were more than friends. She told Augie, *my father has requested to meet you.* When he showed up to her apartment in college for dinner and shook her father's hand she thought, *I always thought Augie had balls – but, showing up like this, to meet one of the most feared men in America – spectacular.*

To battle his nerves, Augie overate at dinner and had too much of the Carlo Rossi handle jug of Chianti. After everyone left, he laid down on her bed and clutched his stomach. She just looked at him lying there, silently suffering, and was more turned on than perhaps he was ready to handle at that moment, still digesting. He suffered, for her. He was brave, for her.

She had never met anyone who even slightly understood her offbeat world and now she met someone who not only was knowledgeable about it, but liked it. She thought she would never meet anyone like this again. He took her source of insecurity and recreated it as an asset. He was powerful.

She remembered his first visit to the racetrack when they were still lovers. They were waiting outside in her father's Cadillac to finally go home. He had endured her gracefully loveable yet uncouth and foul mouthed, degenerate gambler father that whole day. A day in the life...

"So, this is how your father pays for you to go to college" he slowly asked her, as the engine hummed with the heat on.

"Yes," she answered.

"It must be hard for you. Your existence being so dependent on a game of chance."

Was this intimacy? She wondered, instantaneously hit with a desire to tell him that she loved him. He actually understood what no one had ever understood about her before. About how shaky her foundation had always felt. How embarrassed at times she felt. Augie was not like anyone she had ever met. Not like any friend she had ever had. This was the most honest conversation she had ever had. And she wanted more of them.

She did tell him she loved him, later that day, after spontaneous sex on her girlfriend's bed.

While she was taking a nap on the couch, he made a pass at her. Then he moved her in front of a giant gold mirror that rested on a soft carpet in the living room. He took his shirt off and he unbuttoned his pants. He unbuttoned her shirt and her pants. He tried to get her on all fours in front of the giant gold mirror. The room lights were on, so she refused. He begged her to do it. He was angry at her about it, he was getting so frustrated with her inhibitions about her body. He hurled a series of questions at her, why wouldn't she let him look at her? Why couldn't she relax and be herself with him when they were naked together? What's your problem, Benny? What happened to you when you were younger? Why do you act like this?

Benny's spin on the events were a series of moral justifications and self-revelations. She reasoned that he was her guest, staying at her friend's fabulous apartment, for free, by themselves, and in her hometown. Yet she was the one who felt vulnerable, and she was the one living in a glass house on the verge of shattering.

Benny held back a tear as she told him she would rather be upstairs and in the bed. She slowly walked up the spiral staircase slowly to her friend's bedroom, holding her breasts in her hands. They were still big but a little bit smaller from how he remembered when he first went home with her a year prior. Since then, she had lost almost twenty pounds. He probably hadn't noticed the weight loss. She was sure he'd notice everything about her breasts.

All of a sudden, he sprinted from the living room floor and up the stairs, to chase after her. She ran up the last few steps and into her girlfriend's bedroom before he pushed her face down on the edge of the bed. He ripped her jeans and underwear down and began to fuck her immediately, pushing her whole body up against the edge of the bed with such a force that she was stunned and winded. He pulled her hair so far back that she was afraid to move beneath him. She screamed...loudly.

All Augie was thinking was *I want to fuck this girl, I'm going to fuck this girl, I'm fucking this girl.* This girl no longer meant Benny. He was done, he'd had had it, enough was enough! He was fed up with her goddamn insecurity. He wanted her to be confident, to like herself, to like her body not just for her sake, but for his. He thought he had always provided a refuge for her to be uninhibited.

Didn't she know that? Didn't she know that allowing him to see her – under the lights – was for both of their pleasure? For her to get out of her head and feel free? He did want something from Benny. He wanted a lot from Benny. He thought she would rise to this level of greatness he had thought her capable of. She was so smart and strong, overwhelmingly sexy, to him, at least, but so immature, so insecure, and not ready to be his girlfriend. Not ready to deem herself beautiful.

She would always let him lead, let him seduce her, so this is what she was going to get. This is what she wanted. He was going to give it to her. He was going to fuck her, this girl. This painfully insecure girl who trusted him more than she had ever trusted anyone ever in her life. Despite his knowing, he blocked it all out. He had just met her grandmother that day. She introduced him to the Sunday dinner ritual and to her entire family-babies to old folks. They saw him as a potential. A potential something for their innocent Benny, the late bloomer. They were graduating in a month. What more could happen between the two of them? What more could happen?

She remembered how he used to always stare at her when he was inside her, how he used to force her to look into his eyes. He liked to overwhelm and possess her, he knew he was the only man she had ever given herself to. He knew how hard it was for her to say yes to him at all. He ...owned her. This time, she did not look at him and he did not look up at her. They were disconnecting.

He threw her down on her back and started to push into her hard, not looking at her at all. He was hurting her now. She was scared, and no longer turned on. It was chafing. He finished inside of her.

She had not put in any birth control but she didn't care. He didn't care. Her brain still reeled, I love you, I love you, I love you...and it just came out, finally it just came out, I love you. Benny caught her breath, knowing before she even uttered the first syllable that this experiment was over. But she had told him, at least she had told him. She had revealed her true self.

And she was right. He would break up with her within a few hours along with a sleepless night and most uncomfortable shared flight back to school. She sobbed the whole time on his chest. She only associated love with pain from that point forward, never fulfillment, never a higher level and never an *I love you* back. He apologized repeatedly. But what hurt her was that he said they never should have done this. She saw it all differently. It was never just an agreement between two friends. It was romantic. 'I was just kidding myself, thinking I was just your friend, your old friend. Are you one of the only people IN THE WORLD who has not seen **When Harry Met Sally?**' He had convinced her on the swings at Ursuline Academy at midnight that it was better for her that they were friends, and that not being romantic was a good thing. After that first taste of intimacy in the back of her father's Cadillac, all she could think of was *I love him, I love him, I love him.*

9

Benny and Augie walked into the VIP section dressed in their finery. They were given a two top with leather chairs facing the window and the track. Since Belmont Park had the largest track in the country, he delighted in every accouterment of the racetrack. He constantly wanted to convey to her his education and experience when it came to horse racing. Apparently, he had been to many racetracks and he had participated in many notable, high money races over the past twenty odd years. He told her he discussed the Triple Crown race from the Belmont, years ago, when her father used him as a media consultant. At the time, she had asked her father not to tell her one damn thing about their conversation. She wanted to know absolutely nothing and pretended it wasn't happening. She wondered if he spent time on the phone and e-mail with her father because he feared for his life. He actually liked and respected her father a great deal for his talent as a pool player and as a member of the Pool Players Hall of Fame. She wondered if this was the only connection between them.

"Your Dad and I, we talked about the Belmont race at the Triple Crown a few years ago. How I had bet the winning horse that year. Your Dad told me, wait, he told me, "I got there early," he said, laughing and pausing for effect, "I got there early..." trying to mimic her father, "I need to look that race up again to see what year that was."

"I don't know anything that occurred between you and my father. He mentioned he talked to my old boyfriend. See, even my father called you my *old boyfriend*. I told him to not say another word. I didn't want to know. My Dad kept talking and laughing about you and how you were a good kid and I just put my hands over my ears and repeated to him, I don't want to know." She held back telling him that her father had a picture of the two of them up and framed in his house. Then she told him. She found it so odd that her father did this all on his own. It annoyed her to no end to have to see it whenever she visited. She secretly went over to his house while he was out of town and replaced it with a picture of a family member. Her father hadn't mentioned anything to her about it. She told Augie all this, remembering how strong she was back then. She had to shut him out completely in order to be a wife and mother. He even sent her group e-mails which she annoyingly deleted immediately. Then she contacted him. After eight years. She had written a novel that was based on a dream. She didn't tell him that she had a dream about him at least three times a week. The dream always ended with her desperately trying to find his phone number. Sometimes it was just missing the last number. She was so frustrated within the dream, in not being able to find that phone number, that she would kick and scream and cry and punch walls the way she used to as a child when she had a tantrum.

10

Benny and Augie congratulated a couple who had just won the last race at Belmont. The horse was named "Seem Like Old Times," and the number eight. The couple was dressed way too flashy for the Upper East side, but perfect for the VIP Section of the Racetrack, where the dress code was strictly enforced.

The man was named Bobby. He was tanned, around sixty, had Robert Evans slicked back hair, Porsche sunglasses, a sharkskin suit and exotic leather cowboy boots. He only carried one-hundred- dollar bills in his pocket and wore a gold pinky ring with thick gold chains around his neck. He spoke in a Southern accent. Benny and Augie both said "Alabama" aloud at the very same time and Bobby was so impressed he tried to give them each a hundred dollar bill, which they politely turned down, laughing.

Bobby's girlfriend, Casey, was ten years younger and wore a long, hot pink, silk, spaghetti strap dress and high heeled silver sandals. Her blonde hair was up in a bun with bangs covering any forehead wrinkles and framing her heart shaped face. Her caked-on makeup was thick, dark beige and garish. Her heavily applied make-up and giant fake boobs made her look doll-like. Benny wondered if her eyeliner was tattooed on. Benny never wore a lot of makeup and she *never* wore eyeliner. It wasn't intentional, she just never could because of her contact lenses and sensitive eyes. It did help give her a youthful look. At times, she would apply a little glitter shadow and a top layer of mascara. She was jealous that Casey, ten years her senior, could pull off a dress like that *without* a bra. '*So lucky,*' she thought.

Bobby and Casey were dripping in jewels: white and black diamonds, sapphires, rubies, and pearls. The security guards at the door just stared at their table.

Casey cased the joint like a girl who had been around the block and knew her way around a racetrack or any other gambling institution. She kept assessing every person who walked in and out of the VIP section as a potential thief or a potential threat. For some reason, she chose the table Benny and Augie were at to sit down. She must have found the younger couple boring or safe, maybe she knew they were having an affair. Casey seemed to know everything. She even explained to the bartender every ingredient she wanted in her *Top Shelf* Mississippi Mudslide. She could calculate payouts on all the eighth race horses, told Augie he was a fool for betting "Shorty Forty" and that Benny was onto something with "The Girl Who Got Away."

"It's a long shot," Casey told them, "but sometimes I just bet on names. Nothing scientific about it. I just like to go with my gut."

"Let's Quinella it, then Benny. Raise our chances," Augie suggested.

"You just like shouting out combinations to the Teller. Makes you feel cool. Like a seasoned horse man," she teased. "Do you have any idea *how many* of my relatives have been *buried* with a Racing Form in their front pockets? How about a Perfecta instead? Greater risk but a greater reward. " she teased. Casey smirked.

"I do like it, and it's more fun with a variety of bets," he conceded.

"Okay, okay just do it." Benny reached for her clutch to hand him some money, "Here,"

"No, I've got it," he told her.

"But I like to bet my *own* money," she insisted.

"Not this weekend," he told her winking as he walked up to the Teller with Bobby to place their bets. Augie would savor his two minutes at the Teller booth, that was for sure. He would try and show off in front of Bobby who would blow him out of the water with his horse number combinations and the thousands in cash he would lay out at the window. Augie was a bit more generous than usual with his bets. *This is a weekend worth the risks,* he thought.

Benny walked over to the VIP ladies room. Even with the air conditioning, she felt like she needed some cold water on her arms and chest. Maybe she shouldn't have said yes to that Mississippi Mudslide that Casey sent her way.

"I'll join you," Casey told her, grabbing her own giant Chanel bag and following Benny into the powder room. Once through the doors, Benny ran the cold water in the sink while Casey took out her compact and curled her perfect eyelashes.

"So," Casey began.

"So," Benny answered nervously. She wondered what was coming next.

"How long have you and Augie been having an affair?" Casey asked her boldly.

"What?" Benny whispered.

"If those are even your real names?" Casey questioned again. She took a piece of gum out of her purse and offered one to Benny.

"We, we..." she began.

"Oh, spill it," Casey said. "I just paid the attendant a C-note to keep the door closed so I can sneak a smoke. You've got five minutes, entertain me."

"Just this weekend. Although we have known each other for over twenty years. He was.."

"What? He was what? Your boyfriend?"

"My first time."

"Whoa! Really?"

"Yeah."

"What were you like, thirteen, fourteen?" Casey asked, trying to figure out how old Benny was.

"Um, almost twenty-one," Benny answered.

"Jesus Christ. What were you, going to be a nun or somethin'? Did he kidnap you from a goddamn convent?" Casey said as she nearly choked on her gum while puffing away on her cigarette.

"No – college – and believe me, my college was definitely not a convent."

"Did you love him? He's got a nice ass, you know. Sorry if I'm so blunt. I notice these things. As far as I can tell he's hung like a horse. I hope for your sake, I'm right."

Benny started laughing nervously. "Oh, Casey, you don't *know* how right you are."

"So, why now? You both married, had kids?" Casey pushed.

"Actually – just him. He doesn't know I got a divorce. I'm afraid.."

"To tell him because he'll think you're needy."

"Yes. Exactly. It's so much safer when both parties are... spoken for."

"Ain't that the truth. Men are so fickle I tell you, but so are women. We're the same. We got fetishes just like the best of them. We get cagey, too."

"Augie, well, he was my first *everything*, Casey."

"So you *were* in a convent, before you got to college?"

"No, I was just shy."

"He doesn't seem shy."

"He's not."

"But then again you don't seem so shy either."

"But...*I am.*"

"Fuckin' A, you LOVE HIM."

"Well," Benny began, "maybe just the idea..."

"Rule number one, *girlfriend*," Casey implored, as she flushed her cigarette down the toilet and grabbed another piece of gum out of her purse, "You don't have an affair with a man you *love*."

"I like him so much, but I don't know if he deserves me.... certainly not til he's s ingle"

"You mean you haven't slept together yet?"

"No, I mean, almost. There's just this thingy-ma-bob, a, a, voice, inside of me, that's new, and that tells me, I deserve... *things*. I don't know if we're just acting, both of us."

"Listen to that voice, honey. It's called self-esteem, girl-friend. Own that shit!"

"We're just hanging out like w did when we were kids, get-ting to know each other again. But also, it's...been awhile if you know what I'm sayin..."

"Well, then…"

"Didn't you ever want a second chance? A second chance with someone? When you've grown up, *kind of*? When you feel good about yourself? Really, really, good, *finally*?"

"I don't sentimentalize sex, and neither should you. If you're not going to give up the goods to that cutie out there, then the least you can do is have a shot with me before the next race."

Benny begrudgingly did a Tequila shot with Casey at the bar, *Top Shelf of course*, walking back to the table the four of them shared in the VIP room, the race only two minutes away.

Augie shivered and turned to Benny sitting beside him, her throat still hot from the alcohol. He claimed his territory and kissed her on the cheek.

"You okay, there, Ben?" he asked.

"Yep. You bet my horse?" she asked, clearing her throat. She *hated* Tequila.

"Yep," he told her.

"My soon to be winning horse?" she added.

"Well, we'll have to see what happens," he told them.

"Do we win more money if our horses win *together*?" Benny asked Casey, the math whiz, the expert, the woman of the world.

Casey gave them another once-over while Bobby looked out onto the track with his gaudy, bejeweled binoculars at the horses being put in their pens. "In this case…*together*, yes. If you hit the Perfecta you win the most, that's your horse comes in first, Benny, with Augie's in second. Great payday but the odds are against you."

11

"Holy Shit!" Benny yelled.

Augie stood in front of her with a handful of cash, ten thousand dollars to be exact. Even he felt a rush, thinking, '*We are getting lucky this weekend, aren't we?*' He almost suggested they telephone her father to show off. Augie was forty-three years old and married. And not to Benny. Her father would want to kill him. Any affection her father had for him would go right out the window.

Augie remembered twenty years earlier, when he discovered a shovel and a baseball bat in the back of her father's vintage Cadillac and thinking either Benny or her father was definitely planning on killing him at some point during his visit and burying his body in the woods somewhere in Wisconsin.

"Yeah." Augie responded, hands filled with crisp hundred dollar bills "I've never held this much cash before."

"So, it's true, then?" she asked.

"What's true?"

"Leprechauns really exist."

"Benny..." he sneered. He was exceptionally good at *sneering*.

"I've found you, my little Leprechaun, at the end of the rainbow, in Queens, with a Pot of Gold."

"Correction – Pot O' Gold."

"I love you, Augie Baxter!" she screamed at the top of her lungs. She knew that no one acted appropriately when gambling, so a little hysteria did not draw any attention. There they were, mature, handsomely dressed, smiling brightly. Towering over him in her high heels, she grabbed his fat cheeks and kissed him on the mouth.

"I feel like Steve McQueen and Ali McGraw after their big score in **'The Getaway'** when they lay in bed with all that dirty money."

He grabbed her face, cutting her off, and kissed her. Winning all of this money at the racetrack – on The Girl Who Got Away – was a giant adrenaline rush for both of them. Benny stood stunned and flushed as Augie released her mouth, "Movies?" he asked.

"The two of us are the stars of all of my favorite films. Don't you know that?" she told him.

They walked out of the restricted VIP entrance of the racetrack and into their waiting Town Car. As soon as they got inside the car, he started kissing her neck.

"Please don't give me a hickey. It's too hot for me to wear a turtleneck. And I'm forty, not twenty." He started laughing and caressing her body over her dress. She tried to keep his hands at bay to give him a good talking to.

"That's a lot of cash, Augie. Normally my people carry a loaded weapon when transporting that amount, or at the very least a pocket knife. I hope your wrestling moves are still sharp."

"How do you think I am able to pin you down so quickly?" he asked, "Those legs of yours, they shake a lot. Why can't you keep them still?"

"Still is something I will never be around you, Augie."

She moved his face to hers and kissed him deeply with her tongue.

"My god! Why are you such a good kisser now? Wait, don't tell me! I just...I just don't remember us kissing this well together before. Are we *connecting*?" she asked, smiling and proud at this revelation.

"We have a little time to kill before dinner. Are you ready?" he said, panting.

"Ready?" she asked, rubbing her crotch up and down his thigh.

"Sit on my lap" he ordered and patted his lap. He liked to order her around. He liked to tell her to sit on his lap, she liked to oblige.

"Oh, no, Augie. There is something incredibly important you seem to have overlooked."

"Um, birth control? Are you on the pill?" he asked, resuming the licking of her ear lobe and sucking on her neck. Her hair was becoming a disaster.

She was angry for a short second but did not say anything.

Even when she was married and her OB/GYN asked her if she wanted to go on the pill she said no. It made her think of Augie and how she hated him. A few months after they started sleeping together, in college, he had asked her to get on some birth control. She thought that meant she was now his girlfriend. Even Louise admitted to being wrong about Augie, that he did want her as his girlfriend. So, she went to the doctor, got the pills, and before she had the chance to even take one, he broke things off with her, saying they had to go back to just being friends.

She wondered if she was acting like a fool right now. *'Probably.' she thought.* They were *pretending* to be boyfriend and girlfriend. Just for a weekend. *Pretending.* They were pretending. And because they were pretending, she could tell him she loved him whenever she wanted. Just to try it out. Did she love him? She always thought she had, but now at forty, she questioned it. Maybe Louise was right, with her three graduate degrees, Benny had romanticized Augie. Maybe even Augie *was* right. Maybe they *were* just friends that had slept together and maybe they would never be more than that.

"I'll never go on the pill," she told him in the backseat of the Town Car, dazed now, and looking out the tinted back window.

"Why?" Augie asked, interested.

"It's a *long story*," she answered.

She broke free from his clutches and pulled her dress down.

"What is it?" he asked, confused.

"My cut. You owe me seven thousand dollars!" she yelled. It was just like her to all of a sudden begin screaming at him. She didn't care if her screaming upset him or not, this was Benny at forty, and the way she had always been, easily excitable.

"Seven Thousand? No. You get thirty percent. Three grand. I put up the money for the bet. Remember?"

"You insisted on putting up the money for the bet. Your horse, Shorty Forty, *lost*, remember?"

"It came in second, that's how we won the Perfecta!"

"Still, 'The Girl Who Got Away' came in first. I get seventy percent, you get thirty."

"Our horses won together, so, I get at least half of these winnings," he argued.

"Fine, now take me to Madison Avenue. You're buying me a dress."

12

Benny and Augie quickly entered the exclusive store while their driver circled the block. All Augie could think was, '*There are so many beautiful bodies inside here, even the Mannequins.*' All Benny could think was, '*I know the dress I want, I know the dress I want.*' She had been dreaming about this dress ever since she spoke to Augie on the phone that winter. It was a dress she found in Vogue just that week while she was fingering through the magazine during a pedicure. She saw it and *knew* this dress was all a part of her fantasy. Skin tight with cherries on it, it was just like when she was in college and had another dress from Vogue that she wore in her fantasy. She had to have it. It was the dress she wore in her dreams! The one where her hair is teased and her eyes have fake lashes and heavy, liquid black eyeliner – a la – *La Dolce Vita*.

The dreams were shot in black and white. She and Augie walking down Sixth Avenue, past the Little Red Schoolhouse and into Da Silvano's to argue about their mutual existential crises and their love for the singer Rick James. Benny believed she was the R& B singer Teena Marie and that Aggie was Rick James; except without the braids and/or musical talent. Teena and Rick had one of those Teacher/Protégé affairs that never quite ended. Rick was the great love of Teena's life, he was her best friend. She always loved him; even in old age. She wrote many songs about him and after he passed away, she passed away not too soon after. Or, at least that was what Benny recalled from an old TV episode of VH1's "Behind The Music." She was sure Augie would know which episode she was referring to since he was, Mr., I've seen everything that's ever been on television.

Once inside the store, she had decided she would only speak to him in Italian. She loved how fine Italian tailoring could make a *man* out of him. A tight black suit would justifiably show off his soccer thighs and strong back. All it took were the Persols and he was a forty year old, *sort of* Marcello Mastroianni. Her Marcello. Her smoke free Marcello. She realized that the only thing Augie and Marcello shared was their ability to stare at a woman and make her feel *desirable*. He gave that gift to her, whether he knew this or not.

He thought they were only buying her a dress, but she asked the staff to outfit him with a black suit worthy of Fellini's classic film **La Dolce Vita,** tight and tailored – *like an Italian.* He was known for wearing pleated baggy pants because he felt he needed room down there. But she wanted him on complete display. Her vision Included a three-thousand-dollar suit that should be tight around the *coglioni*. She pointed to his crotch in front of the four-foot-eleven tailor named Silvio and said "Grande." Augie laughed as he took a swig of the Campari that a pretty twenty-year-old poured for him. The girl sifted through the CD collection and he pointed to her XX Album.

"Please, play that," he asked. She smiled and said "Of course."

While Augie was dragged through the men's section by another pretty salesperson, Benny told her saleslady - "*Con ciliege. The Cherry dress?*"

" *Si, Si,*" the saleslady answered. She lived in another chic neighborhood that used to be filled with Italians, Brooklyn's Cobble Hill.

"*Aspetta, Aspetta,*" Benny said, grabbing some cash out of her purse and speaking English, "I need a bra and panties, old fashioned, you know, the Dolce & Gabbana style, in black?"

"Yes," the saleslady answered.

Augie and Benny were in side-to-side dressing rooms. This wasn't standard operating procedure at the store, but it was late on Saturday, so the staff obliged. He tried on a suit, which was quickly removed and taken down a hall by the tailor, leaving him alone. He walked over to Benny's side wearing only his boxers, while the seamstress made a few, quick minor adjustments. Benny stood high and over six feet in black platform heels. She was just stepping out of the cherry dress as Augie entered the room.

"Perfect fit," the saleswoman told her.

She was topless and the young saleslady stood behind her and snapped the back of her old fashioned black bra in place. Augie watched.

The saleslady went over to the door, dress in hand, waiting to be excused. Augie stood beside Benny and they looked at themselves in the giant three-way mirror. She wore tight, black panties with a matching bustier and he wore only boxers and bare feet. His sunglasses were still on top of his shaved head.

"Fotographia?" Benny asked the saleslady, who probably found it odd that she was about to take a photo of a very tall woman, speaking Italian to her even though they were both clearly American, wearing underwear next to a shorter man who was barefoot, wearing boxers and had a shaved head. The saleslady took the photo with Benny's tiny pocket camera and quickly closed the curtains. Anything was possible with a little Campari on a Saturday night in your underwear at the store's closing.

"Piace?" Benny asked.

"Yes, I like it. Your..." he hesitated.

"Como se dice in Inglese, *Granny Panties?*"

"Granny panties," he joked.

There was a chair in the corner of the dressing room that he grabbed and placed in front of the three-way mirror.

"Sit," he told her sternly and without emotion. "I was told I had twenty minutes before my suit is ready."

"Oh," she said. The XX song "Heart Skipped a Beat" came on over the speakers. It was one of her favorites because she thought of Augie when she heard it. She contended that, if there was a duet better than **Islands in The Stream** or **Leather and Lace**, this would be it. She hoped he needed her as much as she needed him. She wanted to leverage this weekend of freedom and self-expression for all it's worth.

Augie grabbed one of the ties hanging on a hook on the wall and asked her to put her hands behind her back, behind the chair. She gave him a questioning look but remained quiet. He forced Benny to trust him, emotionally and sexually. He was the only person to ever get her to trust the Unknown and he enjoyed that power over her.

"Si" Benny said quietly and not sure of what was going to happen next. Only a velvet curtain separated the two of them from the hall and the checkout table. The music happened to be particularly loud at the moment, the sales staff was closing and busy walking through the store. There was a vacuum running in the distance. '*Perfect timing.*' Augie decided, ' *Scene ten, take one...*

Action.'

He tied her wrists behind the chair. They had not done *this* before. 'Thank God I bought these panties.' She thought. Every time she looked at herself in the mirror, prostrate in the chair, she had to close her eyes again. This scene, watching herself with him in the three way mirror, pushed a wave of pleasure and slight anxiety through her over and over again.

"I've, um, I've never done this before, Augie," she whispered, swallowing and trying not to feel claustrophobic.

"Tied up?" he asked.

She shook her head yes.

"Okay," he whispered back, "You know I have to gain control, *somehow*, Benny. You keep outshining me and I forget who is in charge here anymore."

"Who is in charge?" she whispered

He walked in front of her. She could see herself in the mirror, tied up and with her face and chest bright red. She suffered from a very serious case of claustrophobia. He knew this. Her physical reactions to him, when they were younger, worried him. He always wondered if someone had hurt her as a child. She had jerking moments when he first touched her. She had an overt physical anxiety if he laid on top of her for too long as she often complained that she couldn't breathe.

"I am," he told her, getting down on his knees, in front of the chair, lifting her ass with both of his hands. He pulled her Granny panties aside and began licking between her legs almost violently.

He told her "Look at yourself in the mirror, Benny. See what I see."

It was almost like their first night together, when he pushed her down on her bed naked and locked his face between her legs, she was excited, frightened and ashamed - all at once. In the dressing room at Dolce & Gabbana, after a huge win at the racetrack, his tongue pushed hard within her and his hands squeezed her bare ass. Just one look of this provocative scene in the three way mirror and Benny had the most power-ful orgasm in all her life. She couldn't believe how quickly she came squirming in the chair, unable to move her arms. With a deep, guttural moan, she called out Augie's name so loudly that he had to stop and put his hand over her mouth as her screams were louder than the music and the vacuum cleaner combined. She continued to jerk forward and convulse, tied onto the chair, until he stood up and lifted his hand off of her mouth, which was wide open and trembling, as he pulled his boxers down around his hips.

"Good," he whispered into her ear "Will you kiss it?" Hearing those words, her entire body tingled - scalp to toes. She thought she might climax a second time in the chair like this, without him touching her. He had done that to her a few times before – just from his soft voice and lightly touching her skin - those first few times they were naked together.

She nodded. He held her chin in his hand and moved his midsection over to her face. He pulled himself out of the hole in his boxers, but did not take the boxers off, in case they were disturbed.

She licked her lips and began to kiss it, Augie's *it*. She did so gently and lovingly, licking the large, mushroom head and then the shaft with her strong and determined tongue. He moaned and when he looked at their reflection in the mirror, he started shaking and flexing his bare feet.

"Open your mouth," he whispered, voice cracking. She attempted to lean in closer to him but was unable to and squeezed her legs together. She opened her mouth and took as much of him as she could inside her mouth, without being able to use her hands. She told herself to try and relax and took him deep within her mouth, deep within her throat.

He jerked as well, looking at the two of them in the mirror, her mouth deeply accepting him.

He didn't last long and produced a very loud moan, slowly pulling out of her shaking, pink glossed lips She squeezed her legs together and lifted her head back and closed her eyes. She was unable to look at herself in the mirror. He tried to catch his breath as he untied her as she leaned forward and quickly wiped her mouth. *This* was the Augie he remembered.

"Should I call the saleslady in again to take another picture?" he asked with a grin on his face, trying to slow his heart rate.

"No...please...*no*."

New Benny enjoyed the pleasure of being tied up, but regretted old Benny's submission. Could she still love herself outside of this bubble? It was intimacy that created love and love that allowed her to be sexual.

"It's the price you pay for those goddamn Grannie panties," he chided.

"You *owe* me," she told him.

"I'm sorry, I couldn't wait. My alter ego is on auto pilot right now."

"I don't know how I feel about *him*. About *you*. I need a drink."

"I'm sorry."

They chugged the rest of their Camparis, dressed slowly into more casual summer wear, stole five of the free Fiji water bottles, and walked out of the infamous shop with at least half of their gambling winnings spent. Their *score* also included a fitted suit and a skin tight cherry print dress for their big date the following night. A big date that Augie had planned. A night he deemed worthy of both of them and their long, unique *friendship*.

13

A ugie and Benny were able to grab the last two seats at the bar, at The Mermaid Lounge on Greenwich Street. They were there for oysters. She loved oysters and he said it reminded him of New Orleans. Plus, she called ahead and they promised to have the Mets game on for him.

"You're just not a guy I see holding a martini glass, is all," she began to tell him as they both looked over the bar menu.

"What?" he asked, insulted, in a good way, *their* way.

"You're more...import beer in a bottle or a pint glass?" she snickered.

"Are you saying I'm not manly enough to drink a martini?" he asked.

"No, of course not, don't be ridiculous," she soothed.

"Then, what are you saying?" he pushed.

"I'm saying I don't see you like that...in *my* fantasies..." she slowly admitted.

He smiled. All he heard was, *'I fantasize about you...a lot.'*

" I'm attracted to your wit and I don't see a guy chugging martinis as having any wit." She continued, "The vision of you, stumbling...drunk...unless it was for you to swear your love to me..."

He swallowed. He thought they weren't going to talk about love.

"Because it would be so hard for you to admit all on your own," she continued, "you'd *need* the alcohol, then I would..."

"You would what?" he interrupted.

"Allow you martinis," she answered.

"I didn't want one," he stated coldly, "but when you tell me I *can't* have something, then all I want is that *one* thing."

"Oh, you're too easily manipulated, Augie. And I'm such a fool for ever telling you that I loved you," she said, "it went straight to your head..."

The bartender, a vacant woman in her early thirties, was being slammed by the Saturday night crowd. "What'll you have?" she asked.

"Two vodka martinis," he answered her quickly.

"I knew you would do this!" Benny joked.

"Two dozen oysters – an assortment," he continued, "we'll try them all."

"You know, you don't need to get me drunk to sleep with you," she informed him.

"There's a lot we haven't done yet," he began and he shifted control back to himself.

"That I've had twenty years to mull over. Was the dressing room the preview?" she asked, quietly.

"I want you ready tonight," he said, looking right at her. He offered no apology for his tone. He looked up toward the Mets game on television, elbowing the older gentleman to his left when the pitcher struck out the batter and nodded his head at him. Benny sat on the stool on his right side and felt hair grow on her scalp and arms. She could not look him in the eye. She remembered the feeling he used to give her – the sharp pains in her privates, the contractions, the twitching, they were back. He didn't even have to lay a hand on her to make it happen. He just had to talk to her, or stare.

She felt his eyes, which occasionally glanced over at her while the game was on, burning a hole into her skin.

"We're going to try these things whether you want to, or not," he whispered in her ear. He surprised her by squeezing her bare thigh with his right hand, then his attention returned to the game, elbowing his new buddy to the left, once more.

"Great arm, this guy," he said to his new baseball buddy.

The goose bumps came quickly. Maybe it was because they were in public and he had most definitely won control. Her eyes hung low and in deep, deep, hiding. She needed to close and lock a door soon or she would go mad. When the bartender arrived with the martini shaker, he started flirting with her. *Augie flirts with everyone* she told herself. *He could so easily be gay and just want ' to get under my skin,'* she thought. *He's fueled by the attention and my angst.*

Augie continued to get louder and more obnoxious, calling out the Yankee fan, who sat at the high table by the window. She stared straight out in front of her at the paper doilies and then, at the silverware. She looked up, only once, and caught Augie's reflection in the mirror behind the bar. He smiled back at his reflection. This relationship was all about mirrors and reflections - *projecting.*

She quickly drank her martini, without looking directly at him. He continued to flirt with the bartender. She overheard him ask her if she was an actress because he swore he had seen her in the latest Judd Apatow comedy.

"Another?" the bartender asked her when she saw her empty glass. Benny nodded so she poured another martini which was drank as quickly as the first. Augie started clapping and high fived the man next to him in response to a home run. Even the bartender decided to lift her hand up for one of Augie's high fives and then asked why the Mets don't have a Designated Hitter? *Flirt.*

The crowd at the bar began to get louder with the excitement of the game and Augie did his best to rile everyone up around him. He leaned over to Benny and said "You know I'd only sleep with her...if you were there to watch." His attention never left the flat screen television, "I'll take a Heineken now," he told the bartender.

Benny still didn't look over at Augie, who smiled and licked his lips.

"I have to pee," she whispered. She slid off her bar stool and walked straight into the rear restroom. It was hard for her to let go and pee. Her head was spinning and her body felt so tight and nervous. But once she finally did, it was a relief. Her friend Tara was right. She was barely able to look at her own reflection in the mirror, *ashamed.* If she thought about it for too long, she would discover a lot to be ashamed of. But all she ever wanted was to be uninhibited with one person, *just one.* For some reason, which continued to baffle her mind, *Augie was that person.* She could be free with him. It was okay, because *it was just with him.* There was something about her exposing her body to him, exposing herself sexually, that gave her a chance to be close to someone, *intimate.* She always wanted to be her whole self with someone, but sexuality, that pushed her limits, was the only way she could ever open up and relax enough to focus on what she cared about most beyond her immediate family, being an artist, being a great writer.

There was a knock at the door. Since she was finished, she opened it. It was Augie. He pushed her back against the wall, locking the door.

"Augie, what are you doing?" she asked, nervously.

"I want to feel you," he whispered into her ear. "It's your turn, remember?"

His hands played with her white cotton bikini underwear straps that were beneath her thin silk dress. She closed her eyes and felt his arousal through his pants. He quickly turned her around to face the wall. As he stood behind her, he told her, "Put your hands up high on the wall and stick your bottom out, toward me." Then, he pulled her panties down to her knees.

"Augie!" she hissed.

"Don't turn around," he ordered.

"Augie!" she begged again as she started to feel disoriented.

"Don't turn around or I'll fuck you right now." It was hard for even him to keep up this act of telling Benny what to do. He knew he was good at it, and he had never found a woman he wanted to do this with before her. He liked winning her over, he got off on it. She got off on being *won*.

He lightly stroked the inside of her thighs, kissing and biting down on her bare shoulder.

"I want to take you right now," he whispered, grinding his shorts on the back of her thigh as she unbuckled his belt and pulled down his zipper. These sounds alone made her want to so much, *but...*

"Augie, no, this isn't what we agreed on. *Not* for the first time. Not yet!" she pleaded. She wanted to convince him. As turned on as she was, it wasn't how the fantasy was supposed to go. Not for their *first time.* There was still a voice, like she had told Casey at the racetrack, that warned her, *no...be careful before you give all of yourself to someone.* Love first, lust second.

"Keep your hands up," he commanded, as he grabbed one of her breasts through the thin fabric and from behind her. He continued to suck on her soft neck and to lick her earlobes. She held back her screams. Elvis Costello's "Clubland" played loudly in the background, but not loud enough.

"Augie!" she sighed.

"With my finger, I can feel everything," he whispered in her ear as she leaned back against him, took her hands off the wall and back behind his freshly shaved head and stuck her tongue in his mouth. As her breathing became erratic, he released her body from his own and took a step backward.

"You can turn around now," he told her softly.

Her hands went right to her face as she turned around. She was bright crimson and crying.

"Oh, Benny, I'm so sorry. Are you okay?" he asked as his heart raced.

"Hold me," she said. He embraced her as she cried on his shoulder for a minute. Her mascara ran onto his white shirt.

"You're still sensitive to me, Benny," he assured. He comforted her, stroking her sweat soaked hair back. "That's a *good* thing." She held her face tightly against his shoulder. He lifted her face for her and looked into her eyes: "Benny, that's a *good* thing," he repeated and smiled up at her.

'I only want to be new Benny,' she thought, *'not old Benny. You don't respect old Benny. I don't respect her.'*

There were knocks on the door. They collected themselves and opened it together. It was the bartender. Benny smiled brightly. Augie smiled too. It was like he was saying, *'It's okay, you're with me. At least this weekend, you're mine.'* They walked out of the room feeling giddy and excited. The oysters they had ordered were ready to eat.

She held his hand under the bar, kissed it every so often - *privately,* while she slurped down the oysters. He put an oyster in his mouth and stuck his tongue out flashing the oyster on the tip of it. They smiled as they swallowed. She kept quiet, she just *listened.* There was something to being possessed by another person, it was just like living in a shared, private world.

Occasionally, she caught him looking at her from the corner of his eye. Even as he made various scenes among the crowded bar area, even a wager or two, he never let go of her hand which remained hidden under the bar. He released it when all of the oysters were eaten and when the Mets had claimed a Dog Day victory.

14

Augie had the driver drop them off on Mulberry Street for their walk back up to the apartment. White lights hung from above and the street was bustling with tourists. Sandwich boards advertised Linguini and Clams. There were a number of tchotchke stands on the street that were run by Asians who tried to get them to buy one thing or another.

"You've got to get this!" Benny pleaded.

"What do I need to get?" he asked.

High above a stand was a cardboard with black tank tops with the Ferrari logo on them.

"That!" she pointed.

"O-kay?" he chuckled. "You like to dress me up, don't you?"

"I'm a sucker for a Dago tee, what can I say?"

The middle-aged Asian man was happy when Augie pointed up high to the shirt and haggled with him over the price. The vendor wanted twenty dollars but he talked him down to sixteen.

"You know how much that turns me on..." Benny began as she helped him remove his Pixies t- shirt and replace it with the tight, black, Ferrari tank top.

"The shirt, right? Benny, I think it's too tight," he answered.

"No, no it's *perfect*. I love the shirt and...the haggling. It shows a great survival instinct," she complimented.

They started to walk toward Mott Street.

"Benny, at least this shirt isn't as offensive as the one your mother bought me during the Clinton campaign."

"Oh, yeah, I don't know if a shaved head and a swastika in place of the S in George H. Bush's name during the 1992 presidential election was the best idea. I can't believe you actually wore it."

"You wanted me to wear it."

"Be honest, YOU wanted to wear it. However benign your pro-Clinton political statement was, you live to be controversial. I don't know, maybe that's the old you..."

"This is about as controversial as I have been in some time. You're bringing that bad boy back out of me."

"Bad boy, huh? Or maybe just attention seeking asshole."

"Hey, don't be mean."

"I can be as mean as I like. You dumped me, remember? Twice."

"Benny."

"Wait, stop."

"What?"

"I think you are standing in the exact spot Vito Corleone was shot in the Godfather....*Respect*."

She looked at the surrounding buildings as she held him in place with her hands.

"I think it was right here...yeah," she added.

He leaned in and kissed her.

"What was that for?" she asked.

"Respect."

"Because I think I know where Vito Corleone got shot?"

"Yes, and because you, for some sick reason, want me to stand in the same exact spot he was shot five times. Benny, did you place a hit on me with Brooklyn Jimmy earlier today?"

She punched him on the shoulder.

"No, but I should have."

"Gelato. Want some?" he asked, spying a gelato vendor.

"No, thanks."

He pulled out some cash and ordered a cup of pistachio.

"Hey, you know maybe you should have an ice instead. Italians try not to mix fish and dairy and we just ate a ton of oysters, and drank vodka."

"I lived abroad for a year, remember? I have an iron stomach, Benny."

"Okay."

They walked down Prince until they hit Elizabeth Street and started to walk toward the Girardi building. They heard loud music and noticed a number of people standing outside the storefront waving a French flag.

"Viva la France!" a slender man in white jeans, no shirt and an Hermes neck scarf yelled above the loud Euro Disco.

"I can't imagine the Girardis would be happy about this," Augie commented as he finished the last scoop of gelato and threw the cup away.

"A-LO!" White Jeans Guy waved to them as they made their way to the front of their building.

"Hi, you must be celebrating France making it to the Quarter Finals in the European Championship?"

"Oui!!! You know football? Come and have a Kir and celebrate with us!"

The eighties' dance song "Hypnotic Tango" began to play inside. Benny started to move her shoulders, she couldn't help herself - *Italian disco*.

"Do the Girardis know you are having a DJ Dance party down here? And by the way I LOVE DJ Dance Parties!" she asked, looking at Augie, a former DJ.

"No, they are in Atlantic City. Madame Girardi, she likes the Ke-no and the Slots."

"Awesome!" she screamed and ran into the dark, crowded store to dance and drink her Kir.

"I am Jacques," White Jeans Guy said to Augie as he waved the flag a few more times, and thoroughly assessed Augie, whose biceps were taut under the too tight Ferrari tank top.

"Augie," he answered as he put his hand out for a shake. Instead, he received a Kir.

"I've been seeing you a lot lately, you visit JR a lot? His wife spends a lot of time in my store."

"Yes, I have been in town a lot, haven't I?"

"Do you live in town?"

"No, I used to, when I was younger. Now I just visit, for work and such. Living here just seems like a big dream..."

"Do you know the Girardis? Do you think there is any chance they would rent the fourth floor to me? How big is it anyway? Wait...don't tell me. No, tell me!" Jacques asked, flirtatiously.

"How big is...?" Augie asked, confused. The Frenchman just laughed.

"The apartment...for now," Jacques answered with a smile.

"Gosh, I don't think the Girardis will rent to anyone they haven't known for like twenty or thirty years. They're old and they don't need the money," he answered, relieved.

"Oh, you can't put in a good word for me?" Jacques asked and batted his eyes.

"Jacques, I would, but it wouldn't do any good, I swear. JR's been there for twenty years. And their son lived there before him. Before that, the Girardis lived up there and their parents lived on the second floor. See, they're very old world and untrusting."

"How many square feet? Just tell me already and break my heart into a million pieces!"

Augie cleared his throat, for...*delivery*.

"Sixteen Hundred Square Feet."

"Sixteen Hundred Square Feet! My God, the rent must be a fortune!"

Jacques chugged his champagne and wiped his brow with his forearm.

"You don't want to know," Augie said as he happily sipped his Kir and watched Benny dance inside with a bunch of French dudes. She may have been the only girl inside. If he had told Jacques that the rent was only fifteen hundred, his heart may have actually burst into a million little pieces.

"Is that, is that your *girlfriend?*" Jacques asked.

"No," Augie answered in record reaction time and then stopped to think about it. His reasoning was two-fold. First, he was married, so he wasn't used to someone asking if someone was his girlfriend, and second, he had never admitted to anyone that Benny was his girlfriend before.

"Oh, are you available?" Jacques said, giving him a look in the tight tank top.

"No, I mean," Augie began nervously, hesitantly, confused.

"No, you're not available?"

"No, I'm *not available*."

"Oh."

"But yes, she is *my girlfriend,*" he answered knowing that Benny would be over the moon to hear him use that word. He thought about telling her this story later, but instead didn't want to lead her on. He was married. They were cheaters. They were having an affair.

"Oh, that's too bad," Jacques said and appeared disappointed, "C'est la vie."

"C'est la vie," Augie echoed and he pushed his way inside to dance with Benny just as the late Divine's eighties' dance club hit "Native Love" came on. *'John Water's muse,'* he thought. *'This is going to get dirty.'* He came up behind her in the heat and she kissed him in front of many disappointed, well-manicured Frenchmen in exquisite footwear. She started jumping up and down, he started jumping up and down. Then all happy Frenchmen started jumping up and down...and then sirens.

They were drenched in sweat and drunk. This time, they fell out of the elevator and onto the floor of the apartment making out like two horny teenagers. His belt was unbuckled and his shorts were falling down. Her underwear were in the elevator heading downstairs right at that moment.

"Oh, no! We have to get it out of there. Ms. Girardi!" she panicked.

"Ms. Girardi does not use the elevator. We'll get them in the morning!" he yelled with slurred speech. He dragged her away from the elevator doors so forcefully that her shoes slid across the wood floor.

"Augie! I'm SO drunk right now. I need to sober up a bit. We weren't drunk the first time. I don't want to be drunk like this. My head is spinning."

"Oh, come here, Benny, let's take your clothes off," he said playfully.

She was twisting and turning and trying to keep her dress on.

"I love you but I'm drunk Augie! I don't want you to overdose on Viagra trying to please me.

Is it possible you have anything *left* after today?" she complained.

"Stand still little girl or I'll be forced to spank you," he said, spontaneously and sternly. It was starting, *again*. If the room wasn't quiet before, it was dead quiet now. Benny swallowed loudly and stood still. She could feel liquid travel down the inside of her thighs. She didn't know if it was sweat or something else. *'Probably something else.'* she thought. She was quivering now and breathing heavily. He pulled her dress over her head. He squeezed her breasts with both his hands- roughly.

"Lay down on the bed and spread your legs," he ordered.

She scooted backwards on the mattress and did as she was told.

"*Spread them wider...*" he directed her.

These were the same instructions he had given her the first night they'd slept together. She put her hands on her knees and spread her legs apart for him to gaze upon her. She felt like one of Egon Schiele's watercolor models back in Vienna. Maybe the painter's lover and favorite muse, Wally who presented herself to a man who wanted to admire and exaggerate that which a woman hid between her legs.

The only sound in the room was the two of them breathing, heavily, waiting to touch, or be touched. Benny's eyes started to feel heavy and sleepy with her head up against a pillow.

"Music! We need music!" he yelled, breaking the silence and her deep throated moans.

"Wait, wait right here!" he pleaded as he slid over to the record player and searched for five minutes in a milk crate until he found Roxy Music's "Avalon" album. He carefully put the needle on the record.

"Benny, don't you remember?" he asked as he turned around.

He found her passed out cold on her stomach, with nothing but her bare ass sticking up in the air. This time *she* was snoring. He rolled his eyes and stripped down to his boxers. Leaving the Ferrari tank top on, he laid down on the bed, turned the TV on low, and passed out five minutes later. *He* snored too.

15

ugie lay asleep on his back on the floor mattress. A mid-evening nap would provide much needed rest from the long day that included an excessive amount of foreplay and cocktails. He hadn't been this hedonistic since Mardi Gras, 1990.

Benny tiptoed over to her backpack and removed a white, black, and gold, classic Hermes scarf. She wrapped the long scarf around the bottom of the cast iron heater against the wall, then wrapped the two scarf ends gently around Augie's wrists. She climbed on top of him, without sitting on him, leaned over, and stuck her tongue in his ear. "You've been asleep long enough," she whispered.

His eyes opened widely and he tried to lift his hands up to her face but they were bound. He jerked backward from the restraints.

"Benny" he said, amused and surprised. His nipples began to harden as she licked them beneath his face.

"Shhh!" she whispered, in an almost childish attempt at seduction, "I'm going to ride you now." She remembered he always used to say "Ride me, Benny" in the throes of passion. She pulled his boxers down to his knees and past a growing erection. She stared at its size and its enormous length and girth. Past experiences involving it had haunted her. She thought it was so big it was going to break her in two.

The night she lost her virginity, she turned white as a ghost and she held onto Augie for dear life. He was just as afraid as she was, afraid to push himself in her any further, as he felt her squeezing his arms so tightly and telling him how badly he was hurting her. He had never had to do this before, be someone's first. It was all new to him, too. She was looking up at him with frightened eyes that appeared to be begging for guidance.

Benny's mind returned to the present and she stared down at a now grown-up Augie. She opened her mouth, desperately wanting to lick him. She hesitated, ' *Not yet.*' She thought, knowing the waiting, as excruciating as it was, worked for both of them.

"Benny," he begged louder, heart racing, increasingly more excited.

"Shut up, or I am going to be forced to gag you," she threatened, trying to impress him. She didn't know if she could last much longer as her legs were twitching and her sweet spots ached. '*It's been such a long wait.*' She thought, wondering how much it was going to hurt her this time.

"Benny, please, listen to me," he said seriously, "I give you an A for effort, but we've waited this long for the first time to finally happen."

"*Again,*" she corrected, slightly annoyed.

"*Happen again,* YES. But I want it to be perfect," he added.

"But, I thought you liked it when I shocked you? Just like you shock me?"

"Yes, I do. I *love*...this...but I love the idea of making love to you for our first time, *more*."

She knew he said *make love*. He knew he said *make love*. Yet, neither one questioned it or acknowledged it. He had never used those words before in front of her. This *was* feeling like a first time.

She wanted to luxuriate in his words but noticed he was sweating *too* much, his face was *too* flushed. These were symptoms she had seen before.

"Benny, please, get off of my stomach," he croaked.

His stomach started making gurgling sounds from beneath her white cotton panties.

"Benny, untie me now!" he gagged. She untied one wrist and he started running toward the bathroom, the long Hermes scarf still tied to one wrist and dragging on the wooden floor.

"Oh, no, the oysters!" she cried.

He slammed the bathroom door, locking it. Benny ran to the door and all she heard were the groaning and retching sounds that precede vomiting. Her most paranoid thoughts were, '*What if I have to call an ambulance? How would Augie explain this to his wife? I can't leave him alone in a New York hospital. I would have to wait, maybe call JR and ask him what to do? I'd have to call him, on his honeymoon? JR is his best friend. He won't ask any questions, he won't rat.*'

Finally, the bathroom went quiet.

"Augie, are you conscious?" she asked nervously, "You're scaring me."

"Food poisoning" he mumbled, throwing up, again, "I'll be fine in a little while," he mumbled between retching.

CATHERINE ADAMI

"You know," she spoke into the door, "I have had many fantasies about killing you, but I have to say, I never had one that involved you shitting yourself."

"Benny..." he yelled. He threw up again.

"I think you brought this upon yourself," she continued, "by flirting with that waitress. Telling her you'd seen her in a Judd Apatow movie. It's just not a Judd Apatow movie without body fluids," she added.

"Please, Benny, get me some soda water, from the fridge."

She went into the kitchen and grabbed a cold Pellegrino. By the time she made it back to the bathroom, the door was ajar. He laid on the shag rug that covered the gray-green granite floor. The Ferrari tank top and her mother's Hermes scarf was covered in vomit.

His eyes were puffy and his face and head was drenched in sweat, he could barely move. He looked like he was in such agony that it hurt to breathe.

Benny squatted and sat on the floor beside him, gently pulling the tank top over his head.

"My head hurts," he groaned.

She gently untied the scarf from his wrist.

"Sorry, about the scarf," he apologized.

After all, it was only a forty year old keepsake given to her by her mother and one of the only thoughtful gifts her father had given her mother. But she didn't tell him that.

"We need to get you cleaned up. You'll feel better," she said.

She took his boxers off and threw them against the wall with the rest of his dirty clothes. She wondered if this is what it would be like to take care of him when he was eighty and handicapped... just like she had imagined. She threw off her nightie and panties and helped him up from the floor. He leaned on her, eyes half open, as they walked together into JR's large shower.

He laid on the floor while she turned the shower handle to the left. She held her hand under the running water until it felt warm enough to soothe him. Then, she sat on the floor with her back upright against the wall, pulled him onto her lap, and stroked his clean shaven head and waited for the steam to cover them both.

"This will purge the poisons out of your body. My son just had the flu last week and I threw him in the steam, too," she told him.

She pumped some soap and started to lather his body. It smelled nice, like mangoes. His skin all soapy and wet felt nice against her palms.

"And to think, this is the first moment we first both get to be completely naked together," she said.

He pushed out a chuckle. "I didn't think it would be like this."

She laughed and wiped the soapy sponge over his strong thigh.

"I'm so sorry..." he repeated.

"You look exactly the same, all of you... and you feel the same..." she said.

He looked up at her and gave her a weak, half smile.

"You look the same, too," he said.

"If you need to throw up again, just do it. If you can't make it back to the toilet, it's okay." she told him.

"I'm sorry," he said, again. He seemed to be saying he was sorry less for his inconvenient and temporary illness and more for the position a vulnerable Augie was putting Benny in, which was that of a temporary wife. He knew that part was *not* fair.

"You know, this is one of the first times you have let me take care of you. When we first started sleeping together, you had the flu and my mother told me to go to your house and nurse you. I was too insecure and nervous about what I meant to you to go over and all of a sudden act like your girlfriend. I was afraid you might reject me in that role even while you were sick in bed. I was too shy to force myself on you. In the end, I think I dropped some orange juice off with JR.

I always attributed that to us not *cementing.*" she finished. She wasn't mad. She was just explaining.

"Benny..." he moaned.

She reached over to the shampoo bottle, squeezed a palm full of the thick liquid into her hand and massaged his scalp with it.

"Okay, I know you have no hair, but, I've never met a man who didn't love a good scalp massage."

He smiled. She kissed the top of his nearly bald head, "Let's put you to bed now."

She turned off the shower and grabbed a towel from the rack. She dried him off and placed a robe that belonged to Stacy and JR on each of them. They felt rich and velvety. Benny found herself liking JR's self-indulging wife more and more.

Leaning on Benny, Augie walked over to the sink. She found his toothbrush and toothpaste and started to brush his teeth since he seemed likely to pass out again at any minute, he didn't resist.

She walked him over to the mattress and propped up a pillow for him. Then she walked over to the wall unit and smacked the twenty year old empty box a few times after turning it on.

"Oh, come on now!" she yelled and all of a sudden the air conditioner made the cry of a Banshee and began to shoot out cold air.

"Victory!" she shouted as she raised her arms-Rocky Balboa style.

She walked around the apartment closing and locking windows. She noticed that Augie was shivering. She put the vanilla Pratesi coverlet over his robe clad body, and grabbed a bucket out of the kitchen, placing it beside him.

"Benny, I can barely lift my arms or my head. What an outrageous day," he told her.

"It's from the gagging, that's why you're so sore. You just need a good night's sleep to recover. Don't you remember when you drank all that Malt Liquor back in college and threw up all over the place? When you wake up in the morning, you'll be famished and we can walk to Houston to Katz's and get you some Latkes."

Then she walked over toward the coffee table, turning on the television and DVD player. '*Yep, I'm a wife now.*' she thought, '*No sex and TV on a Saturday night. Stomach issues. Mothering.*'

She handed him the remote.

"I know you at least have enough energy to change the channel," she joked.

He grinned and took the remote in his hands, glad to be in control. This situation, tonight, was odd for him, Benny wanted to make him feel better about it.

"You're spoiling me, you know that?" he said in a weak voice.

"I always have, haven't I?" she answered, flirtatiously.

She headed over to another crate that was filled with DVDs. Augie checked out all the sports scores on ESPN. She stumbled upon two DVDs and immediately hid them behind her back.

"What do you have?" he asked.

"Judy Garland, **Meet Me In Saint Louis,** because you were gay in a past life."

"I thought you liked my feminine side."

"OR, keeping with tonight's theme, you know how I like to identify *themes,* **Alien.** It's just not a proper film class without a screening of Ridley Scott's famous opening scene."

She took both DVD cases out to show him.

"Please don't make me laugh," he told her, "it hurts."

Not wanting to see the poor boy, "Oops!"...*man,* throw up again, she inserted the musical and laid back down beside him on the mattress. Lounging around in their lavish bath-robes, it was as if they were on honeymoon or as if they were celebrating their 20th wedding anniversary.

Augie slumped down on her chest like a little boy cling-ing to his mother as she sat up on the pillow and stroked his scalp again with her short nails, *spooning* him for a change. Exhausted from the excitement of their incredible day, they fell asleep. They left the TV on.

BOOK III

Sunday

1

Benny woke up first on Sunday morning. No sun came into the apartment and the sky was dark outside the fourth floor windows. The temperature had dropped maybe twenty degrees and it looked like it was about to storm. She wondered if her ex-husband would take the kids school clothes shopping, like she had asked. The Windows-type operating system that ran in the back of her head as a parent was causing pop-up errors. Even though she was enjoying her life in the bubble, she would remember to text a short reminder to her ex during her allotted, private phone time outside this morning.

Augie, who had moved into a fetal position beside her, was restless and talking in his sleep. He was mostly mumbling but he did laugh once, and smile. It reminded her of her son, when he was a baby. *'Cute'* she thought. The only word she could decipher out of his mouth was "pretty." She stood up and opened one of the windows, feeling the cold air. She turned off the air conditioner.

Benny tiptoed in her nightgown to the hall closet and found a baby blue cashmere blanket. She grabbed it and walked back over to Augie, covering him with it now that there was a breeze in the room. She walked over to the kitchen to boil some water for tea. She always kept a variety of tea bags in her purse when she traveled. She had become just like the old ladies in her large Italian family whose purses doubled as stranded island survival kits.

She flipped over two highly decorative tea cups in the dish rack to read the label "Versace," *'This Stacy is ridiculous,'* she thought as she poured the hot water into two different tea cups. There was a Green tea bag for her, and a Chamomile for him. His stomach was probably still queasy after the over indulgences the night before. Benny thought she should be hung-over herself, but remembered how happiness can cure any ailment almost instantly.

Under a phone book, she identified what she thought was a photo album. She heard Augie's big nose snoring now in the other room and decided to open the album, she was going to let him sleep late. *It wouldn't just be sitting out here, if JR didn't mind someone opening it,* she reasoned.

The first few pages were of JR in boarding school. He wore a mean looking crew cut. Next, there were college photos with lots of cute guys in shorts with no shirts and flip flops. *'I love this look,'* she thought. A few pictures uncovered JR's short stint with long hair playing Frisbee with a pretty, hippie girl on the quad. She remembered the girl, but not her name. Anyway, she had always been convinced JR was secretly in love or lust with her roommate Louise. They were all on the same dorm floor freshman year. Augie always seemed to forget that Benny was friends with JR before he was. JR personally helped carry her drunk, out of the elevator of the twelfth floor of Monroe Hall, after she had chugged an entire pitcher of Rum and Cokes following her first Poli Sci exam. She could not get off of the floor of the elevator without assistance and was talking in gibberish. A team of freshman boys had to be recruited to deliver her back to her dorm room. It was only three in the afternoon on a Tuesday, Benny thought she failed the test and was having one of the many identity crises she would have in her life. Since she wasn't the girlfriend type, which was a fact that continued to haunt her, all she had were academics. If she wasn't the good student, she didn't know who she was.

She continued flipping the album pages and sipping her tea until she found one of Augie and JR with their shirts off as usual. This time they were posed on Saint Charles Avenue in front of the Tulane University sign at Gibson Hall, where streetcars passed by and lit up in the evening. The shirtless look in photos became their theme because they attended school in a warm climate. They tied t-shirts to the belt loops on their shorts or they would hang them from their back pockets. There were a few more photos of them sitting beside a keg at their Fraternity house, lifting cups of Natural Lite or whatever beer was cheap.

Augie wheezed from the living room, still asleep on his back, she debated videotaping his strange noises but she didn't have her phone handy. It was hidden in a jeweled box on a fireplace mantel outside the *bubble*.

Near the end of the album JR and Augie's photos' matured. There was a photo of the two of them outside the Girardi Building on Elizabeth Street on moving day, and there was one of the two of them standing on the Brooklyn Bridge. '*Liar*' she thought. Augie walked that bridge before. He called *her* a tourist!

Finally, she came upon a picture of a wedding party. It was Augie's. Just like she imagined, it was small and conservative, taking place under a blue sky, on a spring day at his mother's country club. It appeared tasteful, even with a pregnant bride standing beside him. This was a happy moment and they both smiled. They looked so young! Especially the bride - the woman with his last name - the mother of his beloved babies. Did that woman still love Augie? What was missing in Augie's life that would make him play with his moral compass? That, that wasn't like the Augie that she knew, the one she admired. *'I'm outside the bubble,'* she thought and returned to the present moment. An overwhelming sense of guilt forced her to close the photo album. She replaced it exactly where she found it.

All of a sudden, her stomach convulsed and her chest tightened. She was experiencing a rush, and it wasn't a sexual one. It was absolute and utter dread, despair, and more importantly, shame and disappointment. She ran into the bathroom as quietly as she could and turned the water on in the sink with one hand as she threw up into the toilet. *'Drinking green tea on an empty stomach made me throw up before'* was all she kept telling herself. She wiped her mouth, washed her face, and brushed her teeth, but avoided looking at herself in the mirror.

She turned the shower on, took off her clothes and jumped inside for a few minutes. She always felt safe in showers. She loved the heat and the quiet and how for a few minutes she would actually forget about Augie. Yet, she thought about his wife, who she had never let herself think about for fifteen years, who was sitting in a house somewhere, with his kids. A series of unsettling images replayed in Benny's mind, him putting a ring on his wife's finger. Benny wondered what he said when he found out she was pregnant. How happy and scared he was. How he reassured his wife, in a way he had never reassured her. How he broke the news to his parents and her parents and the collective joy this created in the universe. How for some reason he thought to call Benny at work out of the blue, to tell her he was getting married *and* having a baby. He had called under the pretense of needing to ask her father for a favor, but it felt like it was important for him to tell her.

Benny, remembered being in her office cubicle, phone ringing off the hook, looking at a picture of the sailboats near his Mom's house on the water, unable to say a word. He rambled on about it, uncomfortably. She just said, hoarsely, "That's great news. I'm happy for you." He started talking about something new and she cut him off. "Augie, I have to get off the phone now" and she hung up the phone as slowly as she had ever hung up a phone in her life. She grabbed her coat and walked out the door of her office and went on a very long walk fighting all the sharp pains that attacked her body.

When she returned to the office an hour later, she was a different person. She was no longer a romantic. She put everything she considered romantic in a box in her closet at home – music, movies, letters, pictures. She placed a moratorium on romantic comedies, she couldn't bear to watch two people kiss on screen. It irritated her. She had no interest in touching another person or being touched.

She would never give herself to another human being so intimately ever again.

But she did find happiness after Augie Baxter. It took a long time, but she did find it, and her own, equally beautiful and important family was born. Her friends and family were right, a nice guy did come around and discover her, shortly after Augie's wedding. Perfect timing.

Steaming herself on the floor of the shower, she remembered when Augie showed her a picture of his girlfriend, later wife. They were in the kitchen of his mother's house one weekend, two years out of college, in the suburbs of New York, when they were "just friends." Or at least, that was what Augie thought, and what Benny tried to convince herself. She remembered how happy she had been up to that point, being inside the house that he grew up in and surrounded by pictures of him as a young boy. She'd savored every baby and childhood photo in every album laid out on the dining room table, while she sat, drinking an iced tea. How happy she was, and then, *that* picture. Benny had thought she'd looked so pretty that blue sunny day in Westchester. So pretty that day for him - definitely *girlfriend material*. They sat by the water and watched the boats pass along the Long Island Sound. She was sweet smelling, and tan, in a cleavage baring sun dress with long blonde hair next to Augie looking like a *schlep* in a dirty blue t-shirt.

The picture he showed her – was it incendiary? It caused her to excuse herself immediately and sprint to the restroom where she started to get dizzy and have a panic attack. She considered climbing through the window to get out of that house and thought they might have to call the fire department to carry her out of the bathroom. For a moment, she convinced herself that she was going to spend the rest of her life in that bathroom. '*This is it,*' she told herself. '*Fantasy over.*'

That Sunday morning, Benny had been shocked for the second time with a picture of life outside the bubble. It was also a reminder of her younger and much less confident self.

The one who didn't win Augie over - the one who let things just *happen to her* – Old Benny. The one who always undercut her own value. The one who didn't trust...*anyone*. Was this weekend empowering or was it happening to remind her of the remnants of her older self - the weaker one? She had never, ever been a liar or a cheater of any kind, she was a woman you could trust. Yet, here she was having an affair with a married man, a happily married man outside the *bubble* on Liz Street - for all she knew. *'It's okay if this is just a once in a lifetime event,'* she kept telling herself. *'It's okay. You'll be okay, I swear, you'll be okay. I swear...'* Louise was right. *'She better have that Pinot Grigio waiting for me on Monday,'* she thought, wondering if they had any confessionals at La Guardia?

She sat under the spray of the shower, breathing in the steam to decompress and think.

She heard the bathroom door open. *'Damn, I forgot to lock it.'* She heard Augie relieve himself and flush the toilet. Then, he opened up the shower door, ripped his boxers off and threw them across the bathroom floor to show off in front of her. At that moment, staring below his waist, she remembered two things: Augie was definitely a "shower," not a "grower," and that *she hated him again.*

"Hey Ben, you okay there?" he asked, standing under one of the shower heads.

"Just recovering," she answered, still on the floor.

"Starving!" he yelled, as if happy and excited.

"You know, you are the first person I ever took a shower with?" she said, or at least she thought she did. But he kept rubbing the soap over his body, talking about food, and didn't seem to hear her. They'd washed themselves in front of one another! Did he have any idea how much these first times meant to her? He was the first person to hold her in his arms. The first to sleep in a bed with her. The first one to ever hear her moans.

"Let's go to Freeman's and get brunch?" he suggested.

She sat up, rinsing water through her hair, while he grabbed her by her hips and leaned over smiling, tongue out, and heading toward her breasts.

"We can't. That's where my husband and I eat when we're in town," she answered. She lied because she wanted to shoot a little arrow at Augie. A little arrow because of all the pain JR's photo album had just caused her.

He dropped his hands and she walked out of the shower and dried herself off. She put the thick hotel robe back on, while he switched gears. He started singing Third World's "Ninety-Six Degrees in the Shade."

"We'll eat at the museum, then," he offered, keeping inside the *bubble*.

After her shower, Benny walked in a short silk robe over to the record player that was on the floor. Augie had a towel wrapped around his waist, eating from a bag of stale pretzels as he stared at her.

"May I?" she asked.

"May you?" he asked.

"Touch your records. Something tells me, these are probably all yours and you just kept them here at JR's. Lord knows I like the guy, but the whole reason he became friends with you was to at least appear to be cool and cultured in front of the ladies. Plus, DJs always have the best vinyl."

"DJ-ing is my fallback career." he answered, smartly.

"I'd like to listen to an album while we get dressed. "

"Sure, sure" he agreed, "I'm going to be hot in the suit. So glad the temperature dropped. It's pitch black outside. Better bring umbrellas."

Benny fingered through the albums that were leaning against the brick wall. She found one, and took it out of its sleeve, blowing on it, before she put the needle on the record and walked away. She grabbed a hairbrush out of her bag and stood in front of the mirror. Augie watched all of her movements from the bed with his legs crossed. She noticed that his hair had grown a little within the past two days. As he ate the bag of pretzels, he dropped crumbs and salt crystals all over the bed sheets.

"The crumbs, Augie, the crumbs. I do remember the family of mice that live in this apartment. I did visit you here a few times before you got married."

She wanted that last word to make him feel something, *anything*. At least she wasn't the one married and having an affair. But she had lowered her standards to come to Elizabeth Street. The Benny who would return home on Monday would regret this.

He stood up, walked into the kitchen and put the bag on the counter. He heard his Kate Bush album in the distance.

"Kate Bush, Benny? That's stormy weather music." he told her, "I played this for you, up in my attic bedroom, in college back in the day."

She started to apply moisturizer to her face.

"Yes, I get it, you're a sensitive male. Raised by women. But Kate Bush was on my radar since the eighth grade. *Running Up That Hill* was a make out song. Not that I ever, you know, made out to it." Benny said, "Your know, every time I got up to your attic bedroom, I felt like I was being filmed. Like you were crafting a third rate Paul Schrader film."

She knew that was an arrow.

"Okay, that one hurt. Don't mess with Paul Schrader, you know he's my idol."

"Wait, my God. Did you ever film us, you know, up in the attic? Secretly? I wouldn't put it past you. I always felt like a Roger Corman, busty, bit player in one of your movies, putting on one of your Hollywood fantasies about the more sexually experienced male introducing the uptight virgin to her body, and his body and you know *sex*."

"Finally, you said the word *sex*. It's out in the open, *I want to have sex with you Benny*. Don't you want to have sex with me?" he asked.

She immediately darted her eyes toward the windows and knew. She could feel the heat on her face, she was sure she was blushing.

"And I can film it, if you *want* to," he continued, walking closer to her as she slowed down brushing her hair, "I did want to offer it as an *option*. Don't worry. I have already prepared a soundtrack. It's mostly modern with only a single Rogers and Hammerstein."

He took the brush out of a nubile Benny's hands and he led her to the edge of the mattress where he knelt in front of her. Facing the large, gold, corner mirror, it felt familiar. He slowly pulled all of her hair behind her back and began to brush her hair. Kate Bush's "Watching You Without Me" started playing and Benny closed the top flaps of her robe together tightly as he brushed. She clasped her legs together, not wanting to give him a cheap thrill...yet.

He took time and care brushing her temporary, honey gold locks. He had a hair fetish and he loved long hair-loved Benny's long hair. He liked the way it felt against his chest and against his stomach. He liked to pull it occasionally. He didn't know that she had been growing it out for the past eight months, just for him.

Augie, placid and content with his hair brushing skills, leaned over her and kissed the top of her still slightly wet head. She leaned backward, onto his chest and into his arms, like a little girl and smiled. She liked this feeling. She felt protected and safe, like no matter whatever happened in her life, one person existed who kind of understood her. One person existed who she could be close to. One person knew what made her tick.

"Augie, when we grow old and are both single, *will you chase me again?*" she whined in a child-like voice.

He had always been her security blanket. Like all roads leading to Rome, all roads led to Augie Baxter. He was the one telling her to jump into the water head first, while everyone else told her to just dip her toes in. All Cassandra Bennett wanted was children(accomplished,) to be a great writer(still working on,) and Augie Baxter. That was it. Just three things. One out of three ain't bad. But no matter what, she would hedge her bets and put all her money down on the Trifecta. She just had to try, right? Her life was important to her, she wanted to leave her mark on the world much like the way Augie had already left his with all his trophies. And when you want something badly, as badly as she wanted to be a great and published writer and possibly the *Talk Of The Town*, you seek out those who believe in you. And that, that was Augie. He told her anything was possible, and she believed *him*.

She was not a groupie of Augie Baxter, not anymore. She was his equal, and frankly, now – better looking. She was better, *older*. Even though he was married and this weekend might end badly with a giant broken heart or two, it didn't matter. She would live, no matter what the outcome.

She was with Augie again, in his arms, at only *forty*, watching him be a show off *and* laughing at his jokes. She knew she had been a source of his confidence and his success in life. She just knew this to be true. Even from afar, her love gave him something extra to be adored like he had. At the end of the day, he knew there was this girl who loved him and who thought he was her soul mate. Who thought they were going to grow old together like Fermina Daza and Florentino Ariza from her favorite novel, Gabriel Garcia Marquez's **Love In The Time of Cholera**. It was hard for friends like Louise, who were more experienced, to comprehend that Benny only wanted *him* to be her lover, *Catholic guilt,* she argued.

He didn't let her pretend the way they were pretending now, in New York City. She had to be herself with him. She had never been intimate with anyone *before him*. He was still the only one she had ever been intimate *with*. He said everything she ever wanted to hear, he recognized the person inside of her, the person who had dreams and that was it. It was done, sealed. No one had ever spoken to the person she thought she could be, *knew she could be*, knew *she was*.

Benny decided she was going to savor these last few hours of pure freedom and of hearing words she loved to hear. She had a flight home for tomorrow, her stomach hurt every time she thought about it.

"Let's just stay here like this the rest of the day, *the rest of our lives?*" she asked, softly.

He tried to ignore the *rest of our lives* part and leaned over and whispered in her ear, "But I only have today to make it all up to you, just today. I promise you, you won't be disappointed."

Benny relaxed in his bare arms, body parts kept apart with a towel and a thin silk robe. Augie, still on his knees, leaned over a reclining Benny and looked into her attentive and calm brown eyes and kissed her in such a way - that he could have forced himself inside her at that moment, camera or no camera, soundtrack or no soundtrack.

"You can't ever disappoint me again, Augie Baxter. I won't let you," she whispered and curled her lips up at him.

"May I help you get dressed?" he asked while his right hand stroked the inside of her trembling thigh. Reclined in his lap, she did not remove her eyes from his and she let her head lean against his bare chest.

"Yes."

He continued to caress the inside of her thighs while their eyes connected. He slowly touched her between her legs and she shook. She was caught under a wave of heavy tree sap and unable to move an inch.

"I'm the Director today, Benny, and this is the first part of your perfect day."

He slipped his middle finger inside of her. She loved the way it felt, wanting him like this. She wasn't sure if this meant they were going to sleep together this morning, although, she was ready if he was.

"Relax, Benny. Like when you were asleep on the couch, during Hurricane Andrew, " he continued.

"You remember?"

"I caressed the inside of your thighs, just like this, and stuck my finger inside you, one was all it took, through your short shorts, and you woke up, moaning strangely, stomping my bare foot, on the floor, angry at me. You didn't know what had just happened, what I had just done to you."

"I could barely catch my breath. I was *confused.*"

"You asked, *what was that Augie? What did you just do?*"

"I was angry, *oh Augie, your fingers.*"

"And *shaking.* I could feel the pulsing around my finger inside you."

"You were grinning."

"I had your body first."

"Yes," she gasped. This being exactly what she wanted to hear, his *acknowledgment.*

"It's not hard for you to come *with me, Benny, is it?*"

"Augie."

"Say it."

"Augie…"

"Say, *you made me cum first.*"

"Augie…."

"Say it!"

"Why?"

"It's true, isn't it?"

Benny hesitated for a moment and closed her eyes to just focus on his hand and his voice.

"*Yes,* Benny?" he whispered into her ear. Then he looked right back into her eyes and knelt above her, like a doctor examining a patient. He stroked her hair back and kissed her forehead. He removed his towel and revealed his erection. He kept the rhythm of his fingers moving in and out of her as he massaged the top of her pubic bone with his thumb. Kneeling above her like that, all clean, sweet soap smelling, completely naked and with his soothing voice felt so relaxing to her, made it so easy for her body to finally let go and submit to him.

"*It's happening.... It's happening...*" she gasped into his tiny ear while she moved her body up and down on his fingers, squeezing his shoulders, remaining engulfed in his strong arms. She rested her head on his shoulder as she sucked and bit on his soft neck, not caring if she left a mark one goddamn bit. She was completely and one hundred percent all *his*. He owned her. *Benny, this Benny, once old, now new, his Benny.*

2

enny and Augie helped one another get dressed in their Dolce & Gabbana. It was dark and rainy and she kept telling him that they should just spend the whole day in bed. But, he kept putting her off saying today had to happen just the way he planned it. When it came to being a Director, *Augie was a Type A perfectionist.*

When they finally left the house, they walked across the street to get some Cuban coffees at Café Habana for the car ride to the Upper East Side. He was more self-conscious with how tight the black suit fitted around his *package* than she was - dressed in a skin tight sheath with her bust popping out like Sophia Loren in DeSica's film **"Marriage, Italian Style."**

She ordered a Cafe Con Leche and he had a Cuban coffee with three sugars and a ham and egg sandwich. After the orgasm as powerful as she had this morning, Benny thought she would never be able to walk again, especially in high heels which put her over six feet. Somehow, she managed to put her feet in motion. He begged her to wear the heels, assuring her that it would be a day that she would remember for the rest of her life. He liked knowing he had *that* effect on her, and, well, she had that effect on him, too. He was determined to convince her that her first time with him - after so long, would be unforgettable. He *owed* her, she *deserved* it.

She enjoyed Augie and all of his *begging*, especially in that suit. Jesus Christ, she was going to fuck a White Bread Marcello Mastroianni that night. Talk about a fantasy come true. She had to talk herself out of getting turned on again. It was going to be a long day. She was grateful for the espresso.

She tried to let go of the past and enjoy their last full day together. They were going to her favorite gallery and should timing go right, finally sleep together. They almost did that morning, but Augie told her he'd scheduled it for this evening, after their day of *entertainments*. Benny forgave her younger self and forgave Augie's. She remembered they were just kids. She was so many millions of miles ahead of that younger girl, in part, because of him.

They hopped into the Town Car which circled around and dropped them back off on Prince street in front of her favorite bookstore in the city, McNally Jackson. It was the bookstore that she wanted to read in one day, when she "made it" as a published writer.

"That was quick!" she remarked.

"This will only take a second."

He grabbed her hand and led her out of the car. He opened the front door of the bookstore and brought her to the check-out counter.

"I love this place. Do you want to just stay here all day?" she asked.

"And waste you in this dress? No, not today. I want to show you off. Another day, maybe..." he answered.

'Another day? Did she hear that right?' she thought, *'He wanted to show her off? New Benny, points.'*

A woman in her thirties noticed Augie immediately and said hello.

"Hi, Jessica. This is my friend Benny, the writer I told you about," he said.

"Hi, nice to meet you, I love your store. Big Box bookstores can go fuck themselves," Benny said boldly.

The store manager, Jessica, smirked at her remark.

"As you can tell, Jessica, my friend, Benny here, is very passionate about her writing." Augie interjected.

"I am," Benny concurred.

"It's her dream to do a reading here one day in McNally Jackson," he told Jessica.

"So you've told me," Jessica said. "Benny, this guy can't say enough good things about you. Says you're hilarious, says I should read your blog. A straight, female David Sedaris, he told me."

"Wow, is he exaggerating!" Benny responded, aghast.

"You need to learn to take a compliment!" Augie countered.

"You're even part Greek, no?" Jessica continued.

"I've got the aesthetician on speed dial to prove it. Just ask Tina Fey." Benny answered. "Please, the second you get your book deal," Jessica chuckled, "call me, e-mail or stop by. I'm always here. I'll let you read, *no problem.* I am totally supportive of first-time writers, can't ever age out of *writing.*"

'Can't ever age out of dreams,' Augie thought.

"Thank you, thank you," Benny chanted.

"Thank you. I will give Nonna Girardi your best," he told Jessica.

"Yes, please tell her we love her Italian lemon cookies - delicious. I have an extra batch of Noodle Kugel I'll be sending her way."

This time, Benny reached first to hold Augie's hand on the way out of the bookstore.

"Thank you so much, Augie."

"For what?"

"*For listening.*"

Next, the driver headed to Benny's favorite museum, the Neue Galerie, which was a very small and intimate museum focused on Austrian artists of the late nineteenth/early twentieth century, and owned by Ronald Lauder. The museum was converted from a Gilded Age mansion on the corner of eighty-sixth and fifth avenues. Art by Gustave Klimt and his protégé, Egon Schiele, were the highlights with Klimt's Adele Bloch-Bauer I - the crown jewel.

Since today *was* Augie's day to show off his attributes as a successful TV producer, he had planned everything *to a T*. He thought, *'Today should be award winning, epic. She gave me all her first times, and her love, and I'm going to give her...this.'*

Heading uptown, their driver pulled up to a non-descript little restaurant on Lexington. Augie rolled down the window and pointed.

"Do you know what this place is?" he asked.

"Of course I do. That's Swifty's."

"Benny, you're going to make it in New York."

"I've dreamt about it my whole life, Augie."

"You're going to be sitting at table one."

"Only if you sit beside me."

"Let me be your groupie."

"Yes, it's about time! I'd like that."

"Soon, Benny, soon. Fans, best sellers!"

She couldn't take her eyes off this man. She could hear him talk all day about her and her dreams. He wanted to invest in them.

"You believe in me, don't you?" she asked confidently.

"As an artist, I have always believed in you, Benny. How long have I waited for you to believe in yourself! But you do now, you do, and I see it all coming together, *I see it.* I want this for you, I have always wanted this for you. You've made me happy with your words, your letters, your stories, for the past twenty years. It's time you shared yourself with the rest of the world. They're going to love you, Benny…almost as much as I do."

Okay, he just said he loved me? Benny thought, but told herself to just take it in the context of his pep talk to her. *'He's always been good at pep talks.'*

Did I just tell her I love her? Augie thought. *I did, didn't I? Maybe she won't notice. It was part of the pep talk, yeah, part of the pep talk.*

He rolled up the window.

3

Moments later, Augie and Benny sat in a booth facing Fifth Avenue at Cafe Sbarsky drinking some cold white wine. A couple was seated at a two top next to them and they were quiet enough to hear their conversation. The two strangers had just been set up and decided to grab a drink here after meeting in the park.

"Have you, ever been set up before, Benny?" Augie asked. He didn't want her to be mad at him for asking, he was just curious.

"Well, once. But I swear to God I must have been the fifth girl on her call list. It was a double date and after dinner we're at a bar and the guy, that I'm not attracted to, pulls my bar stool closer to him and whispers into my ear "What are you great at in bed?"

"No? Are you serious?" Augie asked.

"Yes, he's totally serious. I literally had tears streaming down my face. I'm so drunk and laughing at him..."

"No!"

"I'm thinking, A. I am not attracted to you at all physically or intellectually B. At what point in the evening did you receive a signal telling you I would discuss my sexuality with you? Was it when you sucked on your Osso Buco bone and then belched beside me during dinner? When you yelled at the Polish immigrant valet, perhaps? Or, I know, when you blurted out how much you bench press?

At that point I'm just like replaying my favorite episodes from **"Good Times"** in my head to guide me through the rest of the evening. You know the episodes with Janet Jackson?"

"Yes, she was cute back then," he answered, "What happened?"

"I told him the truth."

"Which was?"

"I'm terrible in bed."

"Why would you say that? You know, you're great" he interjected, defensively. It was quick, but awkward, coming out of his mouth, as if he thought it, but didn't mean to say it. All of a sudden she was filled with angst. This wasn't said to her over the phone, thousands of miles across an Ocean, or late at night, under the covers in a dark room. It was revealed in a chic and ultra-civilized art gallery on the Upper East Side with the lights on and an open bottle of seventy-five dollar white wine at forty years old wearing head to toe Dolce and Gabbana.

"How would I know any better?" she exclaimed much too loudly for Cafe Sbarsky. She quickly regretted the words that came from a heartbroken and insecure young woman. A woman who waited way too long to give herself any credit for being the reason why this relationship began in the first place. A boy, *Augie,* liked her, *a lot*; that was the reason she had agreed to this whole weekend. As a more confident adult, she knew how much he had liked her and how grateful she was that those "glass half-empty" days were over. Regardless of all this, she went ahead and said "You were the only person I had slept with up to that point, and you made me feel like I wasn't good enough to be your girlfriend."

"Oh, Benny," he was not in the mood for daggers on this epic day.

Benny nonchalantly resumed her account of the set up exchange.

"Then, to add insult to injury he tells me, as I get up to walk out the door, I was just kidding. I have a girlfriend and she's Asian."

Augie had a serious look on his face.

"*Of course you do*, I thought and caught a cab home. Wonderful – first and last set up. Wonderful first official date. You know, at like twenty six."

"We…hung out," Augie offered.

"Yes, Augie, we *hung out*, but we never went on a real date before this weekend. Not one."

He felt uncomfortable and didn't know if he should get angry or keep his mouth shut.

"By the way, that last remark," she continued, "was not to add any drama to our day, or to make you feel like I was taking a stab at you."

"Benny."

"And, that my good, old friend, is my foray into dating, period."

"I just don't understand…" he asked confused.

"Please, let's not talk of dating, of *boyfriends* and *girlfriends*."

"I thought you would have a lot of boyfriends."

"You said we were *just friends,* remember? Like it was a different category entirely. Then you ended up dating a girl right after me who you told me was *just your friend.* How are you supposed to date someone unless you are friends first? At least you fucked me a few more times after you broke up with her. Started coming back into my bed again, spent my birthday with me – even had dinner with my father. At least you flew home with me, met my friends and family, made me feel a little bit better.

Actually, it made me feel a lot better."

"I'm sorry, that you felt that way."

"How about *I'm sorry I was a fucking asshole* instead of, *I'm sorry you felt that way.*"

"Being your boyfriend..."

"Please Augie, even hearing that word makes my stomach hurt. Once you took me out of that category of *girlfriend,* I could never imagine myself back in it. And I never was back in it, not for a long time. No one waits twenty years to take her clothes off or to have sex with someone and not be their *girlfriend.* You liked me, yes. But you didn't respect me and then, it took ages before I could respect myself."

"I told you that you would fall in love..."

"You told me to fuck other guys, that's different. You wanted me off your back. You didn't want to be my only one. I'm sure that's the same reason you married your wife. She had fucked a lot of guys before you, am I right? No, I bet you were her only one, or near only one. But you kept her. She could belong to you and only you. Well, that's what I wanted."

"This is crossing the line, and no, Benny, you're wrong, dead wrong. I never said that! I told you that you would fall in love and sex would be great for you. That is what I said."

"You made it your job to cross the line with me, Augie. You knew me. You knew how to get right into my head and mind fuck me. You did this countless times! Why in the hell did you say that to me, anyway? That's something you say to patronize someone, or to your little sister. I was anything *but* your little sister! I didn't want to play the field, Augie. That's not me, that's never been me. Maybe you don't know me like I think you do. Like I want you to know me!"

"No, Benny, I don't know everything about you. I forgot your middle name, didn't I? You don't know everything about me, either. What are all of my younger, half siblings names, Benny?"

"Fine, you're right, I don't know them all! But, but *you knew* I only wanted to be special. Why couldn't you have given me that? Just that. I have never seen so much energy wasted trying to convince the world that you don't care about me and that you didn't date me. Why is so much effort necessary? Is it that embarrassing to you? Or is it that you think about me more than you want to admit? You sure like to complain about *me*, why so much? Why say anything at all? If you hated me so much why can't you just shut your goddamn mouth up about me?" Benny finished her wine and quickly stood up.

"You noticed," she continued, "I never said a word for twenty years about this. About not being called your *girlfriend*. But you, you'll make it a point, to strangers. I never once asked you to be my boyfriend, either, did I? NO, never, not once. I just thought you liked me..."

"Yes.." Augie agreed, but kind of reluctantly. He never had to tell her how much he liked her before. It was never necessary for him to do so for her to like him back. But he did like her so very much back then. For years, he had fantasized about her, before he actually *had* her. He had made passes at her that she never acknowledged or noticed. He remembered flirting with her at Les Bon Temps on Magazine-the regular Tulane Thursday night hangout for one dollar beers-when she slapped him across the face for making some sexual comment, and how he went home and thought about her. About how he wanted her, this strange and unusual creature – Benny, with her golden long hair and all her curves and her nervous ticks who he could never tell what her experience was with men...*whatsoever.* She was a tough city girl, but he could catch her eyes for a moment even after her yelling at him for saying something silly and see her eyes dart to the other side of the room. She would think about what he said for a moment, really mull it over - let it affect her and *blush.* Maybe she didn't know she was blushing in a dark bar or at a dark, loud party at a shotgun apartment on Calhoun where they both found themselves at, or at Pocket Park, drinking iced coffees and studying before class, but Augie noticed it.

Maybe she wasn't as tough as she presented herself. Yes, she was independent and good at arguing with him, especially calling him out on every little detail. But she was innocent. Not that it was a secret. Not that he had ever even asked. But her eyes, the way they darted, the glow on her face when he said her name.

"I'm walking upstairs," she said, at last, across the table of a now quiet and introspective Augie, on the first floor of this boutique gallery that he picked just for her, for today. He still thought about her a lot outside the *bubble.* A song could set him off, like on the Nano playlist. There was so much love that she had given him so freely, without ever asking for anything in return but his friendship. He had never had anyone submit to him so completely, naturally, unselfishly, and so *beautifully*. That, *that,* to him, was *Benny.*

As Augie sat in the booth, pouring the remainder of the bottle of white wine in his glass, a few things crossed his mind. First of all, this was supposed to be fun and not a rehashing of the past. Secondly, what if *this* resulted in the end of their weekend? What if she decided to move into a hotel? And thirdly, she was right about everything and he had been a fucking asshole to her. He never really apologized for his actions, just her reactions. He had no idea what an impact he had had on her. He realized that he always spent so much time arguing over the status of their relationship. He brought it up, never her. She never asked that he be her boyfriend. He was older and more experienced, she followed his lead.

He had chosen this museum because of the collection of postcards she had sent him while he was abroad. They were Egon Schiele and Gustav Klimt prints. He still had them in a box at home. He thought that they were her favorite artists, he hoped they were. He threw some cash on the table and made his way upstairs.

4

Augie walked through the second floor looking for Benny. He made his way through each room filled with originals of many of the print postcards that she had sent him through the years. He had never been to this gallery before. He was never on the Upper East Side while in town for work. He only read about it in a Time Out on the floor of a hotel bathroom in Midtown on his last visit. The paintings were so large and looming that they were almost like giant Chess pieces that were coming to life before his eyes. It was only at that moment that he was able to fully appreciate Benny and her love for him. Her love was powerful. She had found a way to express her love for him through this art. He was so stupid back then. He chose this gallery as part of his special day for *her*, but had no idea how special it would be to *him*. It made his heart heavy for the first time in a very long time.

He made his way to an anteroom without windows. It was a very small and intimate room with a rouge colored, backless, velvet bench in the center. Benny was sitting on it and staring straight ahead. There were a number of very small watercolors of Schiele's in front of her. He walked behind the bench and around her, approaching gently.

He sat down beside Benny whose mind was far away into a single picture. He found the one, the only one quite possibly that Benny could look at. Engulfed in a sea of bawdy ladies, wearing too much makeup and their legs spread open, was one woman, who loathed to have her body painted and did her best to cover it up. She wasn't a show off, her body was her *secret*. A secret Schiele captured perfectly on the canvas. That *was Benny*.

He took one of her hands out of her lap. She continued to stare straight ahead, her face covered in quiet tears.

"I can fly home tonight..." she whimpered.

"I remember the first time I saw you," he interrupted.

She did not make a sound and she tried to breathe in as quietly as possible. The Neue Gallery was a quiet and serene place. She did not want to draw any attention to herself. She tried to stand up, feeling she needed to "collect herself" in the restroom, but he immediately pulled her back down to the padded bench.

"Augie," she said swallowing, hoarsely, "I'm a mess."

"You look *beautiful*," he whispered in her ear.

She froze on the settee, looking right into his tiny and delicate eyes, and, for once, *for once*, she allowed herself to believe him. She waited twenty years to hear that word, *beautiful*. He had been selfish with it, he was not selfish with it anymore.

"And...what was I like....when you first saw me...." she began and smiled up at him. He looked so strong and so sure of his feelings for this girl, *Benny*, this silly sweet girl, who was now forty years old, a mother, a one-time wife, and an emerging writer. Regardless of her sexy-only-with-Augie-in-New York City-on Elizabeth Street-in-a-bubble, she was still fresh and unsullied in his eyes. She had made a decision long ago that only Augie Baxter owned the uninhibited side of her personality. This brazen woman, new Benny, who showed up to Elizabeth Street two days ago. He didn't want that back then. He heard that naive and love struck girl plead once more, *Augie, please, you don't understand, I only want to be naked with you.*

Benny, who had always admired him, now felt what it was like to be admired by him. All she wanted to do was kiss him. *'Was that okay?'* They never had to sleep together again, ever again, just kiss, right now. She wanted it to happen in front of her Klimts and her Schieles, in New York City, her favorite city.

No one told a story better than Augie Baxter the Second. She could listen to him speak all day long, *all night long,* it was her opinion that there was no better entertainment than words. Spoken to you, about you, spoken in a familiar, loving and soothing voice. Words from the person you *liked.* She knew that, *for once,* in Augie reciting *this* story, *their* story, that he had remembered *all of hers.*

5

Raoul's on Prince in SOHO was busy for a Sunday night. It was early and summer, so the restaurant was bright and cheery. Augie had a reservation for a table, but Benny told him she was just as happy sitting at the bar. She loved to talk to strangers, as did he, that way he could indulge his sporty side and keep track of the Mets game. There was an excellent chance that they were going to sweep the Cubs.

She looked radiant in the white satin Dolce & Gabbana dress in a cherry print. The dress hugged her curves in all the right places, yet, it was tasteful and age-appropriate since the hem only came above the knee. The fabric revealed her curves without revealing her skin and the cherries were an inside joke they could constantly tease one another about. Even the bartender, who went behind the bar to make them each a Kir Royale, was unknowingly in on the joke. Augie must have asked him at least five times if any of the entrees or desserts had cherries in them. He mentioned that he had eaten duck with cherry sauce before and that his mouth watered every time he remembered it. That meal, as scrumptious as it was, took place a very long time ago. Benny kept talking about how her one and only dream for that night was a giant bowl of Cherries Jubilee that she would share with him.

After taking the first sip of the ice cold champagne, he told the bartender, "I LOVE Cherries Jubilee." Then, Benny leaned over, squeezing his muscular thigh and whispered, "I'm wearing the *Granny panties.*"

One thing they tried to forget out and about in New York was the possibility of running into someone they knew. They had lots of friends and associates in the area, but had just decided that, in their new identities they would not run into anyone. Most of their friends lived in the suburbs or Brooklyn. If they ever did run into someone they knew, they would explain that they were just old friends from college, period. To those outside of the *bubble*, they were still the same people they were outside of New York-married and/or divorced-with kids.

All of a sudden, Benny spotted a guy who was dressed in a conservative Brooks Brothers suit waving her over to his table in the corner. It was her ex-boyfriend, Brad. Her first "real" boyfriend. Augie had never seen her with another man before. Benny, shocked by seeing Brad, with Augie in tow, was slightly...she had to admit it...*pleased.* One of those *when it rains it pours* weekends...She didn't mind the opportunity to prove to Augie that other men desired her. In fact, she thought it was important that he did see it. New Benny required this.

"Oh...wow," she said to Augie, lifting her hand out of his lap.

"Hey, where's your hand going?" he asked as he turned around and noticed a conservative East Coast, ultra-preppy couple sitting at a table across the room. They were being served a bottle of Burgundy.

"Um, I...should say hi," she told him. He wondered who this person was who was smiling so widely at Benny. Brad stood up to welcome her. Benny felt way too glamorous for Brad's conservative, Lily Pulitzer clad wife, and she felt way too *Italian*. '*I'm nouveau riche,*' she thought.

'*deal with it.*'

"Cassandra? Cassandra Bennett. It's been what, like... twelve years?" Brad asked as he continued smiling.

"Oh, at least that," Benny, now Cassandra answered. Brad enthusiastically and gently kissed her on the cheek.

"Cassandra, this is my wife, Jenny. Jenny this is Cassandra. She's friends with Louise from home, they were college roommates."

"Hi, Jenny, pleased to meet you," she replied.

Jenny and Brad both had dark brown hair and glasses. Jenny had a shy smile that Benny could strangely relate to.

"You here for business or pleasure?" Brad asked. This was not a question she was prepared to answer. She looked over to Augie who kept turning around trying to assess the situation. He could not hear Benny's conversation.

"Um..." she looked over to Augie who gave her one of his famous stares, like he was looking at her topless, nipples hard, trembling in her white Agent Provocateur Granny Panties - in front of him and that giant living room mirror.

"*Pleasure,*" she hesitantly answered.

"Is that, is that, *your husband?*" Brad asked. Benny wished she could chug that entire bottle of Burgundy with one gulp. No, maybe a vodka on the rocks.

"*Yes,*" she answered, internally squealing and completely terrified of the mess she had just created and wondering how she would fix it at this point.

"Please, come join us for dinner. You know I never came into New York much, we'd love the company," Brad told her.

"Oh, yes, Cassandra, we have no idea where to go while we are here. We would love some recommendations. We rarely get to go out anywhere anymore with our twin one year olds at home." Benny smiled at Brad's wife and gave her *points*.

Benny fell into a mental rant...*Yes, I understand you are happily married with Brad and even have one year old twins at home. You have claimed your territory. I have not seen or spoken to your husband in well over a decade. Oh, and by the way, Jenny, I'm here in New York having an affair with my college deflowerer who happens to be married with kids – we both have kids! So please, Jenny don't worry. Oh, yeah, and I just lied to you, because he's not my husband, and he's going to kill me when he finds out what I've done.*

"Um," Benny blurted.

"Please, we insist," Jenny said.

Benny slowly walked up to Augie at the bar, who had just finished his Kir Royale.

"So, friends of yours? Are we busted?" he said, joking, but also a little nervous.

"Um, kind of."

"What do you mean, *kind of?*"

Brad started walking across the dining room floor toward them to introduce himself, *good manners, Old Establishment Dutch blood, Knickerbocker Society.*

"He's my ex-boyfriend that I never slept with..."

"Did he put his dick in your mouth?"

"Um, *maybe...* that's not important. He wants us to join him for dinner and also, *wait for it*, he thinks you're my *husband!*"

"Hi!" Brad said cheerily, putting his hand out to Augie, who looked at Benny. He was shocked but not sure which shocked him more. Was it the fact that she lied to this guy and told him they were married, or was it the fact that Benny had an *ex-boyfriend*? He didn't think she had any ex-boyfriends other than him. Wait, he wasn't really her ex-boyfriend. But if she had any, other than her husband, he guessed that technically, it would be him. And this ex-boyfriend was handsome and wore Tiffany cuff links *and* Gucci loafers. A little overkill, he thought. And his wife, well...she kind of looked like Benny - in a weird way. *What had Benny gotten them into? Wait, if Brad was her boyfriend, why hadn't they slept together?*

"Hi, I'm Augie," he said to Brad, putting his hand out and shaking, like a strong man would.

"Please, come. We just opened up a bottle of wine, a Burgundy. Do you like Burgundy?" asked Benny's chivalrous ex-boyfriend *who supposedly never put his penis inside her,* Augie thought.

"I LOVE Burgundy!" Benny answered a little too excitedly in front of Augie who was starting to get annoyed. If they were going to take on different identities this weekend and even go so far as to pretend they were *married,* he was going to have fun with it.

6

"So, Brad grew up with my roommate Louise. You remember her, honey? She dated your roommate JR...for a night *or three?*" Benny told her tablemates.

"Really? You know each other through Louise?" Augie asked.

"Yes. Brad here took Louise to the prom, but they were really more like siblings." Benny said.

"I see," Augie stated.

"So, Benny, what are you and Augie doing in town? How did you two meet?" Brad asked.

"I'll let Augie take this one." Benny said, eating an olive off of his plate, while Augie took a long drink of his glass of Burgundy. He felt uncomfortable, but slightly excited by the challenge this situation presented. He liked to be challenged, and Benny did challenge him, constantly. The rush of surprise from her crazy antics reminded him that he was alive.

"We met at an AA meeting," he began, taking a sip of his wine with relish, "a lot of good it did either of us, though."

Benny wanted to laugh so hard but restrained herself. She didn't want to seem rude in front of Brad who she considered to be a nice guy and a gentleman. He was someone she felt she owed a lot of her current self-respect to.

"My husband is a big joker!" she interrupted, "Used to be an actor, but it's pretty evident that was a pipe dream."

"We met in college," he began, again. This time he was sincere, "We were sophomores. I had just returned after a year off for academic and disciplinary probation. I had to spend the year at home saving money, so I could return and get my scholarship again..."

Benny took a swallow. She wasn't sure how far he was going to go with this, go with, *the truth.*

"I still don't know what he did to get the disciplinary part," she chided, she really didn't know.

"We met at a party. Her roommate was dating one of my old fraternity brothers who was also from New York. She was very shy, but I couldn't stop staring at her," he told them.

"They told me you were a smart ass actor, from New York, had to take a year off from school, drove a taxi..." she added.

"Our first class together was European History. Benny used to sit in the sun and smoke cigarettes, listening to her Walkman and scribbling in her notebook. She was usually alone. I made it a point to try and talk to her." Augie continued.

"You...did." Benny added, softly, touched by Augie's memory. Warmed by her memories, she could hear him calling her name, over and over and over again. First he called her "Bennett", then he changed it to "Benny", or sometimes, if he was in a rush, just "Bent." He had given her a nickname. His very own nickname. *Just for her, just for Benny.* No one else called her this name except Augie. It was two years before he laid a hand on her. Then, as sophomores, studying in the University Center for a History Final, he began to "own" her... unconsciously.

"The problem with Benny back then was that she was so shy that she was either speechless and hiding in a corner behind her big head of hair, or yelling at you ferociously. I knew, from the beginning, this girl could be *loud*," he went on.

"You liked to get under my skin," she added, "you liked to get a rise out of me."

"You're not innocent, Benny. You riled me up, too. Must have insulted me a thousand times, slapped me across the face?" he teased.

"I never knew you *liked me*. I thought we were *just* friends. I thought you liked me as a *person*," she added, softly.

"I did like you...*as more than a friend*," he told her, also softly.

"Wow, that was a long time ago," Jenny interrupted, "*College Sweethearts who found each other later in life?*"

"*Kind of*," Benny answered.

"*Kind of*," Augie concurred.

"I definitely fell in love with him in college," Benny began, "but I had to wait until I was older, much older, before I was confident and happy enough with myself to be in a relationship. When we reconnected, when we were older, we even, *get this*, liked each other *more*."

"And, how did he propose?" Jenny asked.

"I'll let Augie take this one, too," Benny answered, losing her voice a little. '*How can this conversation be happening right now?*' she thought.

"We were in Rome," Augie began as if right on cue. He liked to hear the sound of his own voice, as did she. Benny was lost for a second and couldn't believe what she was hearing.

How did he know that Rome was her favorite city in Italy? How she longed to be a filmmaker's girlfriend in Rome and to pretend she was in **La Dolce Vita**. How she wanted to be in Italy with him so he would have to depend on her for the language and for getting around. For once, *he would be dependent on her,* and he could understand why she was as loud as she was just by eavesdropping on Italians. Rome was like another New York City to her. The two of them looking fabulous and glamorous in Rome was all part of her fantasy. She was Mrs. Gerald August Baxter II, at least here, in this restaurant, in Soho, in New York City for a few delightful hours. She had never allowed herself to even imagine what that would be like and, now? She was...*realizing it.* It felt good.

Augie continued crafting their life together, piece by piece and by gluing together odds and ends she had never thought of. She had always loved his storytelling. She told him over and over...she *loved every word that came out of his mouth....* but there was nothing more exciting to her than hearing his fantasy of their life together. It was *all* brand new to her. She realized that she had always been on his mind, even when they were apart, consciously and more likely unconsciously. Her dreams tended to verge on the ridiculous. But Augie's fiction as related to Brad and Jenny at least, seemed completely plausible. Benny had always been good enough to be Augie Baxter's girlfriend. She had always been good enough to be his wife. Why had she never allowed herself to believe this? To believe in herself?

7

Benny, intoxicated by Augie's masterful storytelling, woke up from this dream life when Brad and Jenny politely excused themselves from the table. They had a show to catch in Midtown and did not want to miss it.

Jenny flipped her Iphone over and Augie caught a glimpse of the twins she had been talking about earlier. He thought about his own twins, boys, at home. Twins with Twin Transfusion Syndrome and how they began life as underweight preemies and were now pudgy, and thriving athletes - just like their Dad. He was sure they were out by the garage right then, shooting hoops and wrestling each other on the lawn. He took a large gulp of some leftover brandy in front of him. He thought of *their* mother - *his* wife. Why did he want to be so far away from her? After everything they had been through. He put his hand on Benny's thigh and squeezed it. His only desire was to be sitting here at this moment – at Raoul's. He did not want to be anywhere else but here. Benny placed her hand on top of Augie's and held it, squeezing it in return.

"Thank you again for all of your New York suggestions," Brad said, rising from his chair, and helping Jenny, out of hers, "Thank you for the company," he added and winked at Benny.

"I'm glad I met you, Jenny," Benny offered. "Enjoy...New York."

The waiter passed by the table and Augie stood up to get his attention. "Please, let me get the check. I'd like to try and give New Yorkers a better name," he began, getting his wallet out of his back pocket.

"It's taken care of," Jenny said, politely.

"Our treat," Brad added.

"Thank you," *Mr. and Mrs. Gerald August Baxter the Second* said in unison and watched the giddy couple disappear out the door of Raoul's in search of a taxi.

Augie sat back down in his chair beside Benny and emptied the contents of a bottle of Sancerre into her goblet. She reached out and held his hand, which he held in his lap, while he dipped his pinky finger in the leftover chocolate sauce from the Profiteroles on her plate. He put it up to his mouth and licked it, smiling, giggling...*blushing*. His face was a ruddy red from too much wine, and too much talking.

"Wow, Augie. I forgot how much you can talk, when you get on a roll," Benny quipped.

"That was very kind of your ex-boyfriend to buy us dinner," he complimented.

"He's generous, yes."

"But not showy."

"Correct. He's old fashioned. But you were never showy. That's one of the many reasons I like you, your modesty. Although you never turned down any of my generosity, did you, Augie?"

"I...took advantage...at times."

"It's in the past, and I let it happen. I didn't even mean to bring it up."

"I must *pale* in comparison to Brad's generosity."

"Pale being the operative word. *Please don't compare yourself to him.* I know I make fun of your television career, but you do know how proud I am of you, right? *I am so proud of you, Augie.* You have a job, *in television.* You made it. People would kill for your job."

"You and Brad...you never?" he asked.

"We *never,*" she answered.

"How long did you date?"

"Six months, but it was really only a handful of weekends. We did not live in the same place. It's one of the reasons we..."

"Didn't sleep together?"

"I liked him a lot and we were, *physically intimate.* He was the first person I was physically intimate with after you."

"That would have been a long time, Benny, if you didn't date him til you were twenty-seven?"

"Yes, a long time. *A very long time.* I felt like it would never happen."

"You waited that long to be intimate with someone?" he asked, slightly drunk and introspective.

"Physically intimate, yes. You know, sharing a bed or bath with someone, waking up and spending the day with them, *yes.*"

"Why so long?"

"Why do you think?" she snapped, even pushing herself forward in the chair and then calming herself, and sitting backward, against the chair, once again.

He said nothing. He just swirled the last ounce of white wine around in his glass and scanned the dining room, which was getting crowded.

"Without Brad coming into my life, I would have never gotten married, probably. He "fixed" me I guess. *Kidnapped me*," she stated.

"Kidnapped you?"

"We met on vacation in New Orleans during the Jazz Festival. Second weekend, I think it was. He was with a group of Louise's friends I knew from her hometown. I was there alone. I merely played the role of little sister that I am so accustomed to. I never suspected Brad liked me. But then again, I never know if a man *likes me*. It wasn't until the last night that he asked if he could stay in with me. It was a beautiful Spring night, a full moon was hanging low outside the balcony windows which faced Jackson Square and Saint Louis Cathedral on St. Ann..."

Augie started to feel uncomfortable. He had never heard Benny speak of another man like this before. She had not said two words to him about her husband, either. He hated that she was a writer and that she remembered so many little details – like *kidnapping* and *full moons*. He did not like to hear Cassandra Bennett romanticize anyone other than himself.

"His wife and he look like a good match, and she looks like you, doesn't she?"

"No," she answered.

"She does, and her name is *Jenny* and yours is *Benny*. Isn't that odd, too?" he pressed.

"Augie, you're being ridiculous. You are the only person in the world who calls me *Benny*."

"I'm not so sure."

"You say I'm the one with the wild imagination? And those stories you told. Where did they come from?"

"You didn't sleep with him? With Brad?" he asked, *again*.

"For the last time, Augie, NO!"

"I am not so sure I can trust you anymore, Benny."

"What? Why would I hide that? He owns half the mid-Atlantic seaboard! Maybe I should have slept with him!"

"You probably did, and you're just embarrassed or something."

"Why would I be embarrassed? He was a perfect gentleman to me. He was the boyfriend I *should have had* before meeting you. He was honest and he treated me like a Princess. Everything *he* ever told me was true."

"And not me?"

"Mostly, but not entirely. In college there were some occasions where I caught you lying. Yes! But I never called you on it. I was too insecure to speak up. I was basically at your mercy back then."

"You never slept with this painfully nice, smart, handsome, well-bred man, Brad?"

"My ex-boyfriend, Brad? I mean don't you think it's odd that I have never been more intimate physically or emotionally with any other human being than you? Yet you take issue with me calling you my *boyfriend?* Brad happily refers to me as his ex-girlfriend, and I never loved him. He never met my Grandmother, or spent Easter with me, or took *Communion* with me in a church. Most importantly, *I never slept with him,* and I'm his ex-girlfriend, *no big deal.* Oh, and he sent me a love letter. It's back at Liz Street, in my suitcase. I carry it with me when I fly."

"What? You carry another man's love letter to come have an affair with me?"

"It's the first love letter I received from *anyone*. The man told me he was beside himself over me, Augie. Imagine that? The letter - it was beautiful!"

"You never slept with him?" he pressed, raising his voice. Some of the diners turned to look over at their table.

"No! I told you!"

"How many men have you slept with, Cassandra?"

"That's none of your business, Augie! And lower your voice. Please!"

"How many?" he asked, softer this time.

"Two, okay! Just two, you and…"

"Your husband," he finished for her.

"Yes, okay. Excuse me if I can only sleep with men I love *or think I love*."

"You didn't sleep with this Brad? He's like fucking Prince Charming, Benny."

"Do you feel guilty or something, that I didn't sleep with more men after you?"

"I just didn't realize…"

"What an impact you had on me?"

"*Yes*," he admitted.

"Brad knows nothing about me. And I hardly know a thing about him, but he saved me. He showed me how a girl should be treated by a man. He insisted on certain standards and he made me expect those same standards. He showed me everything that was missing from you. But…"

"But what?" he asked.

As much wine as she had had to drink, saying this next thing aloud was sobering.

"I never wanted to tell anyone *I love you* again, after I said it to you. It had to mean something.

When I say *I love you* to someone, *to you Augie*, even at forty years old, it should mean *something*."

"I'm sorry I didn't treat you like a Princess when we were younger. I'm sorry the parameters of friend and girlfriend got blurred between us..."

"They were never blurred, Augie."

He slammed his hand down on the marble table.

"I'm going to make up for it, tonight. I promise. This weekend isn't just a do over for you. It's a do over for me, too. Maybe I want the chance for it to be better *for me* this time around. Another car ride!"

8

They drove Uptown. Augie had a scarf, a brand new Hermes scarf, in his hands, that he gave to her.

"Wow, Augie, thank you."

"I'm so sorry about your scarf the other night. I hope you like this new one. I put my faith in the salesperson on the phone. I tried to convey your personality to her, your taste. They delivered it earlier today."

"Okay, so what is my personality, my taste? By the way, where are you taking me?"

"This is a surprise, remember, Benny?"

"*It's our last night together,*" she pouted. Her stomach sank when she said... *last night.* She wondered if his stomach sank, too. She knew what he was looking forward to later that evening when they both made it home. She could refer to Elizabeth Street as *home* now. He did it, so she would do it, too. She wanted him as close to her as two bodies can be. *As two people can possibly be.* But, she just didn't know if that would mean, *sleeping together.* She didn't think she could go through with it, the actual sex part. One night would never be enough for her. She didn't want it to cloud her future, the one she promised Louise that she would commit herself to once she arrived back home.

"Please, let me put the scarf over your eyes," he told her.

"You do know how frightened I am of the dark, don't you? Since I was a little girl? I have an extensive abandonment complex and also a fear of being chopped up into little bits by an axe murderer."

"This is a date. You are in safe hands." He placed the scarf over her eyes. She grabbed his hands and squeezed them.

"Okay, okay. But you have to keep talking into my ear or I will be scared."

"Yes. We are almost there. You wanted to know what I told the saleslady over the phone. Well, I told her you were a romantic. That you talked a big game of being this frank and daring sexual object but at the end of the day you were still the most romantic woman I have ever met. No one has ever read more, or thought of Art in terms of beauty and love, the way you have. You see love in everything. Even inanimate objects, for crying out loud. I...I can't wait for you to get the recognition as a writer that you deserve."

"Thank you, Augie. You don't know how much that means to me, *seriously*."

"You sent me so many letters when we were younger, when I was overseas, or back home. They were so entertaining. You made me laugh, a lot. I overlooked how much of your heart went into writing them to me. But now, that I'm an old man..."

"You'll never be old to me, Augie. You're the same boy in that picture, a pretty boy. Tonight, you're that same boy."

"Now that I'm an old man, I can appreciate all those letters, all those care packages. I'm sorry I ever overlooked them.

I wish I could have instilled as much confidence in you, as you did in me."

"You're a great boyfriend, Augie. Why didn't we try this earlier?"

"I don't know, Benny."

"I mean I think you're a great boyfriend. As I have yet to see your next surprise, I hope I'm not disappointed."

"Like I told the saleslady, you are an old fashioned romantic. A combination of innocence and and old soul. I think this next stop speaks to both of those sides of you, Benny."

She swallowed hard and squeezed his hand again.

"Please, keep talking," she urged.

"Benny, I have one last thing to do and that is to put headphones on you. It's beautiful music. Beethoven. Remember all of the jokes I used to make about the movie **A Room With A View?** How Lucy's passion was fueled by *Too Much Beethoven?*"

"Yes, of course. I used to rewind the scene where George kisses Lucy in the cornflower fields in Tuscany, over and over again when I was in high school. I wanted to be Lucy and I wanted to find my George."

"We're here. Just a few minutes longer, now. Hold tight, I promise, it will be worth it."

He placed the head phones in her ears and over the scarf. It was Beethoven's "Ode to Joy." He stepped out of the car and took her by the hand and led her up a very long set of stairs. There were so many steps that she imagined she was climbing the Spanish Steps in Roma.

Finally, they reached flat land and walked hand in hand in a straight line. She could sense a lot of people around her. She had no idea where she was.

In an instant, Augie removed the headphones off of her. She nearly fell over when she saw, when she heard—They were standing in the candlelight center of a cathedral. Not just any cathedral, but St. John the Divine, above Central Park to the north, the largest cathedral in all of North America. The interior was ornate and enormous and packed with smiling music aficionados who were listening to none other than a symphony orchestra performing, Beethoven – *live*. She looked up to try and catch the ceiling of the cathedral which was nearly impossible. It just went higher and higher and higher. If she had launched a helium balloon it would never stop floating...

Her eyes swilled across the pointed arches, ribbed vaults, stone lace walls and richly colored stained glass windows. She blinked her eyes again and again. It was clear. She was the luckiest forty year old *kind-of* virgin alive.

He was not the same Augie of her youth. He was better, much better. This, tonight, was why she fell in love with him so long ago. He had this in him. For her, for Benny. He always had this in him. As she tingled, truly happy and grateful, he whispered into her ear, "Thank you for being in my life, Benny. Thank you for letting me be your first time. But, most of all, thank you for being my friend."

When the concert ended, he grabbed her hand and dragged her to a shrine that was covered in candles.

"This, this is the perfect place of worship for you. It's a shrine to the world's greatest writers," he told her.

Benny's eyes scanned the names on the slabs of cement highlighted by the candles all around her...F. Scott Fitzgerald, William Faulkner, Edna St. Vincent Millay, Gertrude Stein... it went on and on. A shrine! For writers! In the most beautiful cathedral she had ever seen outside of Europe. In fact, she felt like she was in another country, another world. A shrine for writers, Beethoven, candles... and Augie. This night far surpassed their first night together – the first night they slept together - every night they had ever been together. *This*, this was the best. Augie looked so pleased with himself. He wasn't afraid of making her *too* happy. He wanted her to feel happy, to feel special. The same way she had always gone out of her way to make him feel. Even though he always relegated her to friend. Lingering under the surface, she had always been so much more. A woman worthy of worship, a woman worthy of a shrine.

"One day, Benny, *your name will be on here, too,*" he told her.

She turned and touched his face, his shaved head, the lines in his cheeks, the moles, his big fat nose, his tiny ears and his tiny eyes with her hands and her fingertips. It didn't seem like a night like this could be real, but it was. Older *was* better. How on earth could she ever leave him, now that he had shown her how connected he was to her? How much longer would she have to wait for him to grow old with her, already? She decided not to say another word and just follow him into the dark outside toward the Town Car and one last stop before calling it a night.

9

The two sat quietly in the back of the Town Car which weaved its way down a dark alley in Harlem.

"You constantly joke about how I am going to have you killed..." she began.

"Benny, you did send me a dead fish in college," he reminded.

"Okay, you might have reason to be paranoid."

"I thought my body was going to end up in the East River."

"You're not...going to kill me now? In this alley?"

"Not yet,"

Their Town Car sped up and turned onto Broadway. It made a quick stop in front of a club called Smoke.

"Smoke?" she asked, "I've been to the Lenox Lounge in Harlem before. But never Smoke."

"Smoke used to be called Augie's, not that I planned it like this but.."

"It was meant to be, you taking me here. To a place that used to be called Augie's?"

"Just...follow me."

There were six or seven other Town Cars honking and dropping off guests in front of the jazz club. Their driver came around and opened the car door.

"A night cap," Augie insisted. "Remember, today was my day to plan everything."

He stepped out of the Town Car and grabbed her hand. She hesitantly followed. He dragged her in her skin tight dress and high heels and with her long blonde hair. She thought he looked extremely handsome with the tight black suit, tiny eyes and giant nose as he ran with her across busy Broadway. If he had his sunglasses on, they could pass for a cheap imitation of Marcello Mastroianni and Anouk Aimee from Federico Fellini's film **La Dolce Vita**. Although Benny swore her boobs were not nearly as big, and Augie, whose hair was normally as thick and lustrous as Mastroianni's, had a crewcut, anything was possible tonight.

There was a line to get into Smoke, but Augie walked hurriedly right past the front door and down the front basement stairs where the delivery drivers rolled down fresh produce every day.

"Where are you taking me?" she asked, excited and confused.

"Just wait, you'll figure it out. I just...*I know you will*," he told her, giddy with excitement.

He knocked on the heavy metal door and smiled at her as he waited for it to be opened. A black man in kitchen whites opened the door. Augie put a hundred dollar bill in his hand. The man whistled loudly and had an old fashioned boom box in his hand with a tape player. He pressed play on the tape player and stood behind the well-dressed couple. The Crystals "Then He Kissed Me" began to play loudly.

"Go ahead," the man motioned to the two, shooing them forward and trailing a few steps behind them with the boom box stereo on. Benny squeezed Augie's hand as they made their way through the cavernous kitchen basement. He popped one hundred dollar bills in the hand or pocket of every person he ran into. The man with the boom box followed a few steps behind them, as they passed busy dishwashers, chefs arguing over sizzling steaks and waiters in bow ties yelling for their orders. By the time they made it to the hallway leading to the stage, Augie found two bus boys in a corner who were reading their smart phones, and he said to them, "You two!" using his hands in a dramatic, Italian fashion, then it hit her.

"No?" she said, looking at him telepathically. He continued to lead her in the way she always envisioned a man should lead a woman.

Benny held his hand and was dragged through the last few feet of the long, busy kitchen. It seemed like at least one hundred people worked down there, and they all seemed to know Augie. Or at least they pretended to, as he kept handing out hundreds that had been given to him at the Racetrack after their big win. He must have already given a thousand dollars away! She felt a rush. A rush that he also felt by spending it on her. The speedy thrill Scorsese masterfully conveyed through the wide eyes of the character, Janice in the movie **Goodfellas.** So much to absorb, all at once. The feeling of being led by a powerful man. A man willing to go to such means to impress her. Willing to literally throw money away to spoil her, to give her *art,* to make her romantic dream from the screen *come true.* Feminists be damned. This was one way a man could win over a woman, this was one way a woman could be *won.*

"Here, here" a tall, handsome, older black man in a tuxedo motioned, as he pushed his hands forward and shoved Augie, who had slipped him a one hundred dollar bill and Benny through yet another set of swinging kitchen doors. It was dark. The two of them stood in a throwback room with chic cocktail tables. There were girls in costumes who offered to take their picture. Two younger men, from across the dance floor, rushed to place a small round cocktail table and two chairs in the front row of the dark, Harlem musical lounge. One of the men pulled out Benny's chair from their ringside table, lit a candle in the centerpiece and took a few more hundreds from an extremely showy and ultra proud Augie who was one to never be extravagant with money. The Jazz band was ending the tidbits to "Favorite Things." Benny tried to catch her breath. Augie tried to catch his breath, too. This was invigorating. To *be* art.

"Jesus, Mary and Joseph, Augie!" she said loudly but through her teeth.

"Yes," he answered, contently and as only an award winning producer could for having put on a good show.

"You just gave me **Goodfellas**." she said.

He smiled and cleared his throat.

"The scene with Ray Liotta and Lorraine Bracco? Martin Scorsese's masterpiece, the Steady cam shot? Where he brings her through the kitchen to the front row of the motherfucking Copacabana?"

"I *knew* you would get this…"

"I mean, you gifted me *art*. You *thought about this,* this was a production. This day, *your day*…four stars, Augie, four stars. My God, does this mean I need to put on a turquoise bra and let you sleep with me in a telephone booth and call me Bama? How on earth do I top this, Augie?"

"Titillating offer. I'm up for it, if you are? Tits AND ass, Benny, Tits AND ass. I have *two* favorite things."

"Noted."

"But sadly there are no telephone booths left in New York City. And Tarantino stole most of his good stuff from Scorsese, anyway."

"Yeah. I can't top this, *tonight*," she said softly, smiling brightly.

"Benny, you...you *had your first orgasm during the movie Goodfellas, didn't you?*" he whispered across the table in a shier than normal fashion. He wanted to make sure he was right about all of this. He considered the *layers* of his production. He hadn't hired any fact checkers. Only such a talented mind fuck (with love) like Augie would care about such details. The details that stay with you for years and years and years, until...

Benny's eyes opened wide and she was speechless. The waiter came up to the table and placed two cocktails strewn with fruit garnishes before them.

"Your show is about to start, sir," the waiter told him.

"Thank you," Augie answered.

"Your show? What are you a musical producer now? *Clive fucking Davis?* And, you remembered that detail, you know, that **Goodfellas** was on?" she asked, darting her eyes a bit and not sure if she overestimated his keen observation for more than it was.

"Yes, Benny, *of course I remember.* There was a mobster movie festival on television during the Hurricane."

"I remember you playing with your toenails before I fell asleep. I believe our roommates, JR and Louise, were making out in the couch behind us. I guess the strip poker game we had just finished had gotten them worked up."

"Yes, strip poker."

"I had maybe ten panic attacks before that game began. Louise knew I had never taken my shirt off in front of anyone but you before, and that was in the pitch dark, not in front of a crowd. Louise, God Bless her, threw her shirt off first and the sight of her gigantic *tatas,* took the pressure off. JR made a joke, *it's not like any of us are virgins or anything?* And looked right at me and you squeezed my ass. Thank God that game ended early. Funny, that's the first and last time I have ever played strip poker, with you. Why do you have to be ALL of my firsts? It's *annoying!*"

"After the strip poker game, you fell asleep on the couch, lying with me and I started to touch you."

"Louise told me before we got there, *just be his friend, just be his friend.* I never thought anything would happen again between us, as more than friends, I thought that one night at the end of Junior year when you attacked me, was it."

"I did not attack you," Augie argued.

"You most certainly did. You left me with hickeys and bruises all over my body with flashbacks of your naked body. I had post-traumatic stress syndrome all that summer. You kept popping up in my dreams and made my stomach feel funny."

"You had dreams about me that summer?"

"Yes, Augie. I did. But again, I thought we were just friends. I couldn't even say goodbye to you in the morning, I was so freaked out."

"I...didn't think you liked me after that night. You avoided me. I was glad that you did call, a week later, I think. You were strong, Benny, and a good friend."

"That night, of the Hurricane, first week of school senior year, at your house, I fell asleep...on the couch next to you. I still just thought we were friends..."

"You must have been dreaming about me *or something.*"

"Or *something,*" she said, punching a smiling, show-off-y Augie in the arm of his gorgeous black suit.

"You had a lot of nerve taking advantage of a sleeping virgin wearing short shorts during a Hurricane..."

"During **Goodfellas,**"

"During **Goodfellas,**"

"*I got it.*"

"*You got it.*"

"I'm so glad. Mission accomplished," he pronounced, clapping his hands in self-satisfaction.

"No wonder you won all of those awards. You do know how to put on a great show, Augie. I always thought you would have great talent as a photographer, or a director. You were so good at directing me."

"I was getting worried there, you've been upstaging me almost all weekend, Benny."

"Frank N Furter was on the money when he sang *Don't Dream It, Be It* in **The Rocky Horror Picture Show.**"

"I'm disappointed we didn't get to study **Rocky Horror** or **Grease** in our American Musical Theater class together."

"I know, right? *Robbed.*"

Her heart raced from the excitement of his words and the music until the band finished their song to a packed house crowd on a Sunday night, drinking heavily and looking dapper in suits and dresses. A black woman of around fifty, wearing a long rhinestone dress walked on stage from behind the curtain. Then, *it began,* the dark room of Smoke Jazz Club got quiet and the woman looked straight at their "ringside" table and began to sing Nina Simone's "Sugar in My Bowl." It was on the mix tape that Benny had sent to Augie overseas. He remembered this, too.

They just sat quietly and held hands under the candlelit table and listened. The atmosphere was relaxed and the music was lovely.

When the song ended, she turned to him and said calmly: "You always made me feel like I was the only one with the memory, when, now, you have more than proven that you *remember everything, too.*"

"Well, *some things.*"

"You remembered *everything!* Even things that I had forgotten! Or maybe, *blocked out from embarrassment,* I love you Augie Baxter! *Say it!*"

"Say what?" he asked, quietly.

"You love me, too?" she asked, also quietly and even closing her eyes as if she was both anxious and afraid to receive his reaction.

"Benny..."

"Please, Augie, this weekend, we're *pretending.*"

He was so full of adrenaline and satisfaction that he had pulled this all off for her and he had to admit, *for himself, too.*

"Pretending?" he asked her, knowing she was not pretending when she said those words.

"You've officially made up for the past, Augie. Your karma is back intact. You owe me nothing from this moment forward. Just...tell me you love me, here, now, on our last night..."

Love, to Benny, at forty, was about rising, not falling.

"Benny..."

"Augie, I woke up this morning on the fence about all of this. I know I'm not *your wife*, but in the *bubble* we pretend."

"Benny."

"Don't make me wait until we're eighty!"

"Benny..."

"SAY IT!"

"I....I..."

Right then the waiter walked up to their table.

"Your car is ready for you, Mr. Baxter" is all he said, squashing the moment she had tried to complete. She would survive, it was still a great night. Just like he had promised...*unforgettable*. Even the new Benny knew how hard it was to get someone to say *I love you.*

10

The long ride home in the Town Car was silent and motionless except for the occasional rise and fall of the tires heading south on Broadway. Benny laid her head on Augie's shoulder and she didn't think about anything but feeling good. He enjoyed the silence as well and enjoyed feeling her head on his shoulder and just felt good, too. He was lost in the silence of a happy mind and a happy moment.

They did not speak when they got off the elevator at Elizabeth Street. It had been a long day. A very long day for two forty year olds who had been acting like kids. They had been kids who thought they were the stars of their very own movie. His, a Paul Schrader film. Hers, a Fellini. There was even a soundtrack and Augie put in on. It was Leonard Cohen which was the same album he played the night he deflowered her. The night he made her a *woman.*

He turned off all the lights and lit candles. There was a bit of moonlight streaming in from the large living room windows. He took off his jacket and shoes and sat on the edge of the bed loosening his thin, black **La Dolce Vita** tie. It was finally going to happen *again*. He hoped she would enjoy it more at forty.

As soon as she heard Leonard Cohen, she started to lose it. She thought, *who does this to a girl? On the night you lose your virginity?* He was directing her that night, wasn't he? Something within her wanted to cry. She knew she wasn't twenty anymore. Her breasts were not as big or as perky, and she had some marks, some dimples and lines. She hoped her body felt as good to him as it had in the past once he was inside her. She wondered if she could go through with it. She heard it again - *Don't Dream It, Be It.* It was Frank-N-Furter who pushed her to be confident and brave, to be an artist and to value herself. That Sweet Transvestite told her she *shouldn't, not like this, not like this Benny, you deserve to have it ALL. Don't Dream It, Be It. For Augie to love you – for you to love you - you can't do this.*

"So Long, Marianne" began to play softly, in the candle and moonlight New Benny decided to be daring and to do something in front of Augie that she had never, ever, done before. She would take off all of her clothes while he watched. He had asked her for this so many times when they were younger and she could never do it. She always made him turn the lights out or she would run to his bed and jump completely under the covers and hide her body. Eventually, she would land on all fours or on top of him and he would see all of her anyway. Even when she was on top of him, she put her hands over her face so he could not see her or look into her. She had serious issues with being on display. Now all she wanted was the attention that he had always wanted to pay her.

She stood in front of Augie and stared at him.

"Do you want to look at me?" she asked.

"Yes," he responded, "Yes."

She pushed her chest out front and maneuvered her hands behind her back, unzipping the back of her dress. She pushed the straps off of her cherry print dress for a moment and posed for him. Then, she slowly pivoted around in a circle in front of him. Next, she began to push the skin tight dress down her curves and over her tiny waist and round hips and backside to the floor. She stepped out of the dress in her high heels and walked closer to him. She stood in the white Agent Provocateur Granny panties. She realized that they were so tight on her that he would have to literally rip and pull them off of her. She also wore a plain white push up bra. He stood up and walked behind her, causing her to unconsciously lean her face forward and hide behind her hair. He slowly unhooked her bra and massaged her shoulders as he took it off of her. He worked his strong hands from her shoulders and down to her breasts, squeezing and rubbing and whispering into her ear, "Are you ready to become a woman again?"

She almost lost her balance. He brought her back to her feet.

"Um," was all she could utter.

"Say yes, Cassandra. You said yes before, remember?" he whispered into her ear.

He started to pull the tight, spandex Granny panties down and over her hips and half way down her ass. He stopped pulling down the panties as he liked the way her ass looked with the panties half on and half off. He savored Benny pushing her chest forward, hiding her breasts and face with her hands and hair, not facing him. She waited patiently for him to touch her again. But, he held back. Instead, he slowly took off his own tight ensemble while staring at her perfect ass sticking out right at him, half covered in white spandex and corseted strings. She was *dying. It was* just like it had felt the first time. She started to shake and wobble. He could have pushed her face down on the bed and fucked her on all fours, quickly, just like that, in her two hundred dollar panties and on JR's high-end white sheets. But, he didn't. Instead, he slowly pulled the panties down and threw them across the room. He turned her around to face him and kiss her. Then he lifted the sheet over the bed and told her, *"Let's go to bed, now, Benny"* treating her just as he did twenty years earlier, remembering how shy she could be about her body, and how serious sex and losing her virginity to him was to her. He wanted to let her have her modesty *this* first night. Just like he had let her have it *that* first night. That first night, he did pay attention to her, and he did try to be gentle. She noticed how he had switched gears and wanted her to feel just like the virgin girl of twenty years past. She was touched and it was then that she remembered, as the strong woman now inside her told her, that *sex was serious to her.* She didn't want to do anything more to taint that delicious and delightful possibility for the two of them to have a legitimate relationship *one day.* Like the one they had talked about when they were in their mid-twenties. She had convinced herself that they would be together when they were old. She told him she would spoon feed him pasta and push him in his wheelchair. She would not fear getting older, she would look forward to it because she would have something to look forward to...him. The Wedding Announcements in the New York Times Style section didn't help.

All those old couples who find one another again, thirty, forty or fifty years after they first dated? No, when he thought of her it should be for all *right* reasons and no *wrong* ones. Not for the ones that made him feel guilty.

They both lay naked under the expensive white sheets on the living room mattress. The windows were open and the cool breeze made the sheets billow once in a while. He retrieved one of the Tiffany boxes filled with two giant silver candelabras. He found a stash of old candles and lit them at the top of the mattress.

They faced each other and stared into each other's eyes. Her fingertip traveled over the mole on his face, over and over.

"I love this mole" she said.

Then she put her finger on his big nose.

"I love this nose" she said, her finger moving down to his lips, "I love this mouth, and every single word that comes out of it..."

He leaned over and gently kissed her. Then he touched the skin of her shoulders, and down her forearms, down to her fingers and back up to her breasts. He was starting to get aroused and cleared his throat over the soft music.

"So, how do you feel about this weekend?" she asked.

"I've...loved it." he answered.

"Even though we haven't yet..."

"I've loved it."

"Augie, do you ever think, sometimes it's better, not doing it?"

"Not doing it?"

"I'm worried it's been me who keeps postponing this thing, because I'm not sure about how I'll feel afterward. Or you. What's going on at home, Augie? Seriously, what's wrong with your marriage?"

He held her hand in both of his.

"Benny, I've never done *anything* like this before, and as much as things aren't going too well at home..."

"So they *aren't?*"

"*No.* And as much as sleeping with you would make me very happy... *so happy*, Benny...I don't want to leave this weekend... *devastated.*"

The phrase held different meanings to them. He felt guilty for cheating on his wife, however badly disconnected they had become. She felt guilty for sleeping with a married man that she might *love*. Even if just out of sentimentality, the mutual acknowledgement that they were both worried and were open about it, provided a great moment of closeness for them.

"We were both pretty irresponsible this weekend, but you're technically still married and I'm, I'm...*not*..."she confessed. She waited for a violent reaction from him to this statement but there wasn't one.

"Yes..."

"I thought you'd be shocked!" she said to him in a state of alarm.

"I know you're not married anymore. JR told me," he admitted.

"Have you known this whole time? And you went ahead with all of this? Why? Why?" she demanded.

"I went ahead with all of this because I still wanted this weekend, this fantasy, to happen. I know why you didn't tell me. You were afraid I'd back out."

"I *was* afraid of that. The irony is that it's so much easier to be close to another person when they're in a relationship. When they're single, they're a lot more threatening..."

"Like I said. I didn't care. I still wanted to make this thing happen."

"Like I said, you're still married, I'm not. And if I'm with you, I want it all and it to begin with the greatest of aspirations. I didn't quite make this clear the first time we slept together. You know the fact that I want it all with you. I can't handle sleeping with you and then not having you all to myself again. I just can't bear it and I don't want you to think of me as the woman you cheated with. I want to be the woman you want to grow old with. Well, *older* with,"

"Benny," he said.

"I'm not going to sleep with you, *because I love you, Augie.*"

"You're not going to sleep with me because you love me?"

"Yes. I mean, at least as a *friend*. Someone has to make the sacrifices in this relationship, so I guess it has to be me. And I'm not saying you were an altar boy this weekend, but at least, forgive the term, you didn't go all the way. I'm not claiming a Bill Clinton defense on your part, but it could have been a lot worse."

"Or really, really good.."

"Yeah, like I said, *worse.*"

"Yep. Very, very good."

"As your editor, I have to advise against the use of the word *very* or *really.*"

"Stop it!"

"I foolishly thought, after being with you, that sex was supposed to be the beginning of something. It was supposed to take me to a higher level of consciousness.."

"You're *such* an Air sign…"

"Well, it shouldn't be an ending, Augie, not for us, and you can shut it about Air signs!"

"You're right, Benny."

"There are so many things I've been afraid to ask you about because I was too insecure. But now I want you to talk to me. I want you to be intimate *with me*. It's always been me opening up to you. Will you please open up to me, at long last? Can't you see I'm finally strong enough to handle it? You can tell me everything. Everything I've ever been afraid to hear because my ego was too fragile, because I couldn't just accept you, please. Please tell me your whole life story from the beginning. Make this my perfect night of my perfect weekend. I can't believe I'm saying this, but better than sex to me is feeling like we could be friends again, *talking*. You were *my* best friend once, Augie. Finally, let me be *yours*."

And then he started talking, and she started listening. Benny's "tell" was when she poured herself a glass of wine when he mentioned an old girlfriend or his wife. He noticed this and would slow his speech, not wanting to upset her, but she told him, "Go on, I'm listening. I want to know these things..."

So, he shared, and she listened.

"Tell me, now," he insisted, tired of hearing his own voice, "your stories. There is at least one love story in there that I know of, that I'm not the star of, and I want you to tell it to me. I feel like you always wanted to tell me everything. Like I was the one person in your life you had decided you would tell everything to."

"My security blanket."

"You would share anything from your medical scares, to you masturbating in your office bathroom. Remember that? I remember when you wrote to me about the first time you watched pornography – by yourself. And how it affected you. You, Benny, my Benny, the girl who locked herself in my closet rather than let me see her naked! You, you wanted to *share* that experience with me. How you started to explore your body all on your own, in your twenties, *without me*. How you learned how to give yourself pleasure? *I remember all of that.*"

"God, I was a *late bloomer*," she admitted.

"But you haven't told me anything about your life from the day you told me *never to call you again*, til the day you arrived back on Elizabeth Street. That story is important, it's made you, *you*. This new Benny I have with me today. Please, you can tell me. I still want you to feel like you can tell me anything and everything. I still want to be that person in your life. Now that I'm older, I realize what an honor it is, to be the one person you can confess to and *be yourself...*"

"Myself, huh?" she asked.

"There's so much more to you than just being a late-blooming, pool-hustler with a great rack. Double entendre, definitely. Who reads with pretense.."

"There is a fine line between pretense and pleasure, Augie," she interrupted.

"Agreed."

"You also have a knack for short-jokes and television jokes. Although I believe you secretly watch reality TV when no one is looking."

"I only listen to public radio – seriously!"

"Like I said, *pretentious.*"

"Okay there, Mister let's have casual talks about Dostoyevsky and Kurosawa's greatest hits."

"We're talking about the world's greatest writer and world's greatest filmmaker."

"Yeah, yeah, save it for the NYU kids at Café Wha? with a Daddy complex. You said it yourself – *pretentious.*"

"I'm a victim of my birthday. Generation X."

"*Generation Annoying.*"

"Agreed."

"*You never looked right in a flannel shirt.*"

"Agreed"

"I remember watching the television show **Thirtysomething** as a kid and thinking, Wow! *Those guys are old!* You know, the Baby Boomers?"

"See, you did watch television!"

"Once upon a time, Augie…yes."

"We're older than those Thirtysomethings now."

"I know. And that scares me. I have to live the life that I've dreamed of *now*. There's no more time to waste."

"Do it!" he demanded. He was still the one to push her in the direction she was often too timid or too insecure to follow herself. He provided this to her over and over again, he could still push her along.

"Can I tell you that I want to be as successful as you have been without giving you a big head? You kind of did the uninhibited go for your dreams thing earlier than I did. Lived here on Liz Street with JR, took classes. All steps I wish I had been brave enough to take, and your television isn't total crap. You worked your way up the entertainment ladder in New York City. That's a major accomplishment. Yes, I wish you produced an occasional Masterpiece Theater episode, but every once in a while, the Booty Doctor from the Bronx has an epiphany about beauty and I'm moved. *You did good.*"

"You watch the Booty Doctor from the Bronx?"

"Oh, Augie! I watch all of your shows! Hello! I am interested in your work."

"Thank you. That means a lot coming from you…*my harshest critic.* Even The New Yorker's Emily Nussbaum is kinder, and *yes, you can admire me,*" he said flirtatiously.

"See, I knew this would happen! My point is, and this is coming from someone in a family who lived paycheck to paycheck, can't you write and direct the feature film you always wanted? Can't you take a break from reality TV, sit on a beach somewhere and write? What are you afraid of?"

"It's easier to make reality TV and be judged because I'm not making art. I'm not trying to do anything other than entertain. But a feature, my own creative vision, that is an attempt at art and that will be judged. A million people watch The Booty Doctor of the Bronx. Maybe only five will watch my film, it's different."

"Throw it on YouTube! Someone will watch your movie. I will!"

"I know you would, thank you."

"I mean you had a treatment for this thing years ago. Find it and bring it back to life!"

"You're right. Sometimes it's just easier in life to present yourself as a character, and to experiment with sides of yourself you don't necessarily want to own up to. You can always blame it on the character."

"Much safer, yes. I mean haven't we been doing this all weekend?"

"But, you, I see it, Benny. I see your success. I believe in you. This bold and ambitious you. Well, you've always been ambitious. But, you are so creative, it's ridiculous! And I'm not just saying this because you gave me a hand job in broad daylight in Washington Square Park."

"Get your mind out of the gutter."

"*Washington Square Park!*" he echoed, "I LOVED THAT!"

New Benny, she thought.

She took a deep breath and leaned her head on his shoulder.

"So, what do you want to know?" she asked him while she held him tightly in her arms that were strewn across his pale, bare chest.

He asked her a few probing questions and then she spoke for a little while, sharing a condensed version of her life, the one without him in it. Reciting it made her appreciate how great her life was and how everything happens for a reason. Even not having been Augie Baxter's "official" girlfriend back in college. Even not having been Augie Baxter's *wife.* She realized that she was a late bloomer and that she hadn't been ready for a relationship as intense and uninhibited as this one was *until now.* Until she was a grown-ass forty year old woman. Until she committed herself to being a full-time artist. Until she respected herself despite an affair with a married man which could threaten it all. Until she realized she didn't need any buffers, any characters…unless it was for fun. She realized she was perfectly fine representing herself all on her own.

Timing was everything. Maybe it took twenty years for Augie to appreciate her the way she always wanted to be appreciated by him. Timing let things happen naturally. Nothing between the two of them had to be forced. She was completely committed to them finding one another again if it was meant to be. So many great memories happened between the two of them that occurred naturally, including a Hurricane. There was no reason to mess with a good thing now…

Leonard Cohen's album eventually ended and they started kissing. Just like the first night he forced himself over to her house, they did not sleep together. It was extremely hard to keep them from actually being *inside* each other's body, *torture*. It took every ounce of restraint, but they succeeded in keeping Benny intact. All he could think was, *some man is going to be very lucky to have her.* All she could think was *this might have been my last chance to have sex with him. But it's for the best. I know this is for the best. I need to go home and start over...*

11

At one point, as the sun rose through the windows of the fourth floor apartment on Elizabeth Street, he was behind her and they both looked up into the large golden mirror across from the bed. Their reflections revealed two brand new people and not just the college aged versions of themselves that they were pretending to be, or all of those characters who saw their lives as scenes in a great movie and took risks and pushed. It scared them both to think about who these two people would transform into next, come morning. Exhausted, she rested her face on his shoulder and he rested his on hers as they held one another tightly.

Benny said, as she was prone to do, but especially wanting to at that exact moment, "*I love you, Augie Baxter*," into his ear. Not looking into his face, *not needing to.*

"*I love you, too,*" he whispered back, not looking into her face. He appeared shocked, confused, happy, and exhausted all at the same time. She didn't say another word. If she never heard another word for the rest of her life, she'd have been fine.

Soon, she fell into a deep, deep, happy, relaxed sleep. Stacy's fancy sheets barely covered her naked body. Augie, the night owl, got up and sat at the edge of the bed and watched her. She remained still. He put on Mulatu Astatke's song "Tezeta" on low and grabbed his Leica camera. Recently, she had told him that she enjoyed songs without words or songs with words she didn't understand, like French. He told her he understood exactly what she was saying. That he liked to "shoe gaze." She thought it was because she was older now. She didn't want to be told what she should be thinking when she heard a particular song. She wanted to craft her own story by listening to the song. She just wanted to feel it, not think it. *Like one does when they see a painting, or a photograph. They invent their own story.*

Benny told him she loved this song because it made her happy. It had nothing at all to do with sex or love, she said. She didn't think about anything when she heard it. She just felt...happy all over.

Augie started taking photographs of her with his Leica. More and more, the sun crept into the living room but he just kept on shooting. She just kept on sleeping and the music just kept on playing.

BOOK IV

Monday

1

A few hours after Augie had finished his spontaneous dawn photo shoot, Benny woke up. For once, there was no hint of the abandonment thing. Augie was beside her and she snapped a thousand photographs of him in her head. She was sober when he told her he loved her last night. That *did* happen, didn't it? She must have told him she loved him a hundred times, maybe more. Now he had said it *once.*

She stood up to use the bathroom and looked down at him, sleeping, innocently. He did not look forty three to her. He still looked twenty and like when they first met at his Fraternity brother's party the first week of school during her sophomore year of college. Her roommate warned her "He's an actor, he's from New York, he used to drive a cab, he's a soccer player. Took a year off of school for disciplinary and academic probation. Last but not least, he's a character. He's quick with a one-liner, a smart-ass."

"A smart-ass, huh?" Benny had asked, intrigued.

Somehow, that night, at the party, Augie found Benny. She was the shy, zaftig girl who attended parties with her much more glamorous roommate and her boyfriend. She was the third wheel, the tag a long, who stood or sat by herself in a corner and hid…watching. The budding writer. He noticed her immediately. Cassandra, as she was still called back then, was always politely introduced to all of' her roommate and her boyfriend's friends. But, she never took it seriously that any one she was introduced to actually remembered her name or even wanted to be friends with her. Until…the start of that semester, when she was waiting outside of the History Department with her headphones on and the super long blonde hair that covered her breasts. He came to the bench across from her and smiled and gestured to turn her headphones off. Benny seemed annoyed.

"Cassandra Bennett, right?"

"Yes."

"I'm Augie, remember? I think we're in the same class together. Did I pronounce your last name right, Bennett?"

"Yes," Benny answered. This might have been the longest conversation she had ever had with a boy in college.

"How about I just call you, Benny? Yeah, Benny. I like that. Or, just Bent. No, Benny. Is that okay?"

"Do I have a choice?" she asked him.

"You look annoyed… that I'm talking to you," he told her.

"I'm just…writing," she answered, looking down on her chicken scratch and bubble hearts sprinkled all over her notebook.

"You know, I saw this porno last night," he began.

"What?" she gasped. This was not only the longest conversation she had ever had with a boy in college but also the dirtiest.

"Well, there was this midget…"

She started choking on her saliva and grabbed her backpack to walk over to the other side of the park. There was only the two of them sitting there, on either side of one another now. As soon as she crossed her legs, he crossed his legs. When she turned her head, he turned his head. Mimicking all of her movements was his attempt at flirting. *That was flirting, right?* Then he just stopped and leaned forward on his bench and stared at her breasts from across the park as he continued to talk to her.

"I don't know who you are talking to as you can plainly see I have my headphones on. You… you, *pervert!*" she yelled from across the park, putting her headphones back on and blasting them. She adjusted the volume to allow her the chance to hear him speak again. She liked his voice. She couldn't help it. He intrigued her. He shocked her.

"Benny," he said again.

"Up here!" she said pointing to her face. He just grinned.

"Benny, I love it. You're Benny!"

Uncomfortable, confused, sweating and her heart palpitating, she had just had her first sexual conversation with a man-boy and was made to feel like a sexual object for the first time. She had been given a "nickname" by a practical stranger. The friend of a friend. From New York. Augie. Little did she know that day that Augie Baxter, whether or not they would ever be an actual couple, would always be the great love of her life, and maybe, just maybe, she would be *his*.

When Benny walked into the bathroom that Monday morning, the last morning of her weekend getaway with Augie, she was glowing, content and strong. She was completely secure in her decision. She looked at herself in the mirror and sang *"Don't Dream It, Be It"* and quickly threw a dress on, slid into her flip flops and shoved her stuff in a suitcase. She grabbed her mobile phone out of the jeweled box in the living room on her way out. Seeing her fake wedding band and his real one, she felt justified in her decision. She grabbed her Pink IPOD Nano and threw it in her purse. She would keep the memories of this weekend with her, forever. And most definitely, the music on Augie's playlist. She stood above Augie who was asleep on the floor. She reached to touch him but decided not to. *It's better this way.* She grabbed her suitcase, ran down the stairs and caught a taxi to the airport.

It was not until the vehicle veered off of Elizabeth Street and onto Canal that she allowed herself to cry. She told herself that after she landed, she would take a taxi straight to her ex's to see the kids and for a hug and a kiss. *Mommy just needs one,* she would tell them.

There were a few songs left on the IPOD Nano on her ride to La Guardia. The first was a sweet reminder of their American Musical Theater class that they took together in college "Surrey with the Fringe on Top" from the musical **Oklahoma.** The next song she heard was sexy, Prince's "Sexy Motherfucker." This was the song that he blasted half naked from his attic window the day she delivered a dead fish to his house after the Hurricane, back in college. It was just like him to show off and direct a scene like that one. The last song she heard was kind of melancholy because it made her smile and sob at the same time. It was Chan Marshall aka Cat Power's song "Manhattan." He had put Cat Power on his first mix tape to her. *Another thing he apparently remembered.* Same artist, brand new song. Even Chan Marshall had improved over time...The scary part was that she had put this same song on her playlist for *him.* Maybe they would always be connected. As her taxi slowed midway on the Brooklyn Bridge, she turned around, headphones intact and said goodbye.

2

When Augie woke up late Monday morning, on the final day of his weekend affair in the *bubble* on Liz Street with Benny, he felt around the bed to put his hands on her soft skin. But she wasn't there. He looked around the living room. He didn't see her suitcase.

"Benny?" he called as he stood up and wrapped a sheet around his waist. "Benny?" He walked into the kitchen. There was no tea cup. He scanned the bathroom. There were no toiletries. He walked back to the living room to open JR's jewel encrusted guitar pick box to find her telephone gone. But, for some reason the wedding band was still there. The night before she had told him that she purchased it in the airport before getting on the plane to New York. She had bought the ring to give the appearance that she was still married. There was no reason for her to take it with her when she left Liz Street.

Augie, tired and slightly hung-over, started pacing the floor of the apartment. He walked in and out of every room in case there was some strange chance that she was still there. He had hoped that this was just a bad dream where you missed something, *someone*, more than anyone or anything you had ever missed before in your life. And if you couldn't find them, or any evidence that they existed, you thought you might die inside. It was a dream Benny had had numerous times about Augie, but now it was happening to him. He was *living* it. His futile apartment search was indicative that something significant was missing from his life. The question was, *could he live without it?*

And then he found the note that was pinned under the wedding photo of JR and Stacy:

> *Dear Shorty, My Shorty (or - O, Captain! My, Captain!)*
>
> *The perfect ending to this perfect weekend is for me to leave here The Girl Who Got Away(finally.) I see now that I should have been her all along. It would have saved you a lot of trouble and me a lot of heartache. You never promised me anything more than friendship when we were younger, and I never asked. You were a good friend – and we both had a lot of growing up to do.*
>
> *I love us NOW. Older.*
>
> *If you're ever free, I mean really free, outside the bubble, call me(old fashioned.) Even if we're both really old – like ancient. Even if I'm the one in the wheelchair, even if you technically can't get it up anymore, even if we have to rely on a lot of lube and electronics, even if our relationship consists of my watching you watch a lot of television.*
>
> *I just like you Irish, always have, always will. I thought this was such a complicated relationship*

yet after spending the weekend with you, I know it isn't. It's fairly cut and dry, actually, and simple, the way all good things should be. Like Husker Du's "Diane," like Mulate Astatke's "Tezeta." There's a reason we became friends, there's a reason we were lovers, there's a reason I said yes to you this weekend, but...

I would never want to hurt you, or any one close to you, or interfere with your life, outside the bubble. I want you to be happy. I want your family to thrive.

Liz Street is such a special and magical place! I loved stepping back in time with you and into our collective imaginations. I loved being your co-star. I loved feeling kind of, even, for once? I often feel so alone in my own head.

It's time for me to take a brave step into the future, as a hybrid perhaps, old and new me? Benny XXOO

P.S. You better make a movie, finally, or I'm sending you another dead fish.

After pacing ten minutes, heart racing, he noticed a stack of papers sitting on the floor in front of the elevator door. It was Benny's novel in its entirety and not just the chapter that she sent him last year for his "permission." It was the whole goddamn Opus of their relationship and proof that it was not so hard to convert two very real people into fictional characters, to tell a love story, where there wasn't one. But there was *a love story, he* just never saw it until now.

There was still a half bottle of wine open from the night before. He grabbed it and sat down in front of the elevator door, blocking it. He kept the sheet wrapped around his waist. He drank, and he read.

At noon, there was a loud banging on the door. It was the movers who he was supposed to let in and allow to move the rest of JR's stuff to a new Tribeca apartment. It was the only responsibility he had while JR was on his honeymoon. At first, he ignored the pounding on the door. Then, he stood up in his sheet, bottle in hand and told them there would be no moving today. They were pre-paid weren't they? Then he got his wallet out and put a few hundreds that were left over from the racetrack win into the hands of a guy who was tall, fat and sweaty and who in Augie's opinion would not want to move a guy who was drunk at noon on a Monday and naked under a white sheet. The mover took the money and left.

Augie found himself laughing a lot as he read through the novel. He loved the author's voice, *her voice*. He could hear her in the Beatrice character that she had created. His character, George, was equally as witty. But the more he read, the more he realized that he didn't know Beatrice...Oops!... Benny, as much as he thought that he did. Like him, George had no idea what she had thought of him in many crucial moments. In fact, he didn't even know the moment that she realized that she had fallen in love with him. He had to wait until he saw it happening between Beatrice and George. "*Wow*," he said aloud, opening up a six pack of Brooklyn Lager to fend off the heat.

When he finished reading the novel, he lay down on the mattress. It was late afternoon and he figured Benny was probably on her way home from the airport to her kids. And probably, to her life... far, far away. He wouldn't call. She wanted a fresh start. He was still married and none of this had been a good idea, none of this had been fair. Instead of hopping on the evening train home, as promised, he stayed in bed, with the now-thanks-to-her-working–air-conditioner and watched baseball. He texted his wife to let her know that he was okay but that was it. He said he might be holed up in the city a few more days. He saw no less than ten messages from JR from St. Barths that he did not listen to. He refused to answer the phone when it rang. He ordered in food, drank beer, watched baseball, listened to sad songs and talked to himself. Occasionally, he jerked off while naked under the white sheet for three full days. *Why didn't he sleep with her when he had the chance?* He was stuck in rising quick sand. He needed to take some kind of action. His hair was starting to grow back on his scalp and on his face and he missed *Benny*.

On the fourth day, he bathed and packed his bag to go home. He called JR who immediately began screaming at him.

"I thought I might have to call the cops, and the last thing I want are the cops rummaging through my old dime bags!" JR yelled. "What the fuck is going on? Are you mad I got married? Are you mad that I'm getting rid of the apartment?"

"That's not what's going on. I hardly even know what's happening to me, JR."

"Is this a mid-life crisis? Are you jealous I married such a hottie? What? Tell me!"

"I'm happy for you!" Augie yelled into the phone. "Yes, I'm fucking happy for you. Don't you know that? You have a new beginning, a fresh start with someone. No real responsibilities yet. It's all about friendship and fun. It's hard to keep that going for a long time unless, *it's the one.*"

"Don't be so goddamn serious. How do I know if she's the one I will be with forever? I just like her, you know?"

"Yeah, I do know."

"Listen, I'm going to reschedule the move for Labor Day, okay? I'll be back then, and, honestly, the Girardis haven't found a renter yet. They're pissed I'm leaving, you know how they feel about strangers. "

"Yeah, keeping the apartment longer sounds good. Maybe I will visit again before then."

"What's going on at home, Augie?"

"Nothing, JR."

"Tell me. What happened to you this weekend? Why MIA? Did you, you know, *find a girl?*"

He paused before answering. *He wanted to tell JR....*

"*Yeah,*" he answered in a way that JR knew not to probe any deeper.

"Ok, ok, I understand. I'll call you when I get back home."

"Okay," he answered and closed his phone. He rolled his suitcase into the elevator to descend the four floors of the Elizabeth Street apartment with what now didn't have to be the last time. He could put off saying goodbye for good a little while longer.

3

Augie sat in his car outside the train stop in his enviable New York suburb for at least an hour. Chappaqua, home to the Clintons! Didn't everyone want to live there? Didn't this address mean he'd "made it?" That he could afford to take his single mother and older sister on beach vacations every year and help out with their mortgages? Benny was right, he did come a long way. Like her, he was a scholarship kid, even though you couldn't tell from the outside. He stared at the mammoth colonials and picturesque streets lined with Range Rovers, and populated with six figure salaried nannies. Was this the end of the line? Where did the edge go? He had come back from New York with a brain bursting with new ideas. He couldn't wait to get home and find his old film treatment and read it. Making a film wasn't hopeless. He couldn't wait to jot down all these notes, he didn't want to lose them again.

Benny's novel was visibly in his leather attaché. He kept scrolling down his phone to her phone number. He wanted to press the *send* button, but, he never did. He looked at the photo of them standing in their underwear in the dressing room at Dolce & Gabbana. She had texted it to him before she abandoned him Monday morning. The two of them looked like Mannequins as they stood together with their arms at their sides and blank looks on their faces. Cindy Sherman would have been proud of their super-secret identities caught in a photograph that looked like an old-timey movie still. They could be anyone they wanted to be in that picture. He hesitantly deleted the picture, collected himself, got his "story" together and began his short drive to his own charming colonial.

When he arrived home, his garage door opener did not work so he left the car in the driveway. His front door key did not work either, so he rang the bell. He knew what was going on although it all felt surreal. What he heard, he was, but wasn't, prepared for.

"I want a divorce," his wife said.

He was so tired and emotionally weak from the past weekend that he just slumped up against the doorway and didn't say a word.

"Augie, I know this isn't easy. For either one of us. But I know, I mean, my gut tells me, you don't want to be married anymore, either," she said.

Again, no answer from Augie, who just averted his eyes from his wife. Maybe she was right, maybe not anymore, maybe not forever.

"You and I are not in the same physical place...ever. Our minds aren't even in the same universe. I want someone who knows me better than you do now. Do you understand that?" She added.

He did. Still, he was speechless. It hurt to swallow.

"I've moved most of your stuff to an extended stay hotel in town. We'll have a talk with the kids tomorrow. I think this is better for them, too. I think you should sleep on it, be a bit calmer."

"Calmer, yes," Augie finally spoke up.

"I don't want to fight with you. I just want to be happy," she said, "even if that sounds cliché to you, or unattainable, it's what I want."

"It's not cliché," he admitted, still staring at the doorbell and not at his wife's face. The woman he loved – for a very long time – but maybe not in the right way anymore.

"Do you see, Augie? Do you see why I need to do this?"

"No. Why do you need to do this?"

"I know exactly who I am. Always have. I can't wait for you to figure out who you are."

"I thought…I had."

"And you're not even asking to win me back."

Augie was aware of this and started crying. He put his sunglasses over his eyes and punched the front door. His wife jumped backward and then held his limp body in her arms, even though he did not reciprocate with a hug back. Just more salty swallows and more tears deposited into the corners of his Ray- Bans.

"Tomorrow, we'll sit down with the kids," she whispered into his ear. She was crying now, too. "Be back for breakfast. I want to get this over with. I want to mourn you and move on, please let me move on."

She released her embrace and stepped back into the house and shut the door.

He did not put up much of a fight. He tried to pretend this was a psychological "boot camp." He convinced himself that the next few weeks/months would be excruciating. But at the end of it, he would be a better man, a stronger man. If he wasn't brave enough to make these changes for himself, his soon to be ex-wife would force him to. Over the course of the next two weeks, he looked at his phone, and scrolled down to Benny's name. He did not press "call." The only person he did call was JR who he informed that he was going to take over the lease at Elizabeth Street and that he was moving there over Labor Day. *Just before the San Genarro Festival.. Eleven days of zeppole and sausage and peppers...*he weakly joked, a sharp, salty pain in his throat as he spoke. Liz Street and the apartment waiting there was about the only thing that provided some comfort.

He lived at the extended stay when he had the kids during the school week and on occasion, the kids would come and stay with him in the city. He wondered if his kids knew how hard it was to be an adult and to be a parent. How parents still wanted love, affection, a best friend. How adults still had dreams they wanted to see come true, no matter what their age.

His wife had already been seeing someone on the side while they were married. She did not want or need to know if he had been with anyone. She wanted to release him from any guilt. He wanted to tell her, *no, I was faithful,* but he wasn't. He may not have slept with Benny, but his weekend spent just talking to her and sleeping beside her was more dangerous than just sleeping with a random woman on the PTO. Which he did, just before he moved into the city. She was short and boxy and bossy with long black hair, kind of like his wife. He jumped her in her car one afternoon. It was short and vengeful, and once she found out that he was not getting the house, she told him not to call her.

When Augie lived in the city, he made a practice of getting drunk at Raoul's and basically took home the last woman standing. He slept with them, too, and sent them packing right after. If a barfly tried to kiss him on the lips, he turned his head away and got all *Tomas* on their asses, thinking, *I only kiss women I love.* After his downtown liaisons, he would sit in the shower for hours. Afterwards, he'd scroll down his phone until he saw Benny's name and then he would just stare at it. Eventually, he'd close the phone and watch TV, alone in the living room on Elizabeth Street until he fell asleep.

He started gaining weight, and decided to scale down his production schedule to focus on writing and photography. He had some money saved and some still coming in, so he decided to try to be an artist – to be a filmmaker. He was writing a new feature. He began to hang out in coffee shops like he used to back at college in New Orleans and when he first moved to New York City with JR. Benny had always pushed him to be an artist, not a producer. Producers were more business than creative. She thought Augie was *creative*, and although she hated to admit it, funny.

He hadn't exercised since the summer. He had a decent beard and a bit of his belly came out and over the top of his pants. All that take out deli food from Russ and Daughters and pizza from Artichoke on MacDougal was taking its toll. Even JR was calling him a *fat ass.* He tried to write and headed over to the lobby of the trendy Ace Hotel at twenty-eighth and Broadway. Benny had mentioned that she often sat there and drank the delicious Stumptown coffee and wrote. She said the lobby was packed with writers and other artists. Plus, it was great people watching. They did always both like to *watch.*

Augie sat at the giant wooden table and drank his Stumptown coffee. He wore a button down, khaki pants and some high-top Converse. He wore a New York Giants cap which matted down his messy thick hair.

Augie scanned Twitter and other social media sites on his Mac laptop while he sipped his coffee, The Divine Fits playing overhead. Two young men, one wearing a Yankees cap, the other wearing a Jets hat, took over the two seats next to him at the table and started talking loudly. They both wore Converse, low-tops. They ordered a beer from a young waitress who wore her hair in a Lena Dunham "Girls" style bun. She asked for an ID.

"You giving these guys a hard time?" Augie joked with the waitress, trying to be *cool. Even fifteen years in the suburbs couldn't take away his middle-aged hipster credentials.*

"They look eighteen," she told him.

"We're twenty-five," the one with the Yankees hat told Augie.

"We write for **Saturday Night Live,**" the one with the Jets hat told him.

"What is it – dress like your Dad day?" the waitress joked. "You've all got sports caps and Converse on. It's kind of funny."

"Funny, yeah, yeah," Augie answered, nodding his head. *'No, it isn't funny. These little pricks write for **Saturday Night Live** and I could not be their father!'* he thought, *'I am not that old! I am an award winning television producer. Who cares if it's reality TV! And the Yankees and Jets can kiss my pale Irish ass!'*

Augie closed his laptop and started to walk out of the Ace Hotel – feeling not young, not hip, and without having written one goddamn word. Maybe he wasn't cut out to be a writer, after all. He hopped in a taxi straight to Rudy's Bar and Grill in Hell's Kitchen to start drinking pitchers of draft beer and drown his sorrows. He was in his forties. He was getting a divorce. He always wanted to live in New York City–with a little bit of dough in his pocket–and now he was. Plus, he didn't have to share a bathroom with JR any more. This was his chance to pursue a new career and maybe a fresh start. But instead, he's getting laughed at in the Lobby of the Ace Hotel – *Hipster Central.*

Where was Benny when he needed her? She promised she would *kill anyone who even looked at him funny.* Where was she? He missed her. He always felt young with her, young and understood. When you get to a certain age, being understood counted for a lot. She would understand the cultural irony of twenty-two-year-old writers in New York wearing nearly the same outfit as he was. How that said something. She would understand that we are all connected by shared experiences. *'There are kids who want to be me and all I want to do is be them.'* he thought. He drank his beers with the day crowd at Rudy's and hoped none of his buddies from across the street at the Film Center Building would be outside when he left *sauced.*

Augie built a darkroom on the Girardis' third floor, which was only used for antique storage and started to develop his own photographs. He liked to take pictures of Nolita and of the still visible Italian-American faces that lived in the neighborhood and the remaining authentic Italian-American businesses, like butchers and sandwich shops. He liked to take pictures of churches, Old St. Patrick's being his favorite, of old men playing Bocce-Ball, the many generations of Girardis. He liked to take pictures of New York City, because he loved it. He didn't ever think he would end up living there full time, even though in his heart he always wanted to but now he was. *'That's one upside to this divorce'* he thought.

Maybe his attempts to update and rewrite his childish screenplay about a modern day western in New York City was a bad idea. The story felt empty and uninspired as he reread it. Hadn't Benny always advised him to *write what you know?* Maybe the meaningful film he yearned to make was here – in these photos. Maybe his reality television experience *was* valuable? There a possibility he could transform these photos and some new video into a documentary about Nolita! About Elizabeth Street! Starring Nonna Girardi, of course! How had he been so *blind?* The artist's *passion*, the *fire* he had waited so long for was once again staring him in the face.

The first roll of film he developed was of Benny sleeping. She had always complained that although she had many pictures of him, he had never taken a picture of her, not one. Once, she remarked that he would rather take a picture of a windowsill instead of her. She loved taking pictures of him, she loved catching the way he responded to her adoring him through the camera. Her photos of him said so much. He was happy in that role.

He developed and enlarged the pictures of her sleeping. He hung them to dry and just stared. He thought she looked beautiful in the black and whites when she was naked under the sheets on the mattress on the floor at sunset. He loved that she was a "smiley sleeper." *'Why did I never tell Benny she was beautiful before?'* He knew he held that word back on purpose, just like the camera lens he pointed at a windowsill.

4

Augie called JR late at night and told him, "Remember, that phone number you wanted to give me awhile back?"

JR thought he knew what he was asking for. "Augie, I know I kid about that stuff. It's Bachelor Party fodder. But are you sure? In your state?"

He answered, "I'm sure, JR. It's like you said, I can ask for *anything*?"

It was late November when Augie was tired of Raouls, the hangovers and the women. He waited an entire week before he called and placed an order with the number that JR provided him. One snowy December evening, a woman, around thirty, with long dark hair and glasses, in a flowered sundress, exited the elevator at the fourth floor on Elizabeth Street with a Duane Reade bag in her hand.

He walked the woman into the bathroom and told her to bend over the sink. She told him "Call me, Benny, please."

He put the dye into her hair and massaged it in. He had to pay a lot extra for this. Timer set, he fondled the woman's body over her clothes for a few minutes while she stood there, her brown being stripped-blonde. He rinsed the dye out of the woman's hair, then, sat at the edge of the bathtub to watch while she blew her hair dry.

Afterwards, he watched her comb it. He did not ask to do that for her. She put her probably fake glasses back on and posed for him provocatively. As she was about to push her straps off of her shoulders, in a nasally Slavic accent, she said *"Look at me, I'm Benny, don't you want to fuck me?"*

He felt sick to his stomach and winced. He grimaced in anger and out of shame, "You need to leave *right now.*"

"But?" the woman asked. Her even stronger eastern European accent grated his ears.

"Leave, right now, please." he said again. He stood up and escorted her back to the elevator, closing and locking the door behind her.

He walked right back into the bathroom and jumped into the shower. He tried to fantasize about Benny, the sure-fire hard-on was imagining the night he deflowered her.

That night, she had asked to inspect him as she had never seen a man's naked body up close. She wanted to see "it" under the light. But she was shy, so she asked to put a pillow over his face so he could not watch her watching him. Her asking to see him under the light, with a pillow over his face, was one of the biggest turn-ons he had ever experienced. Before she had even finished her sentence to ask to see him, he had already exclaimed "YES!" He laid down on his back and she placed a pillow over his face. "Hold this," she told him. Slowly and deliberately, she pulled down his boxers and then released *it.* She leaned over his naked body and pulled the lamp light on. She could only look at him down there for one second, that was it. The innocent Benny was still too embarrassed to look at it even with his face covered by a pillow. *Oh My God!* she mouthed to herself. *This boy's going to kill me! He is literally going to kill me!* She quickly turned the light out. Braver, she started to touch him down there with her finger and watched *it move* of all things. Startled, she bent her lips over and started to kiss *it*. He went wild, moaning, and threw the pillow off of his face and down to the floor and jumped on top of Benny, the twenty- year-old virgin. The girl who had only ever seen one man's body...his.

But even this fantasy, this memory recall, could not satisfy him. He could not be satisfied *this* night. Slavic Benny, *the call girl*, just the idea of it, disgusted him a thousand times more than the barflies at Raoul's or the PTO lady in the back of her SUV. He didn't want anything less than the real thing. He wanted the real Benny. '*How could she ever want to be with a man this desperate? This foul?*' Benny had always made him feel heroic.

He dried himself off and crept beneath a blanket. He fell asleep with the TV on hoping he would have a good dream.

BOOK V

December

1

Benny had managed to go on a date every Saturday night after she returned home from New York City. Every friend, neighbor, parent, social networking site, priest and rabbi were on the case. She was going to do the exact opposite of what she did after Augie told her, on the phone, late at night, on her twenty fifth birthday after stringing her along for years, that *they wouldn't be boyfriend and girlfriend.*

She would not be loyal to Augie, she would not be chaste, she would not be devoted. She would not stay home on a Saturday night and cry, destroying furniture like a spoiled child. She was going to do exactly what her therapist told her to do years prior, she was going to mourn him. She was going to pretend he was dead. She was going to pretend he no longer existed. *Correction*, she wasn't going to pretend. She was going to *believe* he no longer existed. When she dreamed of him, as she often did, she would have to muster up the strength to say, "You're not real!" and "Go away!"

This new "break-up," spun her into a totally different mindset. It didn't matter what her date looked like, what he did for a living, if he had anything in common with her, if he were rich or if he were the least bit attractive. None of it mattered. She just wanted a body with a pulse across the table from her. She wanted to know the physics of her actions were leading her in a brand new direction. Away from him, away from Augie, away from memory and toward the future.

Louise, always told her, "Happy Mommy, Happy Kids." She wanted to be happy for her kids.

Innocent, yes. She had always been known as an old fashioned prude, except when it came to Augie. She was completely uninhibited with him. None of her friends or matchmakers would know any better if she just went home *alone* after each of these dates and watched *Masterpiece Theater.* No one knew *what* she could be or *who* she could be when she was with Augie. Hand job in Washington Square Park! Cunnilingus afterhours at Dolce and Gabbana! All she wanted was a date every Saturday night. All she wanted was white noise and a reason to wear a pretty dress. She wanted to be *The Girl Who Got Away,* she *had* to be *The Girl Who Got Away.* She left her Benny identity behind in New York City and returned home once again as *Cassandra.*

After three months of serial dating and repressing her personality, something unusual happened. She was out for coffee with another mom, a "hot" mom, named Josephine, who had happily married a second time. Josephine was a bastion of optimism and town gossip. Benny enjoyed her company. Josephine was someone who rooted for others. She was grounded in her new life, incredibly horny and had a perverted sense of humor, they'd clicked instantly.

As Josephine complained about "no chip" manicures and the various divorcees who flirted with her new hubby, a sweaty

Swiss soccer player rushed into the coffeehouse where they often met. The soccer player looked a few years older than Benny. He was tall and he had a cute smile. As he politely ordered an espresso, he waved to the twosome.

"Maybe Karl should be next!" Josephine suggested. Benny had a blank look on her face that concealed the fact that all soccer uniforms reminded her of Augie. Her heart was in fact beating quickly which was not due to the coffee in front of her, but because of the wave of pleasure Karl waving over to the table, gave her. She refused to share that she was a forty year old *sort-of virgin*. She hadn't slept with anyone in two years since filing for divorce, including Augie. Josephine had never even heard the name "Augie," nor would she, Benny thought, "He's dead."

While waiting for his Espresso, Karl scanned an abandoned New York Times Arts section that was left on a dirty table.

"Hey, Karl!" Josephine called across the coffeehouse, "the boys didn't have practice today, did they?"

Karl, not one to yell across a room, grabbed his espresso that was sitting on the counter and walked over to their table.

"No, no practice for the boys today. I was just making a fool of myself playing in the European, middle-aged football league," he answered with a laugh.

"Oh, Cassandra, Karl here is Swiss," Josephine interjected, "Karl, this is my friend, Cassandra."

"Cassandra Bennett," Benny announced. She hoped she wasn't too eager to respond.

"Cassandra's kids go to private school down the road. She's a writer," Josephine stated as if she were an accomplished salesperson. Benny referred to Josephine's tactics as the classic "hard sell."

"Karl, Karl Rene," he answered, extending his hand to a nodding Benny, who returned the gesture. Benny noticed him look down at her hand, checking for a ring.

"A writer, really?" he began, "Well, I'm a reader. What, may I ask, do you write?"

Benny thought, *I'm always asked this but have yet to come up with a good enough answer.* The answers never seemed witty or charming to her. Being a writer and calling herself a writer was fairly new to her.

"Trash," she answered, "Page-turner trash."

"Trash?" he asked, nodding "I doubt that." He pointed to her backpack on the nearby table with his now empty paper espresso cup as books slid out.

"Sartre, O'Neill, and Dos Passos?" he began, "A little light reading? Never read Dos Passos, but Sartre, of course, and O'Neill...Heart of Darkness, *Brando phase.*"

"Oh, *these*," Benny began, "They are for show, only. Seriously, sometimes I only get through the first chapter."

Then he said something to her in French.

"I don't speak French except when I poorly pronounce a bottle of wine. I'm a sucker for a great Burgundy," she confessed.

"Karl here speaks five languages!" Josephine pushed as she proved her slight intimacy with Karl.

"Not well," he answered, with a more pronounced accent.

"Our boys go to school together. He coaches their soccer team, when he's not too busy betting on currency. European markets," Josephine finished.

"Where do you play?" Benny asked, "with the old timers?" holding back a smile.

"We play at the field at your kids' school. We rent it." He explained, "Games every Saturday, at three. Why not come by sometime, for a good laugh? At least one of us ends up in a brace and crutches."

"I might," Benny answered, softly, "for the laughs."

"Be sure to bring a stack of books, would you?" he continued, "I'd like to know what other authors you don't read."

"Definitely nothing French," she answered. "You can forget about Proust." Benny paused.

"Too pretentious."

"You're killing me here, Cassandra," Karl started, "I do hope we meet again. My son and his dog are waiting in the car, it's our weekend. We like to make the most of it. *American* football and pizza. You know?" Karl told them, "He likes your American hot wings, but I can't stomach them..."

"I love hot wings," Benny told him.

"Of course you, do, Ms. Bennett," Karl said, with a wide smile. "A pleasure to make your acquaintance. I always wanted to meet a writer."

He turned around and exited the coffeehouse. Josephine was intrigued and told Benny, "He was totally flirting with you!"

"No, he didn't," Benny said sternly, quickly changing the subject.

"You gave him a look like *he was* a hot wing." Josephine chided.

Benny forced a half smile and complimented her on her new earrings.

2

Benny was on hand for Karl's soccer game the following weekend. The kids were at their father's and although it was three o'clock, she was slightly drunk. It all started with a glass of wine with Josephine after their Fat Blast Class at the mall. She had the strangest feeling when it came to this man Karl, like she might actually sleep with him. The thought of him gave her a few goose bumps. It was important to her to finally break that connection to Augie "Bastard" Baxter once and for all.

Benny had broken off a second date with an investment banker that night to free up time to be with Karl, just in case they hit it off. She had to admit that there was something to new Benny from New York coming home to Florida that gave her a new confidence and attracted men. Cassandra Bennett was brave. Just as brave as new Benny, she thought. She did enjoy the attention.

Josephine had told her that Karl was an investment banker. Benny hoped that the two bankers did not know each another. Considering it her duty as a friend, Josephine also claimed that Karl was a cheater. She went on to add that he had cheated on his wife which caused her to divorce him. Benny was reminded of the "other side" of an affair. She wondered how Augie was and then stopped herself, he was supposed to be dead so she could get over him.

Even for Josephine, who could vet White House appointees for a living, the details of said cheating were fuzzy. Karl was "private" about it and his wife chose to move to another town. "Anyway," Josephine argued, "The other single moms are wary of Karl, however potent his charm." Benny thought just the opposite. Karl is perfect. For this job.

Karl waved to Benny from the field upon her arrival. He was surprised to see her and even lost his attention for a second, putting his hands on his hips and giving her a contemplative hand on chin as if attempting a Sherlock look. She wore a taupe cashmere turtleneck sweater dress with black wool thigh highs and knee-high rain boots. She imagined she was Lena Olin playing Tomas's mistress in the film **The Unbearable Lightness of Being**. She wanted to be as far away from her old self, the one who idealized sex with love. As she dressed in the locker room after her workout, she thought, *I should wear thigh highs instead of tights. Just pull my panties aside, stick it in and all the while, my legs will stay warm.*

For Florida, in December, it was an unseasonably cold, forty degrees. *Please, just let me get this over with. Let me get out of myself, out of my head, and out of my heart. 'The Girl Who Got Away'* Under no circumstances was it possible for her to confuse sex with love with this stranger...

Benny could tell there were a few other women on the sidelines noticing Karl. She thought he was smart, handsome and charming so she could understand their interest. They could all have their way with him, once she was through with him this afternoon. She didn't want to date Karl, she just wanted to fuck him. She trusted the strength of new Benny, uninhibited, a Dominatrix at times, to get her through this. She wanted to know what it was like to *use* somebody. The Girl Who Got Away always *used* somebody, didn't she?

After the game, Karl invited her out for coffee and then he asked her if he could run home to shower and change. "Only ten minutes," he assured her. She wasn't sure if this was some sort of pick up maneuver as she knew very little about pick up maneuvers, but she did acknowledge that Karl was drenched in mud and sweat and that it was getting colder. She left her car in the parking lot and climbed into Karl's sporty SUV. He opened her door and held her hand as she climbed in, she liked that. He was significantly taller than her and the vehicle's size seemed to fit him. She had never liked a man this tall before, she had never looked up to a man, *this* way.

"So, Cassandra, what books aren't you reading this time?" Karl joked as he pulled out of the parking lot. She pulled out a book from her backpack. It was a book of poetry by Pablo Neruda. She couldn't write poetry to save her life. But she fiercely admired a poet's ability to say so much with so few words.

"I have him, at home, in Spanish," Karl told her. Then he began to talk about how he spent every summer with his family in the coastal town of Marbella and that was where he had learned to speak Spanish. She told him that she had been to Spain, but never to Marbella because it was too expensive. He continued to say how much he loved his family, especially his son, and how much he missed home in Europe. Benny wondered if this was all a maneuver too. He shared that he missed the long summers in Marbella, indulging in wine and sun. He told her that it was the happiest time of his life. He confessed that when he was scared or nervous, he imagined himself as a boy on the beach, in Marbella and how that memory relaxed him. He admitted, "I am not sure why I am telling you this. You probably think I am crazy."

'*I, I do that, too,*' she thought, but didn't say it aloud.

"So, the happiest time of your life was in the past?" she asked just as he pulled up to his enormous McMansion. Benny thought that her literary hero, Howard Roarke from Ayn Rand's **The Fountainhead,** would throw up all over the gaudy architecture. She immediately had this theory that his first wife had bought it and that after the divorce, there was no way he could unload it. She grappled with her obsession with fictionalizing real people.

"Let's just say it was a golden moment in my life, the one I always remember to feel good." Karl finished.

"Oh," she remarked. She was well aware of who she dreamed of, uncontrollably, still.

"Happiness is relative," he began, "I'm happy you came to see me play today, Cassandra. For a moment there, I felt like I was back at University waiting for a girl I casually asked, hoping that she would show up, *and then she does.*"

Then he smiled "Ten minutes. Then maybe I can convert this coffee to an early dinner, yes?"

After closing the door behind them, Karl pressed a few buttons into his alarm code. The vestibule was quiet except for Benny's heavy breathing and the buttons. He turned around, she was staring at him with a blank expression on her face. She leaned in and kissed him, desperately and sloppily on her tiptoes. *Not bad.* He pulled her off of him and she feared that he might reject her. Instead, he stroked her hair back, took her face in his hands and kissed her gently. She was relieved, but also alarmed. The kiss did not feel like a *maneuver.*

She held his hand and walked over to the couch which was slightly worn down. She thought the wife deliberately left this couch here so she could have the chance to purchase a new one. As they sat, they quietly and slowly started to kiss a bit more. First, she sat in his lap and with his big, strong arms he moved her effortlessly from side to side as he kissed her from all angles. She tried to remove her muddy boots while he kissed her, using one boot to push down the other. Then she used one bare foot to push off the remaining boot. Karl finally noticed what she was attempting to do and stopped kissing her for a moment. He took the large, tall, rubber boots off for her. She leaned her back against the couch as he assumed a plank position on top of her. He stared directly at her.

"There's a lot you don't say, Cassandra, intentionally," he whispered. "I think you like to hide."

Dammit, Karl! She thought. *Please stop trying to get me!*

He began to kiss her a little more forcefully until he was laying completely on top of her. She could feel, *everything. Why are you so goddamn big?* she thought. *Like the Jolly Green Giant, for Christ Sake,* she kept thinking as he wiggled a bit and then... *Jesus, you feel even bigger than Augie! Oh my God! Please stop thinking about Augie! Please, just get this sex thing over with, Karl!* She screamed from inside her brain. *Remember you are The Girl Who Got Away!*

She lifted her skirt and took one of his not to be believed gigantic, Swiss hands and pushed a finger between her wool thigh highs. *"Ouch!"* she screamed, when his finger nearly got stuck inside her. He sat up and gave her a strange look.

"Did I hurt you?" he asked.

She sat up, pushed her skirt down and started to rant.

"I'm extremely vocal, Karl. Sorry! If you like fucking crazy, then I am *definitely* your girl. I still, I still have feelings for someone. My first love, from twenty years ago! We were never boyfriend and girlfriend, just friends, that slept together. But I lost my virginity to him. I just saw him this summer, but we didn't. I hoped that maybe if I *started over*, when I came back home, I could forget him. Too much information, perhaps? I told you I was crazy. And pedantic."

"I...I don't know what to say," he responded.

"That was MY golden moment, Karl. The one I dream about, like your *Marbella*."

"Except, I think, the idea of it at least, is incredibly romantic," he answered.

"WHAT?" she screamed.

"Why didn't you, you know, *sleep with him?*"

"He's married. I mean, technically married. He doesn't seem happy."

"Take it from me, people who have affairs *aren't* happy."

" I'm sure you're right, but, it's, *more than that.*"

"Oh."

"I was only number one in a *bubble*. Or, when I was younger, *in my idiot head*. Number one in a *bubble* is fucking meaningless. Sorry, by the way, for the cursing. *American.*"

She recalled Augie's words, *Benny is a passionate Italian woman.*

"You're right. You should never be number two. I didn't want my wife to be number two, either."

"So, we didn't do it and I've just been walking around, restless, *waiting to get this sex thing over with.*"

CATHERINE ADAMI

"*Get it over with?*" he asked, confused.

"Just sleep with me, *please.* I need to stop thinking about my *golden* moment once and for all. I need to forget about it, redefine it, something..."

"Yes, maybe, I don't know," Karl started, "I...like you."

Oh, Brother.

"You don't know the first thing about me, Karl. Nobody does. Seriously, you have no idea. I might be a sexual deviant. You don't know what I'm capable of in a Dolce and Gabbana dressing room!"

Karl's blue eyes opened wide.

Benny started to rant again.

"No! *Just with him*...that one person. He's the one I'm uninhibited with. The one I create multiple personalities for! I like acting and pretending I am another character far too much."

A light bulb went off in Karl's giant head. He snapped his fingers.

"Like Bowie!"

"What?"

"I just saw the David Bowie exhibit in London and...and the point of all of those characters... you know like Ziggy Stardust...was to get a point across. Maybe you go into character to get a point across. Maybe it's easier for you to teach this, this..."

"*Augie.* That's his first name, Augie. Painfully adorable, isn't it?"

"This Augie...about what you like about yourself, about him...in *character.*"

"The crazy part...is that he likes to pretend he is different characters, too. At what point are we just ourselves?

"Listen, if he spent the weekend with you, there has to be something missing in his marriage. Take it from me, I was in couples' therapy for two full years. I could write a book on it."

"Regardless, Karl, it's not how I want to be with someone. Can't I just have it the way I want it, *really* want it, once and for all? At my age, I know what's good and I know what I want!"

"Of course."

"I want to be loved by him. If I can't be that girl, then *I have to be The Girl Who Got Away...*"

"I don't understand this need to be The Girl Who Got Away?"

"Just because I feel connected to him, doesn't mean he does....you know...I don't *trust*...that's why I don't like...Oh, Karl, sometimes even fantasy worlds get *exhausting*..."

"Writers benefit from a fantasy world."

"But forty-year-old divorcees who kind of never want to have sex again, *don't.*"

"You *don't* want to?"

"I shouldn't have started talking. It's my worst attribute, definitely a date-killer."

Benny seemed more stressed than turned on right now. Karl had no idea how much more she was hiding.

"Ten minutes," he continued, "then a proper dinner. Let's start over, *please.*"

With that last remark, and a painfully apparent erection under his muddy shorts that were covered only by a sweatshirt, he stood up and headed toward the bathroom where he threw the sweatshirt on the floor and pulled his soccer jersey over his enormous Hun-like head. For a second, she was reminded of Augie as Karl's thick dirty blonde hair, at least from behind, resembled his. Only he was a much taller Augie. She hated herself for thinking that and hit herself on the head with her fist- multiple times. *Goddamn Augie Baxter!*

She stood up and walked over to Karl's bookshelves. She came across many foreign titles. At one point, she found herself looking at Dostoyevsky's **Brothers Karamazov** in all three romance languages. *Mother Fucker!* Benny thought. *Goddamn Augie Baxter! I've got to get out of here!* Her mind screamed. She put her boots back on, stole an umbrella by the door thinking, *he won't care* and walked out of his door and into his subdivision. She found a patch of trees to hide behind and then started running to the front gate. Once she got to the highway, she started to walk slower and to catch her breath. *Goddamn Augie Baxter! Goddamn Augie Baxter!* she chanted as she walked back to the school parking lot in the drizzling rain. *Just because I love you, doesn't mean you deserve me,* she kept telling herself. *You never deserved me! You could give a flying fuck about me! I was just an entertainment for you. But not anymore....I'm The Girl Who Got Away, The Girl Who Got Away...*

3

It was New Year's Eve and Augie was walking around the Elizabeth Street apartment in his flannel boxers and pajama shirt. He spent Christmas down South visiting his folks with the kids, and had spent the last couple of days reading, listening to music and writing. Sometimes he wandered one block south to the Elizabeth Street Garden for free hot chocolates and apple ciders. He loved how the community rallied around the garden, a respite from the rest of the city spanning from Elizabeth to Mott filled with a grassy lawn and angelic statues. He loved the events that took place there from moon gazing to poetry reading to caroling.

He considered meeting JR and Stacy in Tribeca at DeNiro's restaurant *Locanda Verde*, if he could muster up the energy to take a shower and leave the house. He debated another café con leche from Café Habana.

It was four o'clock, lightly snowing and dark outside. His laptop was open and he was on Twitter. He was listening to Sonic Youth's Carpenter's cover, "Superstar." He decided to look up Benny's page. She had told him long ago, that she would never be connected with him on the Internet- in any way. She was old fashioned and found the whole Internet thing vapid and devoid of romance. She was an old soul when it came to *communicating*. He admittedly took a look on her Facebook page every once in a while. He liked to hear her voice in her sparse snippets on Twitter. She sounded exactly the same and although she never knew it, she made him laugh. He missed her words.

To Augie's surprise, her last post read "At McNally Jackson Bookstore, happy as clam, knowing I might read my book here one day!" He jumped. The post timed in at exactly eight minutes prior.

Benny had planned a New York getaway for herself after Christmas and after the whole Swiss Karl fiasco. Her ex-husband was taking the kids to the beach for the week with his parents, so she had the free time. He nagged her, as lately he was known to do, about making a move to New York. *One call to HR*, he said. She told him sadly, "No." There was no way she would move to New York, so close to Augie, and the memory of Liz Street. No way she would ever move to another state for a man or for him to think she was doing it for him, a married man she was officially done chasing.

Maybe she was being as stubborn about moving to New York as she had been about never going on birth control. It was a big city and he lived in the suburbs. The chances of bumping into one another were slim, right? Plus, as far as she knew, JR had long since vacated the Girardi building, so she could come and go as she pleased. She wished she could explain Augie to her ex. But, she thought it was such a private world the two of them had created and that he would never *get it*. As much as she loved her ex, and the family they had created, she knew, he would never *get her,* either. And that was the not-so-secret reason they were no longer husband and wife. Friends and co-parents, yes. Soul mates, no.

Benny would still always visit. New York was the heart of the publishing world and she planned to write and meet a nice Literary Agent who bit on a query for her new novel that she had updated after her weekend with Augie. *Better ending,* she thought. Ironically, the novel was entitled **The Story of Elizabeth Street.** She had spent the earlier part of the day writing and eating Downtown Cookie Company Peanut Butter cookies at Ninth Street Coffee in the East Village. She had spicy Ramen –hold the egg - at her favorite noodle shop on Fifth Street, *Minca,* which was located around the corner from Tompkins Square Park and she talked about Jazz that related to Coltrane versus Stan Getz with the savvy proprietor there. This was what she considered a perfect holiday in New York. This and seventy percent off at the clothing boutique, Jeffrey, in the Meatpacking District.

Augie threw a hat on over his thick, unwashed hair and raced to put his legs inside his olive green corduroys, which were hard to button thanks to the extra weight. He shoved his feet into some unlaced snow boots. He ran down the four flights of stairs, south on Elizabeth, and south to Prince. He took a sharp right toward the bookstore hoping to catch Benny there. He didn't have a clue as to what on earth he would say to her after four months. She had made it quite clear she didn't want to hear from him, or at least that is how he interpreted her letter. *Should I tell her that I think about her every single day? That I miss our conversations? Miss having someone around to observe me?* Benny was good at observing, and good at shocking.

He would give almost anything to have her slap him across the face, hard, and tell him *he was a piece of shit but that she liked him more than any other person in the world?* The letter she had left him with her novel, back in August, was in his wallet. He would have to read it again, he thought he had memorized it. *Would she still love my moles? My snooty sneers? Would she still be a forty year old kind-of virgin? What if she was in love with someone else?*

These were the thoughts running through his mind as he burst through the door of McNally Jackson Bookstore. He encountered a happy Benny, surveying her two book purchases, "Secretary" writer Mary Gaitskill and Henry Miller's lover, Anais Ninn. She loved reading erotica. '*So much better than porn*', she thought. She was on the verge of lifting an Americano to her mouth…

"Benny!" he yelled across the front of the bookstore as soon as he bolted through the door. He had rushed so quickly trying to catch Benny before she left that he forgot to zip up his corduroys. With the beard and pajama top on under his sweater vest, completely nervous and jumpy and haggard, he did not look like himself but more like a middle-aged slacker.

She jumped just like she did when he first spoke to her sophomore year on the park bench. She spilled her full Americano all over her new purchases.

"Oh, shit!" he yelled, drawing attention to himself again as he ran over to her. She looked perfectly coiffed in a gold Nina Ricci dress and black Jimmy Choo boots.

They worked together to try and clean her table. Neither one had the balls to look the other in the eye. This was life outside the *bubble*, were they going to pretend they were characters again, or were they now okay with who they were on the *inside?* Brave enough and mature enough to be that way, on the *outside?*

She did not know what to say, he did not know what to say. So, she said the first thing to come into her mind.

"Augie, *your zipper...*" she began, "Did you borrow that sweater vest from Pulitzer Prize winner Jeffrey Eugenides? He reads here sometimes, you know?" she finished. "The lead girl in *The Marriage Plot* gets spanked by her college boyfriend. You might like it."

Why am I trying to rile him up? She thought. *Just be yourself.*

The Baristas behind the coffee bar at McNally Jackson bookstore heard Benny's Eugenides quip, turned to look at Augie and laughed. Augie had a grey wool toggle coat on. *A toggle coat? Benny thought. Straight out of the Preppy Handbook! Augie Baxter, why are you so damn cute even with bed head hair???*

"My mother gave me this sweater for Christmas," he explained.

"I like your Mom even more now for her sense of humor."

He stopped wiping the table and grinned as he tried to zip his pants back up. Finally, he relented and pulled his wool LL Bean sweater vest over his pants to hide his bulging boxer shorts. She smiled back at him instinctively. *'My God, it's New Year's Eve and I'm standing in front of Augie Baxter.'* Had all of her praying at her Nora Ephron shrine made this **When Harry Met Sally** meeting possible? Nora's husband, Nicholas Pileggi, wrote the screenplay to her favorite film **Goodfellas**. There had to be a correlation, right? Nora would just love this, New York City, a bookstore, old friends/lovers and New Year's Eve. *'I miss you Nora,'* Benny thought.

"You're here, in New York," he stammered flashing a wide grin under the fluorescent bulbs.

"You're here, too. What, are you working? *As a hobo???*"

He looked at the outfit covering his body and laughed.

"No, I've taken a break from producing to entertain my other interests."

"And just what are those *other interests*, Augie?"

"Writing and Photography. I think I might do what you said, try and write, and…direct."

I am influencing his life, she thought. *Check that. I'm The Girl Who Got Away.*

"That's fantastic!"

"I live here now, on Elizabeth Street."

*WHAT?????*she thought, her brain exploding.

"You do, where?"

"The old apartment. I took it over."

"You took it over? You moved from the suburbs, here *with your whole family?*"

It could not be possible that he was living her dream – their dream – already – with his wife!

She started to get very nervous at this prospect so much so that her throat began to get salty and actually hurt. She quickly calculated how fast she could grab her stuff, run out of the store and run down Prince to Lafayette and catch a taxi to take her far, far away from here. If she happened to buy and shove a few cupcakes in her mouth waiting for the taxi – on New Years' Eve of all days – she would allow herself *that*. She could double book Soul Cycle Classes for the morning from her Smart phone.

"Not exactly," he blurted.

"Not *exactly?*"

"Why are you here?" he asked.

"I met a Literary Agent today, she likes my book, not that that guarantees anything. Did you read it?"

Oh, no, she just transitioned into Joan Rivers mode – manic and throwing zingers.

"Yes, I read it. You know I find time, eventually, to read everything you send my way."

"Well, I made some updates to it, after, our last....what would you call it?"

"Meeting?"

"Okay, sure...*meeting*. Well, I updated it with a new ending, sent out some queries-and someone actually bit."

"They did? They *bit*?"

"Yes, *bit, Don't be so surprised.*"

"I thought I was the only one that liked to bite."

He knew saying this would get her attention.

"You *were*..." she answered, confused. *Please don't flirt with me.*

He pushed forward with his agenda.

"What are you doing right now? Other than needing a brand new espresso? Can I get you to come over? I'll make you one?"

"You'll burn yourself doing that, Augie. And aren't there other people, um, home?" she said. She was terrified at the possibility that his wife might be a whole block and a half away. She was always grateful that they lived far away from one another.

"No, it's *just me.*"

"Oh?" she questioned. "You know, I'm meeting friends for dinner a little later?"

"Where?"

"Lovely Day," she answered, "A burger will be good for my anemia. Keeps me from fainting."

Oh, my gosh, I might faint right now, she thought.

"Oh," he said, *not sure if she was meeting her boyfriend or not, the one who would put his hands all over Benny, his Benny. No, it couldn't be! How many men had she been with since August?*

"Well, it was nice to see you, Augie. You look the same," she said.

She grabbed her two new, coffee stained books out of his hands. He was reluctant to release them to her.

"What time are you meeting your friends?" he pressed.

"*Um, eight o'clock.*"

"Eight o'clock. Benny, it's only five. *You're coming over.*"

"*No, I don't think so.*"

"Yes, yes you are. *You're coming over.*"

"It's better we stay apart Augie. We're lousy as *just friends.*"

"No, *it's okay.* There's a reason why we are connected. There's a reason I still.."

"You're acting crazy."

"See, it's not just you who acts crazy, Benny."

"It's unfair that passionate women, *artists*, who send dead fish get pegged as *crazy.*"

"Yes, I can act crazy, too."

"Like when you begged to come over to my house that first time?"

Okay, she was flirting now. And brave.

"Ah, yes" he nodded, thrilled that she was thinking about him inside her old bedroom. *Maybe she would also imagine his face between her legs.*

"I know you just said you live there alone, but nothing's going to happen, Augie, *nothing.* You understand that, right? I have plans starting at eight, and I still have some revisions due to my agent..."

"Wow! An agent!"

"I know!"

She held back from showing him all of her excitement, from sharing her excitement with him.

"No, I promise, nothing's going to happen. Just come on, let's go! I'll buy you a replacement coffee at Cafe Habana on the way."

"Alright then," she agreed as he quickly helped her get her long arms through her coat sleeves. He even threw all of her books and notebook into her backpack. He took her hand and dragged her the block and a half to Elizabeth Street. He didn't risk a stop to buy her a coffee at Café Habana. He just directed her straight back to his apartment and through the falling snow.

Upon exiting the elevator, Benny was relieved to find no pictures of Augie and his wife. It looked different than when JR lived there. It looked as though it had been used for an episode of TLC's "Hoarders." A woman was definitely not living with him in *that* state of disarray. She remembered how messy he was when he lived up in the attic in college. '*Why was he living here alone?*' Was this just a place where he could have affairs with other women, who weren't Benny, *who actually slept with him?* Would she find a sticky porn DVD on the kitchen counter? Was he still with his wife? There was no wedding ring on his hand, but his fingers may have just gotten too fat to wear one...*he smelled of Peppermint Schnapps...*

He rushed to plug his green IPOD Nano in, the one she gifted him in August and pressed play. Song one was Cat

Power's "Manhattan." *CHAN MARSHALL?* The song they had both put their August "Affair" playlists to one another.

All Benny could think was, *'How dare you, Augie Baxter! You know how I feel about her, and this, this song. It's...us, in New York. "Harlem in a dark black room, dancing to a different tune?" This, this was not playing fair! You put this on my playlist to torture me didn't you? Just like you put Fiona Apple's "Shadowboxer" on your mix tape to me in '95. "Once my lover, now my friend?" Like I wouldn't take those lyrics seriously. Goddamn you, Augie Baxter! FAT Augie Baxter! I need to get out of here.'*

Mind reeling, she started to pace the floor. Her coat was still on but she was shivering. *I'm just paranoid. I only see what I want to see.*

He always showed up at the strangest and most needy moments of her life to reassure her about herself. Sometimes about her writing, her family, her health, her beauty. He saved her, a little bit, those times, you know? A security blanket, but, who needed saving now? Was it Augie?

"You always joke about that night. You know, the night I... touched myself in front of you" she began, as he turned the fireplace on. It was the polar opposite in temperature to when she had visited him there that August. It was freezing. Why didn't he have the heat on? Was he broke? Was he on meds? There were towels on the floor and garbage baskets everywhere stuffed with paper. Was this his writing process? Was he turning into the Cohen Brothers' **Barton Fink**...or Howard Hughes?

"And made me hold your hand?" he answered her, remembering that night, exactly.

"Yes. *That...event.*"

"*Unforgettable.*"

"Did you ever consider how serious that night was to me? I wasn't doing that to entertain you. Do you know how brave I had to be *to do that*? I had never made the first move on a man before. Not that I even consider that a first move. I was in love with you. You were in my fantasy world, and I had to have an orgasm, *attached to you, with you*, because you are an extension of me. An incomprehensible extension of my sexuality. I can't do anything so brave without you by my side. I loved you so much that just you holding my hand... Just you seeing me, *like that*...."

When Benny thought about that night, she pictured herself as the girl in Klimt's painting "Danae." She had sent him at least one postcard with that picture on it. She wanted to *be art*. Danae, with her thick honey blonde hair was touching herself, too. The painting symbolized her arousal by none other than Zeus. It was about divine love and transcendence, Danae didn't have to even be touched by Zeus to be aroused and to feel pleasure. Benny thought love could *transcend* a conventional relationship, and because she was unconventional, *it had to*. It could *transcend* sexual intercourse.

That long ago night Augie always joked about with the two of them in her bed, no longer lovers, in their mid-twenties, was a big deal to her. A *huge* deal to her. And perhaps it was a precursor to their weekend in New York City, fifteen years later when he was married and having an affair. He didn't put two and two together. But she hoped he always would. They weren't mortal in her fantasies. They transcended their bodies, convention and time. *This* would always be the case for her. That's why she was okay with not being conventionally his. Convention was boring and ephemeral. *She wanted to be an immortal like a goddess. The rest of the world would just have to deal.*

"I try not to think of how serious it was. I'm sorry if I've made light of it."

"I had to show you I loved you *somehow*."

"Benny, I have been thinking about you a lot. Since August..."

"Don't tell me that."

"Benny, you...please, let me kiss you..."

"Kiss you? NO."

"Yes, kiss you."

Benny stood up off of the couch and started pacing the floor.

"What is wrong with you? Are you insane? Let's get something straight, Augie. Number one, I THINK I'M IN LOVE WITH YOU! But for real this time, as an ADULT. Number two, I WANT YOU TO BE IN LOVE WITH ME!"

"Benny, I..."

"The inside of me, well, it is one hundred percent committed to the idea that I am supposed to be with you. I AM NOT HAPPY ABOUT THIS!"

"That's what you think?"

"I *distract* myself. In fact I have made an art form out of it. I am in the thick of distracting myself right now."

"How?"

"I'll pretty much go out with anyone who asks."

"How many men?"

"Oh, like forty maybe?"

"You've gone out with forty men since August!"

"At least."

"And you've slept.."

"WHAT? Are you crazy? NO! Never. I don't want to sleep with anyone but you! *Why am I even telling you this???* But I will,

I will sleep with someone else...Sex is meaningless without intimacy, Augie! It's fucking meaningless!"

Augie raged inside of his head, unable to comprehend such a profound anger toward sex. Why was she like this? What had he unintentionally done to make her feel like this? He was supposed to teach her about sex. He wanted her to love it! *Love it!* He loved it – *with her!* But he wanted her to love it without loving him. That was his big mistake. He was an idiot whose ego hurt this girl who loved him and trusted him and who had waited her whole life to trust and love someone and who had decided with *his* help – *his* forceful nature – *his* commitment to her – to *his* chasing her – to *his* dilating eyes staring at her from a corner even if he was with another girl - to trust – *him.* She thought *he* was her best friend. *She still thought this.*

"It's not meaningless!" he screamed.

Why does one always end up screaming when arguing with an Italian?

"Yes, yes it is. Something that I put on a pedestal, of feeling human, of empowerment, is meaningless."

"Don't say that, please, Benny."

"I did not come to New York to see you. I've been coming here for years without ever seeing you. here *all the time* and never see you. I just like it here. I like imagining what my life would be like here. It feeds my soul and inspires my writing."

"Why aren't we Facebook friends?"

"You're kidding, right? I'm the girl who got away, Augie. I'm in a category all on my own!!!"

"Yes, you are unique. I get it."

"Damn straight!"

"I'm getting a divorce!" he yelled at the top of his lungs, invigorated by what she was saying to him and slightly drunk from the earlier shots of Peppermint Schnapps.

"WHAT?" she screamed back at him, eyes nearly popping out of her skull.

"I'm getting a divorce, Benny!"

She started pacing more now, her breath became erratic. She even went into the kitchen and opened and closed the refrigerator door for some unknown, OCD reason. Her high heeled, wooden boots, which caused her to tower over him, made plenty of noise. She marched back and forth, back and forth, as if she was preparing for a long run in Central Park. She was quick to run away from a situation if she got spooked. She was, after all, *The Girl Who Got Away...*

"So? So? What does this mean to me. NOTHING!" she screamed.

"NOTHING?" he yelled back, stunned.

She started walking through the rest of the apartment, opening and shutting the door to the bathroom, walking in and out, opening and shutting the elevator door as if she was about to leave. In and out, opening and shutting the door of his messy bedroom. In and out. She couldn't even allow herself to imagine sleeping in that bed with him. Open and shutting the office door, walking in...and...

"Benny, that's.." he began as he walked up behind her...

She closed and then opened the door to the office, *twice.*

"JESUS, AUGIE!" she screamed angry and overwhelmed, "What's going on?"

Distraught, she was very unlike *The Girl Who Got Away...*

She stood in the center of the room surrounded by large black and white portraits. They were the photographs of herself lying naked under a white sheet on the mattress on the living room floor at sunrise, sleeping and smiling slightly. Did she really smile in her sleep? Wait, he took pictures of her? He had never taken a picture of her before, *'I'm inside his head,' she thought*. She started smiling and shouting expletives in Italian.

"Augie Baxter," she said, curtly, in a military fashion.

"Cassandra Bennett," he answered, also formally, playing with the front of his hair...*shaping it.*

"I finally finished my novel and gave it a title."

"You did? That's great. What's it called?"

"ON ELIZABETH STREET."

This is exactly why I like you, Augie thought.

"I like the name."

"I thought you might."

"The film, I'm working on..."

"You're working on a film?"

"The *documentary*...it's about Liz Street, too..."

"Oh, Augie! That's fantastic!"

"Nonna Girardi is the star, of course. It's about Nolita..."

"I've never been more *proud* of you! What a beautiful tribute to her. To this neighborhood!"

"Benny, come with me to Bryant Park for hot chocolates. Maybe some ice skating?"

"Bryant Park? On New Year's Eve? Isn't that *romantic? Like, like in a movie? Like in the Nora Ephron playbook? Next you'll ask me for a jog on the Highline!*"

"We can eavesdrop on other people's conversations. You know, investment bankers and aspiring actresses slash waitresses having tawdry affairs."

"But we're not having an affair anymore, Augie."

"I know, we're dating now, I hope. You're *my girlfriend, right?*"

"Your *girlfriend?*"

"Yes, that is if you aren't dating anyone? Are you?"

"Maybe."

"*Maybe?*"

"Maybe."

"Well, you'll have to break up with that 'maybe.' You and I, Benny. We were never "maybe" 's he told her as he took out his cell phone. "Give me this guy's phone number right now and I'll tell him this myself."

God he's a bad ass, is all she could think.

"And, *tomorrow?*" she probed.

"What about *tomorrow?*" he asked innocently. He seemed pleased with how tight her dress was on top. It had to be a push-up bra. He couldn't wait to stick his face in between her breasts as he unfastened it.

"Tomorrow's New Year's Day and I have yet to place my Bowl Game bets," she said, seeing how far and how bold he would go to chase her, *The Girl Who Got Away.*

"Got that covered. We'll use my bookie," he answered her rather quickly.

"Augie, what, you have *a bookie,* now?"

"Well, it's JR's. We share the guy. He lives at the Soho House and he's friends with Michael Jordan."

"Number twenty-three? No? Can I meet him?"

"Come on. Stay here tomorrow. Let's not let my living room dual television screens go to waste."

"And what will we do *the day after New Year's?*"

"Anything you want, Benny."

"Anything I want? Augie, *what's wrong with you?*"

"Absolutely nothing, Benny. *I'm perfect.*"

"Perfect? All I ever wanted was to be with one guy, *a charac-ter. A…smart-ass* who made me laugh, kept me on my toes. Was the guy I thought was the smartest guy in the room, even if he wasn't. But this guy, this guy, Augie, he also *loved me.* He was *good to me.* The *best.* More than just *pretending…*"

"One guy?"

"That's what I said, Augie, *One.*"

"He's lucky, Benny. He's so lucky Benny. Because you are a gift. You have always been *a gift.*"

Too much attention, she thought, trying to find a way to change the subject, darting her eyes around the room a few times before they landed just below his belt buckle…*again.*

"Your…dick, Augie?" she blurted.

Where am I going with this? She thought.

"What about…*my dick?*" he asked back.

"Well, what if it's not as big as I think it is? You know, I haven't seen that many."

"*It is.*"

"What?"

"*It's big.*"

"Well, what I'm saying is, we might have to get a ruler and measure. At the same time we can measure how tall you are, because I know for a fact you lied on your Driver's License. I am *at least* two or three inches taller than you."

"We're the same height, Benny…"

"Again, measuring tape."

"Fine, we'll *measure…*"

She walked up to him and looked into his eyes. He looked different. And not just because of the longer hair with a few strands of gray. And not because of the extra twenty pounds or his half zippered corduroy pants or his bookie. He looked different because he only had eyes for her and she knew this. His saggy but pretty tiny eyes told her that he loved her and she had won him, this was more than infatuation. He was vulnerable, the same way she always felt vulnerable. She didn't want to betray his trust in her and hopefully his love for her. His eyes said, *Okay, Benny. You were right all along, but don't punish me for it. Okay, you can punish me a little, um…maybe more than a little.*

They stood in the doorway of his studio surrounded by black and white photos that he had taken hanging on the walls. Photos of *her.* She did not touch him and he did not touch her. But they felt one another *breathing.*

The *new* Benny decided to take advantage of this unique situation she found herself in the only way she knew how, *by teasing.*

"I only want to be with one guy, Augie. One guy who loves me…and…*be his dirty little slut.*"

Excited, he immediately stepped up high on his toes and smiled widely. He loved *this* Benny, *new* and *old* and mixed together *perfectly.*

"*His dirty little slut, huh?*" he asked her as if they were onto some scientific discovery.

"Augie, can you love me? Can you love me and *let me be your dirty little slut?*"

"Yes."

"Say it to me, then."

"Yes, Benny, I can love you and want you to be my dirty little slut, *only mine. I want to own you,*" he said confidently, thinking that this might be the greatest of all their great conversations that they had ever had as a couple.

"Only yours, Augie. I only want to be *yours. I love you.*"

"Is that romantic enough for you, Benny? *Benny, my dirty little slut that I also love?*"

"Gerald August Baxter, the Second, *that's the most romantic thing I've ever heard.*"

4

Benny and Augie started *dating*. Outside the *bubble, real life.* Using Augie's Frequent Flyer miles, she would fly to New York City for a few days every week. In the beginning, they spent a lot of time together, walking through downtown Manhattan, eating and drinking at their favorite bars and just talking. One weekend was spent entirely in their underwear and slippers, watching college basketball on the side-by-side hanging flat screens in the newly upgraded living room while placing various, ridiculous bets with one another. Their usual wagers included, S*uck my toes, Cook me dinner.* He could not cook *anything* without over salting and/or inflicting himself with near third degree burns. During this exploratory process, Benny discovered a brand new pleasure – *spanking* Augie. She liked it, *a lot.* He had always had a large, firm ass. She liked to see the red marks from her hands on his buttocks. When it was her turn to receive, she bit her lip and complained the whole time. "Damn you Michigan State!" she yelled mid-slap, clenching her fists as he laughed, calling out "Blue and Yellow! Blue and Yellow!"

If Benny was there on a Sunday, Mrs. Girardi would invite them to dinner downstairs at her place and they would stuff themselves with pasta in red sauce. She would talk to Mrs. Girardi in Italian and smile at Augie who lounged alongside Mr. Girardi on matching leather Lazy-Boys.

One night, in the bath, Augie read the Sports section on his IPAD while Benny reread Jane Austen's **Persuasion.** She was entranced with the idea that you always end up with the right person... eventually. *If it was meant to be.*

Admiring her concentration, Augie decided to stick his big toe up her bum. She dropped her just-bought-that-morning-from-The Strand Bookstore on Broadway - book in the water. Being a stickler for coveting books in paper form she started screaming.

"Augie!" she yelled, "You ruined my book!"

"I'll buy you a new one."

"That's, you know, *off limits.* I mean, if your toe can cause that much of a stir, I don't even want to imagine."

"Well, *you better,* because it will happen one day."

"No it won't."

"Yes it will."

"No it won't."

"I can be persuasive."

"That's what worries me."

"Need I remind that you are in fact *reading* a book entitled **Persuasion?**"

"I haven't read it in a while, Augie, but I'm pretty sure *it lacks an anal sex scene.*"

He chuckled and put his IPAD down.

"Benny, there's...something you *can do*. You might like it, too. Being in the bath with you, well, it brings out my creative side."

Covered in white bubbles, he grabbed Benny and dragged her over next to him, on his side of the bathtub. He wrapped his arms and legs around her and held her into place.

"Are you going to drown me now? Like Michael Douglas did to Glenn Close in **Fatal Attraction**?" she asked.

"No! Miss Paranoid. Give me your ear," he insisted and then whispered something softly in her ear. She started to get turned on. It was the change in his tone of voice that alerted to her that she was the Submissive. It was that voice that made her nipples tingle and her breath become erratic. She could feel the hairs on the top of her head, her skin was so sensitive...

"Yes, I think I can do that." she softly whispered back. Not even believing she would be into *that*. But it was Augie. And she wanted him to take her places she was too afraid to take herself. That was why she loved *him*. That was why she chose – *him*...He was her *playmate*.

He kissed her on the mouth.

"Seriously?" he asked.

"*Seriously,*" she answered back.

"After the bath?" he pressed.

"After the bath," she promised. She felt some contractions down there just imagining what she would be like...what he would be like. Nothing turned her on more than *fantasy*. Mulling it over in her brain just made the thought of the act that more potent.

"Why do you say yes to me?" he asked her.

"Don't you know by now? *I've been waiting my whole life to say yes to someone, Augie.*"

"Don't always give up a good fight."

"Me? Never! In fact, I'd like you to sign a contract before this all goes down."

He sat up in the tub, blowing bubbles off of his lips.

"A contract? Okay. What terms do I have to agree to?"

"Grab that Village Voice over there and I will write it down."

He stood up in the tub and grabbed the Village Voice and a pen. There was a giant mess when some of the newspaper dissolved into the tub.

She wrote feverishly until she finished writing and looked up at him.

"There, sign there!" she told him.

He grabbed the newspaper and read the contract.

"I, Augie Baxter, do agree to break dance in Times Square wearing a Kongol hat and parachute pants to Grand Master Flash's "The Message" in return for Cassandra Bennett agreeing to, post-bath, put her mouth on *anything* I tell her to..."

"I'm a witness, so I have to sign, too," she told him.

"Fine. I'll do it. Not just for the *fellatio* but for the opportunity for the world to see my dance moves. I will make you proud of me, Benny, and you will be so crazy jealous of all the tourist-clad ass I'm going to get. *The girls, The girls, the girls, they love me.*"

"Oh, we'll just have to see about that!" she exclaimed, pretending to be mad. Actually, mad-as- she-couldn't-bear-to-hear-him-talk-about-other-women-mad, mad-without wanting to leave a bruise somewhere on his body. She started hitting him with the newspaper so he pinned her hands down and laid naked above her naked body. They were both breathing heavy. She could feel his erection pushing hard into the skin of her thighs.

"Benny... I could just do it right now. Just let me do it. Let's...*just do this.*" he moaned to her. Benny, who could not move a muscle was held captive by his expert high school wrestling moves.

"No...no," she whispered back, shaking her head back and forth.

"Benny, *you're turning into a Blue Baller!*" he yelled, frustrated.

"*I'm not a Blue Baller!*" she yelled back.

"I thought you wanted to say yes to me. *Say yes to me, Benny.*" he asked, looking down from above her. His tiny eyes seemed desperate.

"*Just a little longer, okay?*" she teased. He had an icy look on his face. She kissed his cheeks and then he warmed up again.

"You're my *girlfriend*, now, Benny," he told her. That word would never get old, *girlfriend*. "Now, I signed your damn contract, so *get to work.*"

He released her. She pulled the drain out of the tub and stood up and found a towel. She put her hand out for him. He grabbed it and she helped balance him while he stepped out of the tub. She took the towel and started drying off his taut body. Appearing clean and dry, she stood behind him. She was still taller than him. She would always be taller. Then, she whispered into his ear: "Tell me what to do, Augie...I'm listening..."

5

ugie came to visit Benny only once in Florida when he stayed at a nearby hotel. During what started out to be a relaxing picnic on a patch of grass ocean side, turned into an incident that resulted in a swollen ankle that resembled Mike Meyers' neck bulging out of his Scotsman fat suit. He had been attacked by an army of red ants during a nap while Benny was putting her feet in the water. He was forced to endure an allergy shot and to ingest golf ball sized anti-inflammatory pills for the rest of that visit.

The two of them holed up in his trendy South Beach hotel room, leveraging the "Still in Theaters" movies option the rest of that weekend. They only left the hotel room once en-route to the airport Sunday morning so he could catch his flight back to New York. He asked her to take him to get a cup of coffee and to pick up the New York Times. Arriving at the coffeehouse, he almost fell over and onto Benny because he was unaccustomed to the crutches that the doctor had given him to use to keep pressure off of his still swollen ankle. She did her best to position him carefully on a chair under an umbrella. When she walked into the coffeehouse, she noticed Karl, the Swiss Banker. His face was buried deep into The Wall Street Journal. He had noticed her, but he didn't let on. She smiled. He smiled back at her, pointed to his soccer shoes, and then nodded over toward Augie, who was checking into his flight on his IPAD. Augie was also wearing soccer shoes. She nodded, acknowledging Karl's observation. Karl mouthed "That's him?" She nodded. Then, Karl mouthed "Golden Moment."

As the weeks passed, they spent less and less time alone together. In order for them to be *themselves*, they had to take time to be alone. Independence was key to who Benny was, so some days she would spend the whole day at Variety coffeehouse on Graham Avenue off the L stop, in Williamsburg just to people watch, as Augie had encouraged her to do. She might spend three or four hours at a yoga class and/or at the NYU library, just *observing*. She had to feed her need to *watch* and learn the details of not only Augie, but of all strangers. Augie reassured her that *watching* would keep her a good writer. He started writing, too, about Nolita, about Nonna Girardi and her family. He began to fill a cork board in the kitchen at Liz Street with index cards for the documentary that he was slowly bringing to life. It was the one he would finally make, *or else*, Benny warned him. To give himself more free time, he handed half his shows over to a young hot shot who was a kid that reminded him of himself. It felt good to let go of those reins.

He dragged her to the Village Cinema a lot and he told her he couldn't wait until winter ended and the handball courts across Sixth Avenue would be jumping again. *A gambler's paradise,* he told her. They attended an Abel Ferrara film retrospective at Village Cinema. Augie took an inordinate amount of pleasure describing the masturbation scene from Ferrara's **Bad Lieutenant** to her when they were younger.

He enjoyed telling this to her with almost as much relish as he had in explaining to her how some people liked to be strangled *only slightly*, while having an orgasm. This was back at Tulane and resulted in her slapping him across his face in front of the post office on McAlister Drive. It was only nine in the morning! Still a virgin, and just friends, at the time, she was shocked by him even re-enacting a "jerk-off" while smiling at her. He called it "auto-eroticism" and said she could *look it up*.

During the Abel Ferrara event, they happened to run into the actor Harvey Keitel at the concession stand. Augie had just ordered popcorn and Benny had just ordered Twizzlers. She thought Augie might try to tongue kiss the guy, he was in such awe. "It's gotta be a short-guy thing" she teased him. "You're welcome to invite him back to Elizabeth Street with you. I could kill time with a mani-pedi." The new Benny hadn't entirely lost her generosity.

Augie also needed time by himself. Whether it was doing research at the Tenement Museum, going to Midtown for meetings and editing, watching "abhorrent" (as Benny called it) television and movies, enjoying the pleasure of a brand new album download at home, jerking off against the granite walls of the Elizabeth Street shower or fantasizing about a young Catherine Deneuve in "The Umbrellas of Cherbourg," he liked "flying solo" from time to time.

Louise, was still in shock that the two of them were dating at the age of forty. She was annoyed that when she called the apartment, Augie would answer. He was *still* a show-off. It was like the two of them were back in college again and Louise was still pissed that he had pulled their phone cord out of the wall socket so that she would stop interrupting them while they were fooling around.

The shocking truth behind this new, adult relationship between them was that *they hadn't slept together yet.* They would come so close, over and over again. But he never pushed it except for the times after too much wine. He would even point to her ass as an option and then she would raise her fist up at him. But, *they didn't.* They were forty, they shared children with other partners and they did not live in the same place. This was *delicate.* She was strong but *delicate.* They had become best friends and not in a *bubble.* Now that he was in her life all day every day, in one virtual way or another, she couldn't imagine her life without him.

Grown-up issues were facing them. Benny's divorce settlement would be running out soon as well as her severance package from her old consulting job and, if she didn't make a living as a writer, she would have to go back to corporate America. So much was resting on her novel and a publishing contract. She was extremely stressed out about this. She *wanted* to earn money, she *needed* to earn money. Plus, they still hadn't met each other's' children yet. They asked around to divorced friends with kids how they did it, and when was the right time. They all answered the same, "Only introduce if you think the relationship is going somewhere serious." At times, she felt downright disoriented. Augie? Her kids? Herself? Liz Street? Her writings? The bubble? Now? Forever?

Augie's divorce was not finalized and he was showing signs of exhaustion from travel back and forth from the suburbs. She always knew he would be more quiet than usual if he had gone more than five days without seeing his kids.

He would send her texts like "HELP!" when the kids would come and stay in his apartment in the city and when he was forced to feed them something other than Ray's pizza. He felt like he failed in the whole marriage thing and he always wanted to do better than his divorced parents had done. "We all think that way," she told him, "And, don't you think our parents, when they divorced felt just like you feel right now?" She hoped her girlfriend's "Happy Mommy, Happy Kids" mantra extended to Dads, too.

They had not even discussed their children meeting. They had only been dating two months, when she made it clear that this issue was off the table for at least at least six months no matter who she was dating... even Gerald August Baxter the Second. Her fantasy life did not extend to their children.

Augie loved to mind fuck not only Benny, but JR. When he asked JR and Stacy for a double date at The Farm on Adderley in Brooklyn, JR nearly had a heart attack when he found him standing next to Benny, *crazy Benny*, the *virgin*. JR whispered "cliche" in his ear when they hugged and then popped a cho-lesterol pill before cutting into his rare cooked steak.

"Wait, you haven't fucked her yet?" JR asked him, flabber-gasted, at the Carroll Gardens bar, inside the Brooklyn Social, while playing a game of pool.

"No," Augie answered.

"Then why are you with her? Aren't you *horny*?" JR asked.

"I'm always horny, but, she, Benny, my *girlfriend*..." Augie always felt a heart string pull when he said that word, *girlfriend*, as if it was still hard to believe. "We find other ways, you know I always had to be different. I get bored with anything tradi-tional. I am always looking for something new and unique."

"What, she's blowing you regularly? Is that...enough?" JR asked, perplexed.

"It is, for now. We're friends first, lovers second."

"Um, I call bullshit!"

"We both have to get used to this. It's been almost twenty years since the last time..."

"You *fucked?* Yeah, I remember that weekend. I was asleep on the couch downstairs remember? The bedroom above me had a balcony and I heard every word. Excuse me, grunt and groan. You are one dirty, dirty, short bastard," JR finished.

"Wow! I forgot you were there," Augie said, talking himself out of remembering that night. It would make him incredibly horny and he didn't want to risk getting caught in the storage room half naked in Brooklyn Social with Benny...*again.*

"Wanna know what I think?" JR said.

"Not really, JR. But I have a feeling you are going to tell me any way," Augie answered.

"You're afraid. It won't be as good," JR said.

He just liked her. He liked talking to her. He liked pushing her buttons. He liked the way she moaned when he first touched her under the covers and when he whispered in her ear, in the morning.

Benny bridged the gap between old and new Augie.

Once, she told him that if she ever needed to disassemble a bomb to save the world he would have to tell her the instructions. She could do it. His voice could talk her through it. His powerful, unique voice and they could save the world, *together.*

There was something about him telling her what to do that she liked. Was it his tone? Was it his cocky confidence? Silly words? Provocative words? And looks? So many looks. Or, was it that he had seduced her with *words?* He liked the way she looked at him. Like she was committed...committed to him, and desperate to hear every word come out of his mouth. And how she had bloomed all on her own. And how he swore to God, she was literally blooming, *in front of his eyes.* Her writing and her ideas were growing like Ivy all over him and the brick apartment walls on Elizabeth Street. Her dream to be an artist was not a dream anymore. She had talent. She had passion. She had...*confidence.*

"I am scared, I admit. But not about that, *the sex.* I'm afraid I want to spend the rest of my life with her." Augie confided to JR.

"What the hell, Augie? You have *changed.*" JR responded, astonished.

"Well, so has she. I don't know. She grew up and she doesn't need me." he added.

"Whatever makes you happy? You were always a dirty little freak anyway...." JR joked.

"No matter what happens, no one will ever look at me the way she does. *No one.* Like, I'm *the one.* Her *one.* I took advantage of this fact when we were younger and she clearly calls me out on it in *her novel,*" Augie explained, swigging his beer and smiling to a waving Benny who was sending him a telepathic signal, "SAVE ME FROM THIS CRAZY ASS GIRL STACY AT ONCE!"

"Novel. She wrote a novel?" JR asked.

"Yep. And you're in it, too. Be prepared," Augie told his buddy.

"That's actually kind of *cool,*" JR thought.

"She does make you look manly and all. Carrying a case of beer and a bottle of Jack through a hurricane..." Augie began.

"Do you love her? Benny, the *virgin?* The Mafia Princess?" JR interrupted.

Augie didn't answer JR. He didn't want him to think that he was moving too fast after getting divorced or that he was a pussy. But he did, he did love her. Benny, the Mafia Princess. She was the girl who had threatened to slit his throat on more than one occasion. Yes, he loved her and she would always love him. A year had passed since they had planned their little August affair. Yet, he remembered that she told him that they would always be connected and that she would love him the rest of her life, regardless.

Augie and Benny went straight to sleep that night. No TV. Just a little music, on low. As much as she was afraid of finally sleeping with him, she wanted to, more than she would admit. She dreamed that she had crawled on top of a sleeping Augie and started rubbing up against him naked until he got hard and then grabbed his dick and stuck the head inside her before sitting violently on top of it. She sat up and down on his member, until she saw blood covering his waist and blood running down her leg. It hurt her but at the same time, it felt good. Better than she had ever felt before from another person's body, *from another person.* An orgasm started from her warm waist down to her tingling toes. She woke up, *moaning.* Her eyes opened but she did not wake him up. A minute later, she fell asleep.

Augie dreamed that he woke up in bed alone and searched the Elizabeth Street apartment for any piece or memorabilia of Benny's. Anything she may have left there, anything that would prove she had been there with him. And, that she existed. He tried to remember her phone number to call her, but it was the middle of the night and he kept having trouble pressing the phone keys. He was accidentally pressing the wrong numbers or forgetting the last number. He was angry, frustrated and scared. He was starting to cry. He threw the phone across the room and the crashing sound woke him up. His heart was racing. He jumped and looked down to find Benny, her long hair covering his bare chest, sleeping, smiling.

He wiped a tear. It took at least an hour before he was able to fall asleep again.

6

Augie was walking around the apartment in his flannel boxers and an old, gray Connecticut t-shirt, drinking a glass of dark red wine. The fireplace was on and so were the two televisions in the living room. It was dinner time, dark and cold outside. There were hot aluminum boxes sitting on the counter in the kitchen in a giant paper bag. There was also a French Country Apple Pie. *Yes,* he admitted, *I am now privy to the fact that apple pies come in a variety.*

Benny rolled into the Elizabeth Street apartment, out of the elevator, taking her heavy black backpack off and sitting on the edge of the new couch in the living room. She was dressed in wool argyle tights, a short black skirt, a white button down of Augie's and his brown leather belt at the waist. The belt was at least twenty years old. She wore a plain, black headband. She wanted to look East Coast, preppy, and slutty. Now that she was forty, she liked to play with her appearance. Sometimes, she even wore wigs or changed her name when meeting strangers. She told Augie that he had unlocked her creative side. She felt she could become *any one,* if he was beside her. She just wanted to be a working writer, and if costumes helped, like they did for Oscar Wilde, then, she was okay with that. Dressing up let her feel like a little girl again, with her whole life in front of her. *Opportunity.* She was not ashamed to admit she wanted to be with a man who made her feel like his *little girl.*

"I'm exhausted!" she complained, as she threw her boots across the room and cuddled up on the couch and snuggled under a blanket.

He walked into the living room, turning the TVs off and smiling down at her.

"Exhausted? From sitting all day drinking coffee and writing?"

"Yes, writing," she answered, "it's exhausting picking font styles and sizes."

He handed her a thick manila envelope and started walking toward the kitchen.

"What, you're reading my mail now?" she asked.

"I thought it was a tape I was waiting on," he explained.

Benny sat up slowly.

"When we wake up tomorrow, can we pretend we live in Australia?"

"O..kay" he answered from the kitchen.

"Seriously, we'll make some Shrimp on the Barbee."

"It's thirty degrees"

"We'll wear really big hats, quote Keith Urban and Men At Work songs while searching the Lower East side for Vegimite."

"Whatever you say, Benny. Although I prefer Kylie Minogue. "Two of Hearts" is a great pop song."

"NO, NO, NO! **Mad Max** for you, I 'm thinking. Leather pants – YES! We can try the 'tween section at Macy's to find your size. Or no, wait for it, Russell Crowe as Buddy in **LA Confidential**. You know, before he became a misogynist? Oh, Jesus, Augie, his crew cut in that movie used to drive me..."

"You thought of me?" he yelled into the living room. She deliberately ignored his question.

"You know once I start my new job I won't be able to have these long, selfish days at the coffeehouse with my Vegan, Communist friends. Our weeks together will be shortened to week- ends, I'm sure my vacation day allotment will be mini-mal in the beginning."

She heard a pop sound from the kitchen. *Was Augie singing?*

"I don't know what you have in there, but it smells delicious and comforting. I need comfort right now. Hey! Can we watch **Valley Girl** tonight? "she asked in a daze.

"Sure. Anything," he answered from the kitchen.

"You know, maybe I can get a job at Ninth Street Coffee in the East Village? I love that place.

I'm lousy handling an Espresso machine but I think I could be good at Pour-overs?"

"*The best.*"

"Maybe we should shave your head tonight. Tomorrow is *technically* the first day of Spring. It makes me happy seeing you like that. Your eyes, ears and nose pop out. Did I ever tell you that your shaved head reminded me of my grandfathers? They both had hair so thick that they had to get crew cuts well into their nineties..."

She slowly pulled out a piece of paper from the envelope he had given her. It said "Contract for Publication."

"Oh my God!" Benny screamed, "It happened! It finally happened! I mean, Alaskans do have publishing houses!"

She looked up to see him standing in front of her with two glasses of champagne in fine Irish Crystal.

"Yes, they do," he answered, handing her a glass.

"I'm not just some divorcee having a midlife crisis, pretending she's a writer, dating a short, excuse me, *really short,* television producer," she explained.

"No. Now I'm just a short television producer dating a published writer. *A novelist.* Although I can't say you're free from litigation from my people. The way you portray me, in your book, is not always rosy," he lectured.

She could feel every hair on her head and she could feel her heart beating out of her chest.

"I've waited over twenty years for this! *Over* twenty years, for you, too, Augie, I can't believe this is all happening. I'm floating, Augie, I'm *floating,*" she whispered.

"*I'm floating, too,*" he told her.

Benny had read that soul mates were like two balloons that floated *together.*

"Ever since that first night, when you begged to come over," she began.

"Begged is a strong word," he argued.

"Begged," she repeated, "Ever since that night, well, you've had a giant impact on my life. *Even from afar.*"

He appreciated the acknowledgment which built up his courage.

"I always wanted to make an impact on your life, too. Maybe that's why I always sent you so many letters. Why I tried to shock you.... If not, we would never be *even,* we would never have a chance to be..." she continued. Still, she couldn't even admit what she wanted from him. What she *really* wanted from him. She wasn't that confident...*yet.*

"Live with me" he interrupted.

"What?" she asked. Her eyes widened and her jaw dropped.

"Live with me, here, on Elizabeth Street. I talked to Mrs. Girardi and she said we could duplex down the third floor apartment. All I have to do is sell all the antiques she's storing down there on Ebay. She doesn't know how to use the Internet. Five kids under the same roof in Manhattan. I'll feel like Al Pacino in **Author, Author**," he explained.

Benny thought that one of the Commie Vegan Baristas had spiked her coffee as a "joke" today.

Everything she saw out of her glasses seemed surreal, like in Dr. Seuss's **Wacky Wednesday.** Something had to be wrong with this picture, was a painting upside down?

"Augie, we have responsibilities," she countered as her mind swirled. *Was this really happening???*

"Living in New York and being a writer is your dream, right?" he asked.

"Well, yeah, of course," she agreed.

"Well my dream is you living your dream beside me," he said.

"Augie, *my* family, *your* family. This would take some time..." she argued.

Benny remembered the text from her ex-husband just that morning. It was a photo of her kids wearing the I heart New York t-shirts she had bought for them at LaGuardia that summer. The text read, "You love New York, don't you?" The one observation about Benny's true self that her ex was aware of. She wanted to live in New York. He had offered to move there for her *so they could co- parent there together.* Passive aggressively, he kind of wanted her to force him to move. He liked that she was pushy and he knew that there was a fresh start, and opportunity both personal and career-wise waiting for him in New York. *If she would only say yes.* Benny had to allow herself all of these Yesses. Yesses were a new life direction. She deserved them.

"All good things are worth waiting for. Aren't they? Cassandra? Isn't that what you always said? Don't you believe that?" Augie asked.

Benny told herself not to forget this moment. She promised herself to remember every single tiny detail of it and answered him in a soft voice and with her head raised, "YES."

He took the glass of champagne out of her hand and started to slowly undress her in the near quiet of the dark living room.

"I have a game I'd like for us to play," he whispered wetly into her ear as he stood behind her. He noticed she was trembling.

"A game, huh? Just what is this game you speak of, and, more importantly, *will I be any good at it?"* she asked.

"You'll be great. Don't worry. It's a game I like to call, *my penis inside your vagina.* We've *played it before."*

She swallowed hard and took a few steps forward, away from him. She was nervous, shaking and *blushing.* He had not seen her blush in a long time. He felt her pull away. The same way she used to pull away when they first started sleeping together so long ago.

"Augie..." she began.

"Benny, I'm ready. I think you're ready." he said in a soft voice. He took a few steps forward and kissed her bare shoulder.

"Au...." she could barely slide his name out. She was *that* nervous.

He pulled her around, toward him, facing him, but she looked away. She went someplace else... Where, he didn't know.

"Cassandra...Cassandra! Look at me! Please look at me, it's alright!" he consoled her. The pink blush on her face was replaced with an ashen, white hue. Her emotions became mixed, scattered. She was turned on but scared as hell. She needed to reveal her secret...she needed to release.

"Please, Cassandra. What is it?" he asked.

"It doesn't have anything to do with you. It's just me. I DON'T TRUST ANYONE."

That was it. The truth came out *finally*. She could spew out all the "I love you" 's in the world, but when it came to trusting another human being, to truly relaxing with another person, it hadn't happened like that yet. Sex was just *too* serious. She wanted it to be *so* much. She wanted it to be about finally trusting someone with her true self. To being brave enough to *let go* and to feel an out-of- body experience.

"Benny, we're not going to leave this apartment until you do. Your new job as a pizza delivery driver for Papa John's is just going to have to be put on hold."

For a second, she cried and then, laughed.

"I just...I just...I need to know *I am inside you.* Theoretically, *before you are inside me.* Do you understand what I'm saying? *Theoretically.* This...union...was already...an idea. A theoretical idea, that...I had found my match. That I could make you as happy as you make me."

"I understand, *ideas.*"

"I never, ever told you what I wanted from you. I wasn't honest. So I'm trying to be honest now. It's the way I wanted it...that first time, but wasn't courageous enough to tell you. *I wanted you to be in love with me, Augie, when you slept with me. I didn't want to just be friends."*

"Benny..." he interrupted, knowing how true her words were and how these words were always hinted at. But she never told to him *straight out.* She just pretended that everything was okay and that she was okay with what he had to offer. She had never put up a fight about the details of their relationship or their agreement, she never said a word to the contrary. She never admitted she actually liked him or had feelings for him as anything more than a friend. Until it was too late. And then she had turned into a silly, lovesick girl, who had become confused, distraught and unsure of what had just happened to her and what he had brought out of her. He made her *uneasy.* But the ones that make you uneasy and that take you out of your comfort zone, are the ones you never forget – *like Augie, like Benny.*

"I wanted to make you happy. I know our reuniting began as sentiment, an entertainment, perhaps. But I want you to want me, the right way. There is no other for me, when it comes to you, this time. It's all or nothing, Augie. I cannot even move a muscle in your direction unless I *have it all* this time..."

"You trust me don't you? *Please,* tell me you trust me, Benny. It's important to me. *You* are important to me. I want to get to that higher level *with* you. I'm so glad we waited this time. I'm so glad we know one another as *adults.* Please, I won't hurt you, Benny. I love you. I love you. You've had an impact on *me... on me,* Benny...I'm writing a goddamn movie!"

"You're the only person I let get close to me. You're the only person...*ever...*Don't you know that? Don't you know that?" she sobbed.

"Benny, I...I see the person you've always wanted to be. *I see the person you truly are...*"

"I want to be Irene Adler to your Sherlock, you know, *the woman?* And the Dominique Francon to your Howard Roarke. I want you to love me, to need me for my *thoughts.* I want to be your *greatest match.*"

"Benny, you don't have to be a fictional character for me to love you, to want to be with you.

Write your fiction all day long, but please, please don't *be* fiction. Just be *you.* Okay, *just you.* I want to be with *you, Benny...* You are more than interesting and challenging enough all on *your* own. You are a *keeper,* Benny, a *keeper.*"

"You! An extremely short, well hung, straight man who loves American Musical Theater?"

The new Benny emerged again and given *her voice.*

"YES. Let me *keep* you!"

Augie lay on top of Benny, not inside her yet, but *almost,* just staring down at her and her look of openness, as if her heart was exposed, gazing up at him. It had been a long wait. There was no music just the sound of their pounding hearts and the rhythm of their breaths.

"It's not the same as the first time," he moaned, as he shook his head.

"It...isn't? I'm sorry. What can I do? Tell me," she said as she grimaced and shook.

"I feel different," he moaned again.

"You're a man now Augie, and I'm a woman," Benny said. She placed her hands on his face and gently stroked his cheeks.

Then, she kissed him along his jawline. He just stared down in silence. His chest heaved and she felt how hard he was. Her legs shook beneath him as she waited for him to enter her, just like the first time so very long ago.

It was his turn to get lost.

"*Your vulnerability is really freaking me out right now,*" she whispered.

His frightened look turned into a smile. She kept talking about how their weekend in August was perfect. Yet, at this very moment, snowflakes stuck and melted down the vintage windows of the fourth floor on Elizabeth Street. To them, everything seemed absolutely perfect...*again*.

"You're quoting a Scorsese film, **The Departed**?" he asked.

"Yes, I pay attention" she whispered

"*I love you.*" he said as he looked into her eyes. Then he kissed her. It was *different*. It was *more*.

She stopped his kisses for a brief moment to confirm his remark. She said something she had been *not-so-secretly* holding back ever since they started dating as the two old-friend-slash-forty-year- olds.

"Augie, I love you. I, I just wanted to make sure. I mean I *like* everything about you, you short son-of-a-bitch. *You're it, for me, period.* I knew you were special, and that's why I could never entirely let go."

Unlike the first time, he pushed all the way inside her. Hungry for air from the force of his thrust, she gasped and closed her eyes. He continued kissing her as she moaned.

"Augie!"

"Shhh," He pushed faster as if relishing every second. "Please."

Just like the first time, her eyes were tearing.

"Does it feel good?" he asked.

"Yes," she confessed. All at once, that *yes* covered a lot of territory.

"I love you Benny..." he grunted.

She bent her head and looked below to their waists to watch their bodies join. This was *really* happening. She remembered making him let her watch him go in and out of her when they were younger. She would whisper to him over and over, *I want to see, I want to see,* and he would lift up his chest and she would look down and...*watch.* She loved to *watch.*

At that moment, her mind completely left her body. It was her from above, looking at herself. Of them...as *one.* For her entire adult life, she had wondered what it was like to get to a higher level with another human being. This was it. She saw the two helium balloons, side by side, *rising.*

"Sorry, I can't hold it..."

"Go ahead, please..."

He looked into her welcoming eyes and kissed her again. He let out a moan that was similar, but different than the one he let out the first night that they had slept together. He leaned over onto her, laid his face between her breasts and caught his breath. Her legs felt sore. Yet she kept them spread as her body twitched as if in shock. She kissed his forehead as she caressed the thick, dirty blonde hair on his head.

A little later, after a short rest, she straddled on top of him and pinned his hands down as she assumed the *dominant* position.

"Say it," she whispered in his ear and roughly rubbed her body against him.

"No," he responded. His mouth widened and he was sweating.

"Say it," she ordered with a louder voice.

"*I like it when you fuck me, Benny,*" he croaked. Then, he sat up, grabbed her in his arms and wrapped her legs around his legs as the two old friends *first*, and as the two lovers *second* came together *perfectly*.

They took turns being in control, making sure it was *even*; intimate and hopeful, until they unknowingly fell asleep together, hard, sore, smiley, sticky and incredibly *satisfied*.

In the background was the sound of a needle skipping on John Coltrane's "My Favorite Things" record. Earlier in the day, Augie bought the album from a sidewalk vendor on Prince Street in Soho. He had just completed a long journey to and from Margo, the French Patisserie in Brooklyn to pick up croissants and blackberry jam for breakfast on Sunday morning. Benny *loved* jam. She told him that she would like to *rub it all over* his body, and then, *lick it off*. So, he bought an entire shelf load of it. *Just in case.* His hopes were high that this would happen. The olive oil fantasy Benny had mentioned in Washington Square Park last August had never stopped percolating in his brain. *Yes. You are inside me,* he thought. He grinned as he unloaded a gluttonous number of pretty, artisan jam jars on the breakfast counter.

There was also a gift wrapped print sitting in the closet, back on Elizabeth Street, which he *almost felt like a college kid buying it for his dorm room wall.* This was the *after we do it* gift. He had returned to the Upper East Side and the Neue Gallery the day before to pick it up. It was a copy of Gustav Klimt's painting "Fulfillment." Benny, like Augie, *had to be different.* She couldn't like Klimt's painting "The Kiss." "Too commercial," she said. But this Klimt, "Fulfillment," screamed *Benny* and represented a man and woman in perfect physical and spiritual harmony. She must have sent him a postcard overseas or to New York with this print on it a dozen or more times. She had purchased it from the gift store at the Art Institute of Chicago, where she often sat on the stone steps, pen in hand, ending her letter with "Miss you, *Benny*." She ended every phone call and letter to him, "Miss you." She had missed him. She always felt that he held something dear to her that she could never quite get back, not her virginity, or her girlhood, but - *a piece of her heart.*

"My Favorite Things" was the *perfect* opening song, he thought, as he walked back home to the Elizabeth Street apartment with the two, heavy shopping bags filled with dark, sticky sweet deliciousness for the new music playlist he was making, for *them,* for *home.* Fifteen years ago, Benny had put "My Favorite Things" on the first mix tape she had sent him overseas. Coltrane's version had no words, just music, and it offered her a chance to not think for a few precious moments...*to just feel good...to just listen...to just be...together...quietly. And... just be...one...*

That night, as they held hands in the dark, side by side, *spooning,* they were lulled to sleep by *their favorite things.*

Augie and Benny, *old* friends, and *brand new* lovers, finally had the same dream.

THE END

AUGIE'S PLAYLIST

She's Always in My Hair	Prince
Diane	Husker Du
Hawaii Five O Theme Song	
Running Up that Hill	Kate Bush
And then he kissed me	The Crystals
Shadowboxer	Fiona Apple
Favorite Things	John Coltrane
96 Degrees	Third World
Tones on Tails	Go
Clubland	Elvis Costello
Shake It for Me	Howlin Wolf
Can't Hardly Wait	The Replacements
To Turn You On	Roxy Music
Our House	Steel Pulse
It's a Mistake	Men at Work
Dirty Mind	Prince
Teenage Riot	Sonic Youth
Temptation	New Order
Manhattan	Cat Power

BENNY'S PLAYLIST

Native Love	Divine
Sugar Walls	Sheena Easton
Surrey with the Fringe on Top	Oklahoma
Don't Let Me Down	Charlotte Dada
Sugar In My Bowl	Nina Simone
Tezeta	Mulatu Astake
It	Prince
Avalon	Roxy Music
Be Happy	Mary J Blige
Never as Good as the First	TimeSade
Breathless	Nick Cave
So Long, Marianne	Leonard Cohen
La Vie En Rose	Grace Jones
Hypnotic Tango	My Mine
Heart Skipped a Beat	XX
Spirit of 76	Ween
Brain Dead	Red Red Meat
Deeper Into Movies	Yo La Tengo
Manhattan	Cat Power

ACKNOWLEDGEMENTS

My parents – for loving me and supporting me in every en-
deavor and providing me with an exceptional education. My
husband, Jeven Adami, for supporting my writer's life and
blessing me with my two beautiful children, Andrew and
Francesca. Thank you to my Auntie Karen and Auntie Sharon
for your meticulous copy edits. Marianne Strong, my friend
and agent who taught me the publishing industry and made
me feel hope. Agent Marcia Wolfson for your professionalism
and believing in me. Frank Filerino for introducing me to my
agents, promotion and pushing me to complete the manuscript. Columnist and icon Ann Gerber for supporting this
book and writing exquisite coverage of my late father and I.
Norena Mikicic for hosting me numerous times in New York
City. Danielle Klinenberg for hosting my first reading and
emotionally and pragmatically supporting my life as an artist.
Eric Klinenberg for introducing me to NYU's Fiction writing
program and for letters of recommendation. Tony Frenzel, for
creating a beautiful cover! Alicia Senior-Saywell for her hard
work on my launch and pushing me to publish this damn book

already! To all of my Patrons of the Arts who helped send me to LaMuse Inn writer's retreat in Labistide, France. Editors Janet Steed and Rebecca Collazzo. My NYU Patron of the Arts, Big Brother, and friend for life, Gregory Swanson. To New York City and New Orleans for inspiring me with your beauty, excitement and energy. Thank you to Chicago's Newberry Library for providing affordable, wonderful writing classes for me over the past twenty years. Thank you to my Tulane gals, Ellie Bailer, Gale Morrison and Tesa Baum for listening to me and supporting my wacky dreams all these years. Thank you to my Parker community for not thinking any goal is too far-fetched and expecting great things of me. Thank you to the Francis W. Parker School of Chicago for nurturing and educating my children and for my former teachers there like Paul Druzinsky for inspiring a love of reading through Tennessee Williams plays in Drama I, Bonnie Seebold for overseeing my first painful attempts at writing class, to Bob Merrick for making storytelling click for me and wanting to be a storyteller, to Bill Duffy for introducing me to my favorite writers such as James Joyce and Graham Greene, and last, but not least, to my muse, the late great, Dr. Marie K. Stone who made me promise her that I would be a writer one day and who taught me to "throw some sex in there" so the audience will remember you.

Thank you to my favorite artist of all time, the late Prince, for showing me how to be bold and to believe in yourself, no matter what(like, even in your underwear on an album cover.)

Thank you to my late father, Freddy 'the Beard' Bentivegna and my Great Uncle Raymond Biamonte, for being the two greatest storytellers of all time.

Thank you universe, for all of the "good" magic out there and for always looking out for me.

Made in the USA
Middletown, DE
21 September 2016